# ECHOES OF THE DEAD

**ALSO BY SPENCER KOPE**

*Shadows of the Dead*

*Whispers of the Dead*

*Collecting the Dead*

# ECHOES OF THE DEAD

Spencer Kope

MINOTAUR
BOOKS
NEW YORK

This is a work of fiction. All of the characters, organizations, and events portrayed in this novel are either products of the author's imagination or are used fictitiously.

First published in the United States by Minotaur Books, an imprint of St. Martin's Publishing Group



www.minotaurbooks.com

Library of Congress Cataloging-in-Publication Data

Names: Kope, Spencer, author.
Title: Echoes of the dead / Spencer Kope.
Description: First edition. | New York : Minotaur Books, 2021.
Identifiers: LCCN 2021015897 | ISBN 9781250179401 (hardcover) | ISBN 9781250179449 (ebook)
Subjects: GSAFD: Mystery fiction. | Suspense fiction.
Classification: LCC PS3561.O63 E28 2021 | DDC 813/.54—dc23
LC record available at https://lccn.loc.gov/2021015897



First Edition: 2021

10 9 8 7 6 5 4 3 2 1

To my family, friends, and fans. It's hard to believe that I've been writing for almost forty years. If there's one thing I know for certain, it's that I couldn't have done it without you. Thank you.

# ECHOES OF THE DEAD

# 1

*Now I lay me down to sleep. . . .*

Dreams are like runaway trains, and we, their passengers. It's a simple truth of dreams that we may ride the train and see the worlds and visions it opens to us, but we are helpless to change its speed or divert it from its course. Dreams go where they will.

Sadly, or perhaps blessedly, most of the adventures presented to us on these nightly forays are lost upon waking, wiped clean by the churnings of the conscious mind, which demands control and has no patience for the train. Yet some small fragments may linger: a feeling of joy or terror, an image, a sound.

Lucid dreams are different.

Unlike their relentless yet forgettable cousins, lucid dreams are remarkably memorable.

Within the realm of lucid dreams, the normal rules do not apply, allowing some to take control. Like a Hollywood director, they can script their actions on the fly, reveling in the godlike freedom to create, enjoy, or destroy at will. The greater the capacity to imagine and create, the more powerful they become, like mages and demigods from some video game, spinning the world to their liking.

The laws of nature are no obstacle within a lucid dream. In such a state, one might soar over snowcapped mountains, scuba dive in blue Caribbean water, or walk in space. Magic abounds. In a lucid dream, the dreamer is in control.

Jason Norris has never had a lucid dream.

As cofounder of the prestigious Norris & Lambert, an accounting firm in San Jose with offices in New York and Houston, he's rarely been accused of showing even the slightest hint of imagination. He reads voraciously, but never fiction. He plays games, but only those that are numbers based. He collects coins and bills, but only because they speak to the history of ledgers and counting.

His wife, Alice, says he likes his spreadsheets more than the spread of her legs.

It's not *entirely* true—they do have two daughters.

Despite his machinelike brain, Jason enjoys fly-fishing. He was introduced to it in college, and it's the only sport-related activity he was ever good at. It's no surprise then that in this, his first lucid dream, he finds himself at a favorite spot on the Upper Kern River, a fly rod in his hand. He knows every bend, pool, glide, and riffle for miles—yet instead of fishing, he finds himself standing at the edge of the water, perplexed.

This is not the river he remembers, this place beyond sleep.

*I pray the Lord my soul to keep. . . .*

The hills are the same, as are the trees and the collections of riprap gathered here and there, forming pockets of still water. Even the air smells of the wild just before spring, as the Upper Kern so often does. Yet, as comfortable and familiar as these things are, Jason finds himself distracted by something . . . unfamiliar.

There's blood in the water.

It seems to start at his feet—just the surface spread from a few translucent drops, resembling a thin sheen of oil. But as he watches, the red grows deeper, expanding out. It doesn't wash away as one would expect, diluted by the river, but instead defies gravity and spreads in all directions. Soon, the stain reaches across the entire breadth of the river. Some of it washes downstream, but more seems to move upstream, like a dark mass of spawning trout.

*No, that's wrong,* Jason thinks. Not spawning salmon—shadows, undefinable darkness upon the river that only he can see.

Jason doesn't believe in God.

The divine isn't something you can quantify and calculate. God multiplied by creation does not equal *life*, at least not in his perfectly ordered brain. Still, when he hears the rustle of feet next to him and turns, he half expects to see Moses with his staff extended to the water, turning all the Kern to blood in a lesson to Pharaoh.

It's not Moses.

It's something else.

As Jason opens his mouth to scream, the dream ends abruptly. He awakens to darkness, utter and complete. Even the comforting glow of the night-light is gone. The bulb must have burned out, he tells himself; either that or Alice moved it. The air is stifling, the bedroom claustrophobic.

*If I die before I wake . . .*

As he starts to jerk upright, his head strikes something and he flops back down. Attempting to lift his hands to feel for the obstruction, he discovers that they too are blocked, as if someone had built a low ceiling over him while he slept.

It only takes a moment for realization to settle heavily in

his chest, a bowling ball resting on his sternum: this is not his bed.

Fear begins to take over and Jason claws at the obstruction and pushes it with all his might. His breathing grows short and shallow as a sense of claustrophobia rises within. "No, no, no!" he pants, the words giving way to whimpers. He searches his pockets for a match, a lighter—anything that'll shed light on his situation, but finds them as empty as a promise.

The truth finds him slowly and then all at once, like a fast-approaching train that leaves him in a Doppler wake. When it has come and gone, he lies trembling for a long moment, utterly quiet and still. Terror simmers within him, growing to a boil. An immaterial creature seeking release.

Then the screaming begins in earnest as his mind breaks.

*I pray the Lord my soul to take.*

# 2

*Sunday, March 8*

Call me Steps, everyone does.

As a man-tracker for the FBI's elite Special Tracking Unit, I spend a good deal of my time traveling the country with my partner, Special Agent Jimmy Donovan. We look for the lost, bring justice to the dead, and hunt some of the sickest minds our society has produced, which is no small task.

The dental and medical plans are excellent.

Because of my spur-of-the-moment lifestyle, choosing the date for a wedding is challenging enough. Choosing the date for an *outdoor* wedding in the Pacific Northwest adds a whole new level of difficulty. It's a lot like running rapids in a partially deflated raft: you know you're going to get wet, you just don't know how bad the soaking is going to be. The odds don't start to weigh in your favor until about mid-July, and then you have about a month and a half of fairly dependable sun before things get sketchy again.

"How about August twenty-second?" Heather suggests.

"Is that a Saturday?"

"It is."

"And that works for you?"

She smiles. "It does."

Her eyes are dancing the way I love, and she immediately notices that I'm noticing. The smile blooms into something grand and beautiful, a look that could slay a man in his tracks or raise the dead. She's killed me a thousand times.

Heather and I are taking high tea in Fairhaven, a historic district within the city limits of Bellingham, Washington, not far from my home on Chuckanut Drive.

With its Victorian-era architecture, fine restaurants, quaint art shops, and magnificent bookstores, Fairhaven is popular with both locals and tourists. There's a lot to discover, including the Big Ben Tea Room on Eleventh Street, where you can take high tea in a British-inspired atmosphere.

It's one of Heather's favorite places.

Diane Parker introduced her to the place. Diane is the third and final member of our exclusive unit and serves as our intelligence analyst. In her mind, that makes her the most important member of the team. Jimmy and I like to remind her that she's old enough to be our mother.

It's raw ageism, I know, but it's the only thing that shuts her up.

If we told her the truth, that she's smarter than the both of us combined, it would be like pouring endless quantities of gasoline on an already-searing fire.

Diane never goes on the road with us. She rarely leaves her office.

I've never quite figured out what she does or how she goes about doing it, but she somehow conjures up this weird analytical voodoo that helps solve cases in such places as California, Alaska, or on the other side of the Continental Divide, all from the comfort of her office. It's freaky weird and the closest thing to magic I've seen. I'd swear she keeps chicken feet and casting bones somewhere in her desk, probably next to a vial of virgin's blood.

Diane sees more of Heather than I do, and the two of them

are like sisters born thirty years apart. I once said they were like mother and daughter, but that earned me a voluminous stink eye from Diane, so I never said it again. I learn quickly like that.

"What happens if you get a call?" Heather asks.

It's a fair question. Jimmy and I tend to live out of small luggage and homogenized motel rooms. We spend a lot of time moving from city to city, from case to case—wherever someone might be missing, or a body turns up under unusual circumstances. It's the kind of job you love and hate and despise all in the same breath.

"Jimmy won't let that happen," I say, pretty sure that it's true. Lifting my cup and pointing it at her, as if for emphasis, I say, "That falls under the duties of the best man, after all, and you know how seriously he takes his responsibilities. He'll make sure everything goes off without a hitch, you'll see."

"Yeah, well, most grooms don't have access to a corporate jet"—she lowers her voice and leans in—"or bodies dropping around them like candy from a fat kid's pocket."

"Technically speaking," I whisper back, "they're not dropping *around* me; they're already dead when we get the call."

"You know what I mean."

I do, unfortunately. "What about you?"

"Me?"

"Yeah, do you think you can abstain from any enticing crime stories until after the wedding?" I'm teasing, but only somewhat.

Heather's job is as demanding as mine, but without the budget. While still in college, she founded a news blog focused specifically on crime. It quickly became profitable and gained her some small measure of recognition, enough to get her signed by *Newsweek* after she completed her master's.

When her short stint as a bona fide *Newsweek* reporter came to an abrupt end—on her terms—she returned to the blog full-time and has steadily built it into a going concern.

It now employs three people—well, Heather plus two others, and one of them is part-time.

"Don't worry about me," Heather replies. "Charles Manson could rise from the dead and offer an exclusive interview and it wouldn't lure me away." She cocks her head to the side and gives me a funny little smirk, eyes twinkling. "I might consider sending him an invitation, though. That way we could chat during the reception. . . ."

"As long as he's available for family photos," I shoot back.

She crinkles up her nose. "Creepy."

I had an ulterior motive when I asked Heather to tea this morning. I have a secret I've kept from her for almost a year and a half, and if we're to be married, it's not something I can keep hidden. It wouldn't be right.

For months I've been trying to think of a way to tell her, but I'm so afraid of how she'll react that every time I gather the courage it drains out the bottom of my shoes. My gut tells me she'll accept my peculiar condition well enough, but other parts of me think she'll freak out and view me as either completely mad or, worse, a monster.

That's why I can't tell her in the teahouse.

If she freaks, I'd rather it be in private.

As we finish our tea and make our way out onto Eleventh Street, I find the sidewalks busier than anticipated. It's a nice day for early March, and it seems the sun—which locals jokingly refer to as the strange glowing thing in the sky—has pulled a lot of people from winter hibernation and drawn them to Fairhaven. There won't be any private conversations on these streets, not today.

As we pass the British-style double-decker bus that sells fish and chips at the corner of Harris and Eleventh, a thought occurs to me. "Want to take the boardwalk up to Boulevard Park?"

"Sure. Since I have you all to myself, might as well make the most of it."

Kitty-corner from the Village Green, we find the entrance to a short trail and follow it north to the Taylor Avenue Dock, which juts straight out from shore. After walking along the dock for a couple hundred feet, we are connected to the Fairhaven boardwalk, which parallels the shoreline north to Boulevard Park. By this time, we're a good two hundred feet from shore and perhaps a dozen feet above the water.

The whole thing is a marvel.

About every two hundred feet a small platform extends out from the side of the boardwalk with a bench facing the water and the distant islands. Plenty of people are on the boardwalk, but it's by no means crowded. Most seem too absorbed in their conversations to pay much notice to a couple walking along slowly, hand in hand.

Halfway across the boardwalk, I decide that this is as good a place as any, and, before I lose my nerve, I pull Heather aside to one of the benches and ask her to have a seat. Feeling much like Dr. Jekyll on the verge of revealing Mr. Hyde, I take a seat next to her but turned sideways on the bench so that I'm facing her.

"I need to tell you something. Something you need to know before we get married; something I should have told you a long time ago."

She says nothing, but watches me, more curious than concerned.

"Remember when we first met, when you were embedded with the tracking unit for three or four weeks?"

"Three weeks," she corrects. "And, yes, I remember."

"Do you remember calling me a fraud after one of the cases?"

She snorts as if it's an old joke.

"So, you do remember?"

She studies me a moment, then puts her hand on my cheek. "It was very sweet. No one ever followed a fake track for me before, but there are better ways of impressing me."

"You think it was a fake track?"

"Of course, it was." She sees the look on my face and smiles. "What? Do you think I didn't bone up on man-tracking before I joined a man-tracking team? I did. At least enough to know that with terrain like that, there's no way *anyone* could have tracked—" She suddenly covers her mouth. "I forgot his name. It was Jerrod something, wasn't it?" She snaps her fingers. "Anderson . . . Jerrod Anderson."

"Andreasen," I correct.

Her mouth scrunches up in disappointment. "Close."

I take a deep breath. "What if I told you it wasn't a fake track?"

She starts to shake her head, then sees that I'm perfectly serious.

"Promise you won't judge until you've heard the whole thing."

"I promise," she says in a soft, uncomfortable voice.

There's no backing out now, so I plunge ahead. She'd already heard about the time I got lost in the Cascade mountains when I was eight, how I froze to death and was found just in time to be revived. That's where she thinks the story ends, but it was just the beginning of an entirely new story.

"When I woke in the hospital, there was a . . . haze, over my mom's face. And then I noticed the same thing on other people. It was light at first, almost imperceptible, but in the coming weeks it grew more pronounced, and it wasn't just on people. It was on anything someone touched: footprints, thumbprints, handprints. If someone brushed up against a wall, it left a mark. The problem was, I was the only one who could see it. At first, I thought the hypothermia had damaged my eyes somehow, but as the haze grew deeper and more colorful, I began to think I was losing my mind. Imagine that, an eight-year-old kid thinking he's going crazy."

As I fall into silence, Heather studies my face. "Go on."

"You think—"

"No—" she cuts me off.

"I don't blame you," I say quickly. "That's why I didn't want to tell you."

"It's fine," she insists. Reaching out, she takes my hand in her own, then looks me in the eye. "Tell me the rest."

I do. Over the next few minutes, I tell her everything, the good, the bad, and the unbelievable.

"So, this aura you see on people—what did you call it?"

"Shine."

"And it's different for every person?"

"As far as I know. At least I've never seen two that are exactly alike."

"It stays on everything someone touches?"

"Yes . . . well, kind of. Footprints are a bit weaker when shine has to penetrate through shoes, but it's still there. It may have something to do with the compression of the foot against the ground."

I can tell she's confused. Slipping off my shoe, I hold it up. "If the sole of my shoe is a half inch thick, it still leaves a nice print on the ground when I walk around. Shine is left not only on the shoe but on the ground. Odd thing is, if I just hold my foot the same distance from the ground without touching"—I extend my foot and demonstrate—"there's no shine."

I pause and slip the shoe back on, glancing at her nervously as I do. Part of me still expects her to jump up and race down the boardwalk, screaming as she goes and pointing at the monster on the bench.

"Go on," she says in a whisper.

I nod, and she squeezes my hand.

"The only thing I can figure is that some type of pressure

is required, even if it's minute. As long as there's physical contact, it'll leave shine behind, even if it's through a shoe or a coat or a glove." I fall silent as a large group draws near and then passes by, college students from Western Washington University by the looks of them.

After they pass, I continue in a lower voice, "Blood, urine, semen, and other bodily oils and fluid—even skin cells—are a different story. They retain their shine, even when separated from the body."

"Separated from the body," Heather parrots with a shiver. "Sounds ominous."

As she grows quiet, deep in thought, I leave her to it. When she rises from the bench and walks to the rail, staring out over Bellingham Bay, I give her a moment before following. "It's a gift," she whispers at length, coming to terms with the idea and its implications.

"It's a curse."

"No," she says, more forceful this time. "And it's not as freakish as you try to make it out." Extending a hand, she draws me to her side. "Did you know that bees and a lot of other insects see using ultraviolet light? How's that much different from what you're describing?"

"They're insects," I say flatly.

She smiles patiently. "But it's not magical or freakish or paranormal. It's just the way they see, like living in a world of black lights. Then there are bats, of course, which use sound waves to see the world as they flit about. Snakes use infrared, cats have night vision, and Steps sees shine. How is one stranger than any of the others?"

"Cats are pretty strange," I point out with a smirk.

"I'm serious."

"So am I. Besides, the others were born that way, I wasn't."

"As I said, it's a gift."

I want to argue with her, but I can't. I'm just thankful she's taking it so well, that she hasn't called 911 and requested an involuntary mental hold.

She says slowly, "If everyone has their own color and texture—"

"Windex."

"What?"

"You were going to ask me what color your shine is. It's Windex . . . or, I suppose I should say it *reminds* me of Windex. You know, kind of a luminous aqua blue?"

"So, I'm window cleaner?"

"I just read the shine, I don't choose it."

Slipping my glasses off, I hand them to her. "Give these a try."

She's curious but doesn't question the odd request. A moment later, glasses perched on her nose, she looks at me, confused.

"Expecting the world to look fuzzy?"

"That's generally what happens when I wear someone else's glasses." She slips them off and studies them.

"They're lead crystal; the only thing that'll block the shine."

"Lead crystal?"

"Something I discovered when I was ten. I was with Mom and Dad at one of those glass shops, the ones where they have a furnace and they blow wineglasses and fancy Christmas ornaments while you watch. I just happened to glance through a lead crystal platter and realized I couldn't see the shine on the other side. Dad ordered a pair of lead crystal glasses the next day."

"Did your mom know?"

I shake my head. "Still doesn't. Trust me, it's better that way."

Heather is just about to fire something back when my phone rings. I check the caller ID. "It's Diane." I want to let it go to voice mail, but Diane doesn't call for trivial things.

"Go ahead and take it."

I give Heather an apologetic smile and connect the call.

Before I have time to utter a greeting, Diane says, "I hate to interrupt tea, but something's come up."

"Where?"

"Northeast of Bakersfield, California. Sometime over the last twenty-four to thirty-six hours, four men went missing from the Upper Kern River. Search and Rescue was activated at eight this morning, and they have about seventy volunteers running a grid search. So far there's nothing." Diane pauses as if to lend weight to the coming words. "The director himself called a few minutes ago. He wants you and Jimmy down there as soon as possible."

"From what you've described, this only barely qualifies as a mission requiring our type of expertise, so why would the director of the FBI call? What aren't you telling me?"

Diane sighs. "I'll have the details when you get to the hangar. Speaking of which—how soon can you be here?"

I look at Heather and just shake my head.

This wasn't supposed to be how today ended. High tea was meant to soften Heather up for the long-overdue revelation about my special ability, my curse. After that—provided the outcome was favorable—I thought we'd take in a movie and then have dinner at the Hearthfire Grill. This development is disappointing, but then, after six years with the Special Tracking Unit, I've grown accustomed to disappointments.

"Give me an hour," I say.

# 3

Hangar 7 sits at the southern end of Bellingham International Airport.

The facility itself is within the extensive security fence protecting the runways, hangars, and scattered outbuildings, but due to its special status, the cipher-protected door at the southeast corner building opens onto a small but private parking lot beyond the security perimeter.

Most would look at the hangar with little interest, unaware of what lies within. It's taller and wider than many of the surrounding hangars, those that house Cessna, Beechcraft, and Piper aircraft, among others. In a previous incarnation, Hangar 7 had a completely open floor plan, looking more like an empty warehouse. It was rented out to corporate clients and could house two private jets at once.

The FBI paid $300,000 for the empty building and spent another $120,000 building the two-story complex that hugs the inside of the western wall. The upper floor has three offices that empty onto a mezzanine.

Aside from providing office space and a spot on the hangar floor for the foosball table, Hangar 7 is also home to Betsy, the Special Tracking Unit's Gulfstream G100 corporate jet, the only real perk that comes with the job. Les is our contract pilot, and Marty is his copilot. At fifty-three years of age, Les is everyone's image of a calm and seasoned pilot, right down to his salt-and-pepper hair and his aviator sunglasses.

Marty is twenty years younger and reminds me of a Chihuahua on a caffeine binge. Most of the time, he has a thrilled, half-crazed look on his face—but in a fun way. If the wind happens to kick up and ruffle his hair the wrong way, he starts to resemble someone who just walked out of a psych ward.

He's a good guy. Just don't get him talking about aquariums.

Jimmy and Diane are waiting for me in the conference room when I arrive, and as I take my seat, I notice that Diane has a map displayed on the flat-screen television hanging on the back wall.

"Kern River?" I ask.

"Correct. I was just explaining to Jimmy that the men you'll be searching for usually camp at this bend"—she circles an area with her pointing stick—"but they were known to fish locations up to a mile from their base camp, which widens the search area considerably."

"And we're sure these guys are missing?" Jimmy presses. "I only ask because it seems like a hard place to get lost unless it's on purpose. What if they found a new fishing spot farther away or set up a secondary camp somewhere upriver?" He shrugs. "What if it's just guys out fishing? You know, out in the wilderness, living in the moment. Sometimes it's easy to lose track of time."

"All of them had prearranged call times with either spouses or associates," Diane replies, "and none of them made yesterday's call-in."

Jimmy and I exchange a look.

"There could be a hundred reasons for that," he finally says, though with less conviction. "What about local Search and Rescue? What are they saying?"

"Kern Valley Search and Rescue has been on the scene since eight A.M. They know the area well, so the fact that they haven't found anything is concerning."

"What's the rest of the story?" Jimmy suddenly asks, leaning forward on his forearms and eyeing her suspiciously, as if she's been holding out. "Why did we get the call, and how did this land in the director's lap in the first place?"

Diane purses her lips and then—uncharacteristically—takes a seat at the conference table next to Jimmy. "Are you familiar with second-term congressman Marco Perez out of Bakersfield?" She reaches out and clicks the mouse on her laptop.

The image of a smiling white man in his early forties fills the center of the television screen. Though it's just a press photo, his intense eyes stare down and find me in my chair, holding me in place, as if his gaze alone can transfix and constrain. He looks vaguely familiar, but I don't follow politics.

"I've heard of him," Jimmy confesses. "Is he one of the missing?"

"He is, which is why the director got a call from Secret Service this morning. Right now, it's being treated like any other case of missing or overdue campers, but if they don't find him soon, things will ramp up. The director asked that you and Steps get down there as quickly as possible and see what you can see. Or in his words, *do your thing*—whatever that's supposed to mean."

"How do you go missing on a fishing trip?" I wonder aloud. "Rivers are usually close to civilization, and if they're not, you just have to follow them downstream and you're bound to find a bridge or a road."

"Oh, trust me, it gets more intriguing," Diane says. "Congressman Perez was on a fly-fishing trip on the Kern River with three of his college friends. This is an annual event for them, something they've done since their days at USC."

"The fly-fishing on the Kern part or just fishing in general?" I ask.

"The Kern part. More specifically, the Upper Kern, at least according to the congressman's sister. It has something to do with their experiences together in college, but she didn't elaborate. They all met in Bakersfield Thursday morning and were fishing by that afternoon. Marco checked in with his sister on Thursday at three, the agreed-upon time, and then again at the same time on Friday.

"When he didn't call on Saturday, she tried calling him, but it kept going to voice mail. By eight that night, none of the men had been heard from in almost thirty hours, and a lot of people were starting to get concerned." Diane clears her throat. "When I say a lot of people started getting concerned, I'm talking about more than friends and family. I'm talking business associates, powerful political figures, and titans of industry."

"For one congressman?" I ask skeptically.

Diane nods slowly, but not in agreement. "If only it were that simple." She clicks the mouse again.

The image of a stern white man in his midforties pops up and fills the television screen. His look is so severe that one might think he ate glass shards for breakfast two days earlier and is now having a hard time passing them. He's wearing an off-the-rack suit and a generic military haircut that reminds me of the colonel from the movie *Avatar*, but that was an actor. This guy is the real deal, and every edge of the man is sharp and hard.

"Meet Wade Winchell," Diane says. "Forty-five years of age, and the deputy district attorney out of Los Angeles County in charge of Major Crimes. He just finished a big case involving several senior members of La eMe, better known as the Mexican Mafia. In the course of his career, he's been shot at, had a Molotov cocktail tossed through the sunroof of his car, and been the victim of two targeted assaults, one of which broke his jaw and the other fractured two ribs and cracked three others." She pauses to let this sink in. "Not exactly the kind of guy we can afford to misplace."

The next slide depicts a Black male around the same age, but with a softer, more cultured look. His haircut came from a salon. His suit is tailor-made.

"This is Jason Norris, cofounder of Norris and Lambert, an accounting firm with offices in San Jose, Houston, and New York. No gangbangers in his history, but he has a string of lawyers that'll tear you a new one if you end up in a legal dispute with him. From what I can tell, his net worth is about ten million dollars, and he donates generously to both political parties."

Jimmy lets out a low whistle.

"And this"—Diane clicks to the next image—"is Noah Long, cofounder of Ascot and Long, a hedge fund out of New York with seven billion dollars under management. I don't even want to guess what his net worth is, but it probably puts Mr. Norris to shame."

She pulls up a final image showing all four men together and leaves it on the screen. The wealth, power, and influence represented by the four figures is daunting, and I feel something creeping up my spine that feels a lot like anxiety, or perhaps just dread.

Clicking back to the map, Diane sits in silence.

"How old is the congressman?" I ask after a long pause.

"Forty-three."

"You said they've been fishing the same river since college, let's say about twenty years, give or take. That means they probably know the area well."

Jimmy picks up on my train of thought. "You're wondering how they could have gotten lost in an area so familiar."

I point at him dramatically, as if he'd just revealed some inescapable truth.

"That's exactly why his sister is concerned," Diane says, ignoring the theatrics. "Besides"—she gestures at the map—"you said it yourself: there aren't many places you can get lost without getting unlost in short order. I think the main worry is that they stumbled into an old mine or fell down an embankment."

"The trees look thick enough around the river," Jimmy observes, "but they're pretty sparse on the hills. If you were lost, all you'd have to do is climb one of the low hills and get your bearings." He begins to strum his fingers on the table. "This is an annual male-bonding experience, right? So maybe they got drunk and decided to climb a hill in the middle of the night. By the time the sun came up, they could have been pretty disoriented."

"Bit of a stretch," Diane says. "Besides, the congressman is a teetotaler."

"What about the rest of them?"

"The deputy DA drinks like a fish, or at least that's the rumor."

Leaning toward Jimmy, I mutter, "Mexican Mafia," implying that we'd all drink prodigiously if a powerful prison gang wanted us dead.

He chuckles darkly and then turns back to Diane. "What about Noah and the other guy?" He snaps his fingers a couple of times, trying to remember.

"Jason Norris," Diane says.

"Right. Norris. Do either of them drink or indulge in recreational herbs?"

"I don't know."

When Jimmy throws his hands up in mock frustration, Diane gives him a long stare. "I've only had the names for the last hour," she says, carefully enunciating each word and wrapping it tightly in a hard shell. "I know you might find this difficult to believe, but even I have my limitations."

"It's okay," I say to Jimmy, holding up a consoling palm, "we should be getting our real analyst in a few weeks. Until then, we'll just have to make do."

Diane lowers her head and glares at me over the top of her reading glasses.

Contemptuous loathing doesn't come naturally to her, but it is one of her favorite costumes, and she wears it well. With a scowl the size of West Texas, she continues the stare down, shifting her gaze between Jimmy and me. We grin back like a pair of dyspeptic Cheshire cats. After casting her eyes back and forth a few more times, her face reverts to an unimpressed smirk.

She sighs and adjusts the papers in front of her. "You should know that the press has already gotten wind of this. ZeroHedge, an online financial blog, ran an article a few hours ago, mostly focused on Noah and the implications for his hedge fund. There's also a news van parked outside the congressman's office, and another one making its way to the Upper Kern."

"Great," I mutter, tossing a pencil onto the table.

"Tell me honestly," Jimmy says. "How sure are you that this is going to be a straight-up search and rescue?"

"Pretty sure," Diane replies softly. Then she meets his gaze. "If not . . ."

The unspoken words hang in the room like wing-wrapped bats, a slumbering colony of terrifying possibilities.

Ten minutes later we're in the air and climbing to thirty-nine thousand feet for the two-hour-and-twenty-minute flight to Meadows Field Airport, which is just three miles northwest of downtown Bakersfield. Digging out a worn paperback copy of *Ready Player One* from my early-1900s-style travel bag, I turn to the bookmark and dive in. Two pages later I can't remember a thing I've just read and close the book in frustration.

*It's just a search and rescue,* I tell myself.

I try to push my concern aside, but I can't answer the one question that's searing a hole into the back of my skull: How do you go missing in a place as familiar as your own backyard?

# 4

Meadows Field Airport was built north of Bakersfield by the Kern County Chamber of Commerce in 1926 and quickly became a stop for the fledgling US Air Mail service, which had been established just eight years earlier. In 1935, Kern County purchased the airport from the Chamber of Commerce, and Meadows Field became the first county-owned airport in the nation.

It was simple as airports go: one runway, one terminal building, and a few hangars and support buildings. But then, planes and pilots weren't as plentiful as they are today, so a single runway was more than enough.

Times change.

According to the interactive map on my iPhone, it's supposed to be an hour-and-thirteen-minute drive from Meadows Field to the town of Kernville. Somehow, we make it in fifty-seven minutes. I'm not saying the yellow Mustang convertible we got as a rental had anything to do with it, but Jimmy had a nonstop grin on his face from the moment we left Bakersfield.

"Ahead on your right," I say, pointing as the Sequoia Shopping Center comes into view.

Jimmy slows and then slows some more.

There's no traffic behind us, which is fortunate because we're soon doing barely five miles an hour as Jimmy stares ahead at our destination. A mix of disgust and disappointment is on his face, and his eyes dart frantically about, no doubt searching for a Starbucks—though I suspect that any coffee shop will do at this point.

When at last he turns into the parking lot, he comes to a complete stop, blocking the entrance, and just stares at the long building stretched out before us. Most of the shopping center seems to be composed of the Sequoia Market, with a gas station just to the north.

"Not much of a shopping center," Jimmy mutters.

"Maybe it's seasonal."

Releasing the brake, he pulls ahead and noses into a parking space facing Sierra Way. Shifting into neutral and applying the emergency brake, Jimmy lets the Mustang idle for a minute before finally shutting it down. He leaves the radio on, playing low in the background. I don't recognize the song, but it has a nice beat.

Checking his watch and seeing that we have time to spare, he opens the door and steps out. "I'm going to see if they at least have coffee," he says, thumbing at the market. "Want anything?"

When I shake my head, he just nods and hurries off in search of caffeine.

Five minutes later he's back with a twenty-ounce cup of bitter black and a decidedly better disposition. "You should go in and check the place out. Not bad for the middle of nowhere."

"Well, *middle of nowhere* is a bit of a stretch. It's not like we're in the middle of the Olympic Peninsula or Montana." As if to make my point, I gesture to the surrounding hills. "Check out the landscape. There's no way four guys go missing on those hills. They'd have to be either stoned or as dumb as the rocks they're walking over."

The satellite imagery we'd studied back at Hangar 7 suggested as much, but now, seeing it with my own eyes, I have a sudden sinking feeling deep in my gut. It's been two weeks since I've had to look down at a dead body. I'd prefer that the trend continue.

Jimmy takes a moment to glance at the hills to the east and west as he sips gingerly at the hot coffee. The peaks are barren and rocky, some of them as bald as Jean-Luc Picard's head on shaving day.

The longer we sit, the more time the caffeine in Jimmy's coffee has time to work through his system, eventually making it to his brain. You can almost see the moment of its arrival because he begins to glance around with renewed purpose, his eyes suddenly coordinating with his brain as the latter calculates the odds and probabilities of a simple search and rescue.

When he finally looks at me, his eyebrows are knit. "Doesn't seem to fit, does it? Too many landmarks and observation points for someone to get lost. Even if you got turned around and found yourself ten miles from where you started, it wouldn't take much to figure out what direction to go."

"Not like back home."

He shakes his head. "What's the name of our contact?"

"Sergeant Joe"—I pick up the packet Diane dutifully prepared and rifle through it quickly—"Mingo," I finish a moment later. "Joe Mingo. Says here that he's the SAR coordinator for the Tulare County Sheriff's Office." I glance at Jimmy. "I thought Diane said this was going to be a Kern County operation?"

"It's kind of a multijurisdictional thing. We're in Kern County right now, but a half mile north, the Sequoia National Forest begins, and about a mile and a half beyond that is the county line. Seems our missing gents were camped up the river quite a bit farther. For now, the Tulare County Sheriff's Office is handling the search and rescue."

I nod my understanding. "Let's hope it doesn't get any more complicated than that." Glancing at my black Movado, I note the time. "Mingo should be here any minute."

Waiting is always worse when things are most urgent.

When the sergeant finally arrives a half hour later, he's behind the wheel of a thundering white military Humvee with Tulare County Sheriff's Office markings on the side and a light bar overhead. Pulling up to the Mustang in a cloud of dust and exhaust, he jumps out almost before the rig comes to a stop and comes around the front to greet us.

"Sorry to keep you waiting." He pumps Jimmy's hand, then mine. "One of the teams found something down by the river. I'm guessing it's just fish blood, but it took us a while to get it sorted out." Gesturing toward the Hummer, he says, "You guys wanna ride with me or follow in your car?"

"Oh, we'll ride with you," I reply before Jimmy has a chance to say anything. I've never ridden in a Hummer, and I'm getting windburn from the convertible.

Just north of Kernville, we enter the Sequoia National Forest, which seems a misnomer because forests generally require trees. The only trees I see are at the base of the hills, and most of those are scraggly-looking things next to the river.

It's not out of some Pacific Northwest snobbery that I make this observation. Yes, our forests are thick with towering green titans, and they tend to be expansive, the kind of place where you can get lost for real and never found. Mount Baker–Snoqualmie National Forest, which is our backyard, is almost 2 million acres. By comparison, these bare hills are, well, they're not a forest.

I loathe forests.

Not that I have anything against individual trees; as long as they mind their business, I'll mind mine. It's just that I suffer from something called hylophobia, which is an unreasonable fear of forests. It's the result of trauma from my youth, the same incident that gave me the ability to see shine when I was eight. I guess that's what happens when you get lost in a *real* forest only to be overtaken by a wicked-cold blizzard that freezes the life out of your tiny body.

That we're driving through Sequoia National Forest and I'm perfectly at ease in the rear passenger seat of the Humvee is proof positive that this is not a forest.

"The camp is another five miles," Joe explains as he brings us up to speed on the search. "Or at least what we think was the camp. It's a spot they've used frequently, and the congressman's sister seems to think it's the right place. They all came together in the same SUV, but damned if we can find it. We've checked all the pull-offs, the trailheads, even the remote camping sites. It's just gone; same with all their gear. It's like they packed up to go home and just never arrived."

"Only they weren't scheduled to go home yet," Jimmy observes.

"Exactly. And the sister insists that it would have taken a national emergency to get them to quit their trip early, and even if they had, they would have called home." Joe downshifts into a corner. "We pinged his phone a few hours ago with no luck, so the battery is either dead or it's turned off. The last tower hit was Friday evening and suggests the phone was likely in the campsite or parking lot."

Joe downshifts again as an ungainly RV lumbers onto the road just ahead, accelerating with all the speed and grace of an oil tanker.

"So, whatever we're dealing with, it probably started either Friday night or Saturday morning," I surmise. "Are there any caves or old mines—maybe a ghost town? Someplace they might have wanted to explore that didn't involve fishing?"

"There are a handful of places within a thirty-mile radius, but they've already been checked by either deputies or SAR members." Joe shakes his head. "I can understand losing four men, but an SUV?"

Jimmy studies him from the passenger seat. "How long have you been the SAR coordinator?"

"Seven years."

"And how many people have gotten lost in these hills during that time?"

Joe glances over. "Along the Upper Kern . . . ?" He thinks a moment, then shakes his head. "I can't think of a single one. We get reports of lost people regularly, but most of those are drowning victims. In some areas you've got to watch for rockslides; those can break bones or kill you quickly, but most are smart enough to either stay clear or stick to the established paths. All you have to do is look at the side of some of these hills and you can tell which ones are dangerous."

"Is there any evidence of a recent slide near the campground?" I ask.

"None—and if there had been, we would have heard about it."

"So," Jimmy muses, "we're back to four men missing in an area where they couldn't possibly be missing."

"Just our kind of show," I mutter to myself.

When Joe turns off the road minutes later, we find ourselves wheeling through a patch of dust and dirt tucked alongside the silver-hued river. The area is hemmed in by a string of large boulders that seem to assign boundaries on three sides. Vehicles are scattered about, which suggests the place is a parking lot, though, as far as parking lots go, this one looks like it landed here by accident. Like the god of structures and byways was reaching into his pocket while stepping across the mountain peaks and accidentally dropped a dusty parking lot without noticing.

It happens.

I do it all the time with loose change and pocket lint.

A single porta potty and a large green dumpster occupy the center of the lot, while the right corner—the northwest corner—is occupied by a large RV marked TULARE COUNTY COMMAND VEHICLE. Eighteen or twenty private vehicles are clustered around the RV, most of them displaying a Search and Rescue sticker in the rear window. Several have colorful bumper stickers with the words THAT OTHERS MAY LIVE emblazoned across them; a common motto for SAR units.

The Special Tracking Unit also has a motto: *We save the ones we can*. Not quite as optimistic as the SAR motto, and not available on bumper stickers, but it'll do.

Parking the Humvee alongside the command vehicle, Joe shuts it down and then points to the north. "We think they camped next to the river about a hundred yards up the path. After a cursory search first thing this morning, we did a sound-sweep search, and then around ten o'clock, we started a more systematic grid search using four teams of six each. That's two teams on each side of the river heading away from each other."

Removing my special glasses, I place them carefully in their case, then Jimmy and I follow Joe's lead as he exits the Humvee. We start across the parking lot without a word. As Joe steps through the Maginot Line of boulders containing the parking lot, he glances back and with a sweep of his head says, "The camp is this way."

A well-trodden path lies before us, ripe with shine of every hue and color. It snakes off to the north, mimicking the nearby river in its motions.

It's here that I pause.

Glancing back at the parking lot, I take in the army of footprints stacked one upon the other as they crisscross, mix, and cover every inch of the packed earth. Any hope of ferreting out the specific shine of the four missing men seems beyond reach. With no car, no tents, no sleeping bags—not even a firm idea where they pitched their tents or fished the river, all we're left with are assumptions and the vagaries of happenstance.

Sergeant Joe Mingo waits patiently as I take everything in. He, better than most, understands the importance of getting the lay of the land.

"Do a lot of people fish the river?" I ask.

"This time of the year it's pretty quiet, but, yeah, it's a popular place. And not just for fishing. There's rafting, swimming, hiking, horseback riding, even panning for gold, if that's your thing. The hottest days of summer are the most popular. Air-conditioning may be a blessing, but there's nothing like being in the shade of a tree next to a river when the temperature grows unbearable."

"Amen," Jimmy says.

*I'll take the air-conditioning,* I think, then ask, "How long until your teams are done with the grid search?"

"Shouldn't take long." Joe sweeps an arm at the scrabble of trees and low brush. "The vegetation is tame enough that we can space our searchers out as they walk the grid. In areas like this, we can put them forty feet apart. A good stretch of the Kern follows a narrow valley between the hills; most of it is barely three hundred feet from the base of one hill to the base of the other hill, and that includes the river and the road."

"Where are your teams now?" Jimmy asks.

"Two or three miles north and south of us. We passed the southbound teams on the way in." He grins. "You didn't see them, did you?" Before we can answer, he says, "I probably wouldn't have noticed them either, if I hadn't known what to look for. They were in an area where the valley widens considerably. Vegetation is still relatively sparse, especially compared to what you're used to up north, but there's still enough brush to hide someone."

"Including our missing men?" Jimmy suggests.

Joe nods. "Including them."

"If you're two miles into the search," I ask, "how much farther do you intend to go?"

"Five miles in each direction. I can't imagine them going that far, but you never know. If that doesn't do it, we're expecting a helicopter with FLIR this afternoon."

"And the SUV that's missing, it belonged to the congressman?"

"Yeah, a 2015 BMW X5. The DMV database doesn't list the color, but his sister said it's a bright midrange metallic blue—Long Beach Blue. She said it really pops."

The *really pops* part of his statement digs at me and sets me to wondering why we can't find a bright blue SUV among the abundant tans and sparse greens that constitute the Sequoia National Forest. There are only so many side roads they could have traveled.

More ominously, where are the men that came in that vehicle? How could they have disappeared in an area with one road in and one road out? And not just disappeared but vanished utterly and completely. I feel my stomach pitch at the thought, and a sudden rush of fear washes over me. Not fear for myself, but fear for Marco Perez, Wade Winchell, Jason Norris, and Noah Long.

Fear for what might come.

"This is a disaster," I whisper to Jimmy after just a few minutes.

He nods his understanding.

The Upper Kern appears to harbor as many former campsites as it does gnats, and they tend to cluster together in the same manner. The ground is a kaleidoscope of shine, crossing and recrossing and trailing off into all 360 degrees of the compass. Most tracks appear to be more recent—less than a year old. The soil here goes to dust in the dry season, and dust tends to shift and move, dismantling shine and scattering it to oblivion.

The oldest tracks are buried under layers of newer shine and survive because they've attached themselves to the more resilient sedimentary rocks and granite that give structure to the valley and its mountains. These tracks are decades old, perhaps centuries.

They won't last forever, though.

I've found that with rock, cement, and other hard surfaces, shine penetrates about a half inch. It takes a long time for wind and rain to erode a half inch of stone, but if I've learned one thing in my short years, it's that there are two unstoppable forces in the world: time and decay.

Among the new tracks scattered about are the shine of fifty or so park rangers, deputies, and search and rescue personnel who have flocked to the area since last night. Had I arrived before them, I may have had a shot at identifying the tracks of Marco Perez and his companions. I might have been able to follow those tracks and perhaps gain insight into the odd disappearance of the four men, but it's not to be. The area is a jumble of color that even I can't sort through.

Almost all of the prints I see pulse gently with life's energy, but a few lie flat and still, marking those who no longer walk the earth. I notice that the dead shine is mostly among the older prints, giving me hope that the congressman and his comrades are still alive.

Turning to our guide, Jimmy asks, "What about that blood you mentioned?"

Joe Mingo nods and points to a spot downstream. "I'll show you."

Jimmy and I have some well-established protocols, one of which involves distraction. As he falls in behind the sergeant and follows him to the river's edge, I get to work—doing what the director calls my *thing*. This mostly involves studying the ground, vegetation, and any physical evidence left behind. To an observer, it would look like what one would expect of a man-tracker, but not always.

That's when misdirection is sometimes required.

Jimmy's good at keeping the locals busy while I hunt for shine, and as the two of them walk away, I hear him ask Joe how long he's been at the sheriff's office. Other questions will follow, and my gregarious partner will learn that the sergeant has a wife, Carol, and two strapping boys. They own a nice home with a pool just outside the Bakersfield city limits, a place they bought cheap after the bottom fell out of the housing market in 2008—a financial move that Joe seems particularly proud of, though *cheap* in California seems a relative term.

When Jimmy relays all this to me later, he seems most impressed that Joe was an Eagle Scout, and that he competed in three Spartan Races—once qualifying for the regional championship.

When I ask what a Spartan Race is, Jimmy just rolls his eyes and walks away.

He's sensitive that way.

As I continue my search and find nothing, my thoughts turn dark, to the more sinister explanations for such a disappearance. An accident seems unlikely, only because the odds that all four men were incapacitated and rendered incapable of seeking help at the same time and by the same means seems remote.

They may have skidded off a road, been caught up in a landslide, or had a spelunking mishap. They may even have gone swimming after dinner without waiting the required half hour, resulting in the disaster our mothers always warned us about.

All of these are possibilities, I suppose, but then where are their tents and sleeping bags? Where'd they put the outdoor stove and the large skillet for cooking up bacon and eggs at first light? And what about their fishing poles and tackle boxes? These were wealthy and powerful men devoted to fishing. A $500 pole and a $700 reel would be expected, along with at least one backup pole and reel.

I'm no outdoorsman, but I do know you don't go camping without a cooler filled with melting ice and an assortment of sodas and beer. I don't see such a cooler. Nor do I see marks on the ground where a cooler was placed.

For all the evidence I *don't* see, a UFO may as well have flown in from nearby Area 51 and spirited them away in their sleep—tents and all. Which would mean they also stole the BMW.

"Where are you?" I mutter to the desert wind, but the wind has no answer.

When I join Jimmy at the river, he leads me to an apple-sized patch of blood on a rock near the water's edge. Like everything else in my macabre world, the decay of spilled blood is something that can be measured and analyzed. It's not a perfect science, and variables like the thickness of the blood pool and environmental conditions come into play.

But the process is always the same.

Once hemoglobin—blood—is exposed to oxygen, it becomes oxyhemoglobin and displays the bright red we're all familiar with from the many times we've cut, scraped, and punctured ourselves since childhood. The oxyhemoglobin is short-lived and converts to the darker red of methemoglobin within a few hours. This, in turn, fades to the dark brown of hemichrome, usually within forty-eight hours.

In reflectance spectroscopy, white light is directed at a blood sample, and the amount of absorption and reflection is measured to create a reflection spectrum. This spectrum identifies the amount of oxyhemoglobin, methemoglobin, and hemichrome in the sample and helps establish its age.

This process is often combined with spectral imaging to aid in detecting and identifying bloodstains at a crime scene.

"What do you figure," I say to Jimmy after kneeling to examine the stain, "twenty-four hours?"

He nods. "No more than forty-eight."

"That puts it within the window of the disappearance."

"It does." He glances over at Joe, who's twenty feet away, conferring with one of the SAR team leaders over the radio. "Is it human?" Jimmy asks in a low voice that's close to a whisper.

It's my turn to nod. "The shine looks like pewter."

Animals don't have shine.

Or maybe they do, but I can't see it. Regardless, the revelation tells Jimmy what he needs to know. He thinks on this for a moment but doesn't seem overly concerned. "There are a lot of ways to cut yourself with fishing gear," he eventually says. "Kind of goes with the territory."

"Right, but this is more than a scrape or a fingertip poke from a hook," I say, indicating the small pool.

"I know, I'm just saying let's not get ahead of ourselves."

"I'm not," I say firmly, "but you tell me how any of this makes sense? Marco's sister said that this was the spot he called from on Friday. So, where is he? Where's his car, his gear, his sleeping bag?"

"They must have moved camp."

"Not without telling his sister."

Our discussion hasn't carried us any closer to a conclusion by the time Sergeant Joe Mingo returns with a sour look on his face.

"Any news?" Jimmy asks.

The sergeant gives a defeated shake of his head. "I thought they'd have found the car by now . . . or at least some campers who remembered seeing the men. The river's just . . . quiet." He stares off at the silver ribbon of water as if somewhere upstream might lie the answers we seek.

"Any theories?" I ask.

Joe shakes his head, then stoops to pick up a flat rock from the bank of the river. Weighing it in his hand, as if it were a thought rather than a stone, he reels back and flings it across the surface of the water, skipping it twice before the unsteady surface grabs it and drags it down. "The only theory I have is that we're searching in the wrong place."

"You think the sister misunderstood where they were camping?"

Joe shrugs. "She seemed pretty sure of it, but"—he holds his arms wide and twists to the left and right—"here we are."

Jimmy opens his mouth to reply, perhaps to provide a theory, or simply offer up the hope that we all seem to be missing, but before he can speak, his phone rings.

It's Diane.

I know this because Jimmy has separate ringtones for everyone. He's organized and dysfunctional that way. Diane's calls always arrive with the theme from *The Pink Panther*, which now blares from the speaker.

He presses the phone to his ear. "Hi, Diane. What's up?"

As he listens intently, I notice his body stiffen slightly and his face transitions through a dozen expressions, as if unsure which one to wear. "On a bench?" he mutters. "What about the others?"

He nods to the phone, pauses, then nods again. As sophisticated as the iPhone is, I'm pretty sure it can't translate his body movements into English and transmit it back to Diane's ear a thousand miles away in Hangar 7.

Motioning for a pen and paper, he quickly jots down what looks like an address, then says, "Let them know we're on our way."

He ends the call and slides the phone back into his pocket, muttering a curse under his breath. The profanity, though mild, is startling coming from his mouth, and I suddenly fear what has yet to be spoken.

"Bad news?" I ask.

Glancing around at the parking lot, then at the hills rising before us, he shakes his head in a defeated, confused manner. "We need to get back to Bakersfield." Before I can ask the obvious, he turns to Joe. "Can you run us back to our car?"

"Sure," the sergeant replies, a bit confused himself. "Let me stick my head into the command vehicle and let them know where I'll be." He points across the parking lot with his chin. "I'll meet you at the Hummer."

A minute later, we're rolling south toward Kernville, and Jimmy still hasn't hinted at the content of the call, or the urgency for our return to Bakersfield. I'm giving him his space because I know how he is when he's got something to chew on, but as the miles and minutes tick by and the Sequoia Market draws near, my patience finally wears thin.

It's clear from his posture and movement that Joe is just as interested in the answer as I am. The sergeant hasn't said a word since leaving the parking lot, but his eyes keep wandering toward Jimmy, either watching him in his peripheral vision or by way of glances meant to be noticed.

The effort's wasted. Jimmy notices nothing.

I've been his partner for just over six years, so I know that he gets this way from time to time. What concerns me is that it usually happens right around the time someone pulls the carpet out from under our feet. That this reflective silence follows his outburst of quiet profanity is like the punch that follows the jab: the two together spell trouble.

"What's in Bakersfield, Jimmy?" My tone is meant to remind him that this is the Jimmy and Steps show, and not some solo act where he can just tune out and keep the facts of the case to himself.

When his answer comes, there's an edge to the words. "They found Jason Norris."

*Found.*

The word is so specific in its meaning, so straightforward and honest. Lost keys can be found, love can be found, loose change can be found.

A person . . . can be found.

Yet as soon as the words are out of Jimmy's mouth, I know that our simple search and rescue just became much more complex.

"Alive?" I ask.

Stiffening in his seat, Jimmy glances back at me and shakes his head. "He was found on a park bench. He'd been sitting there since sometime last night."

"Cause of death?"

"Unknown. We're heading to the coroner's office. They're waiting until we get there to start the autopsy."

*That's nice of them,* I think, trying to remember what I had for breakfast and wondering if I'll see it again.

# 5

Over the years, I've found that the offices of most coroners and medical examiners are located at or near a hospital. This makes sense, since, in a lot of cases, the subject may have been transported to the hospital before expiring. That, and I imagine it's considered poor taste to wheel a cloth-draped body through the parking lot of a strip mall while mom, dad, and junior are picking up a family-sized pepperoni pizza from Little Caesars.

In Kern County, this observed pattern repeats, and we find the coroner's office located on College Avenue, right behind Kern Medical Center.

As for the coroner, it seems that in addition to his duties as the chief law enforcement official in the county, or CLEO, the elected sheriff also serves as both coroner and public administrator. This means that if you die, his deputy coroners and forensic pathologists will try to figure out why, and if you died without a will or executor, his public administration people will figure out what to do with your estate.

It's a full-service operation.

"Special Agent James Donovan," Jimmy says, flashing his credentials at the woman perched behind the elevated reception desk. According to the standard-issue government nameplate at the edge of the desk, her name is Lori and she's a Pisces. I don't know for *certain* that she's a Pisces, but she has stickers of various fish stuck around her etched name.

"We have an appointment with Dr. Herrera," Jimmy explains.

"What time is your appointment?"

"Now."

"You have an appointment for four thirty-nine P.M.?" she asks skeptically.

"Yes," Jimmy replies slowly.

She raises her eyebrows at that and picks up the phone. Punching a single button, she waits a moment, then passes Jimmy's name to the person on the other end, along with his dubious claim to have an appointment.

"Okay," she says into the mouthpiece a moment later, sounding a bit deflated. Hanging up the phone, she forces a smile. "He'll be with you shortly."

When Dr. Benjamin Herrera makes his entrance two minutes later, he's wiping his hands dry on a paper towel, which he then wads up and swooshes into the garbage can near the door, a solid ten-foot shot. He's at least six-two, and between his height and the Harlem Globetrotters–style dunk, it's not hard to imagine that he's a pretty good basketball player.

As we take turns shaking hands, he says, "Call me Ben." His palm is still sticky-moist, and I wipe the transfer off discretely on my pants, hoping that it's just from washing up, and not from something autopsy related.

"This way," Ben says cheerily, holding the door open.

We follow him down the main corridor, then to the right, and finally left into a large sterile autopsy room accented in copious amounts of stainless steel. It's well lit and contains three workstations, each outfitted identically with a long stainless-steel sink, additional stainless countertops and cupboards, and an autopsy table mounted to the floor.

Each table is identical and state-of-the-art.

The stainless-steel tabletops have an array of small holes lining the outer edges on all four sides, which, when activated, provide downdraft ventilation—basically a vacuum system that sucks up all the bad odors and pipes them away from the work space to someplace where they can be filtered and released back into the environment.

It's a godsend when a body has been percolating too long.

A narrow hose extends from the underside of the table, which is attached to a handheld sprayer used to wash away contaminants during the autopsy. The table itself is mounted onto a thick anti-wobble pedestal that allows the attending pathologist to raise, lower, and rotate the table as needed.

Two of the three workstations are empty, but the third, the one nearest the door, hints at recent activity. And when I say *hints,* I mean an adult figure is lying on the table. I can't make out his features because he's completely covered in a thick white cloth, but it doesn't take much puzzle-piecing to figure out whom we're looking at.

I stop just inside the door. "Jason Norris, I presume."

"Yes, so it would seem," Ben replies slowly—then his demeanor changes and he steps off toward the table with brisk strides filled with energy and purpose. "It seems that we have a bit of a problem with Mr. Norris, one that I'm afraid we didn't clue into until just before your arrival."

"What kind of problem?"

"Well, it seems he's dead."

Jimmy and I both smile politely at the lame joke—until we realize Ben's not kidding.

"It seems this poor stiff died last week and was buried on Saturday." Ben steps to the head of the table and grasps the corner of the white sheet as if preparing for some grand reveal like they do on the reality shows. "There's more, I'm afraid, but I think it best for you to *see* the next part. It's so much more telling, a picture being worth a thousand words, and all that."

With a smooth, practiced flow, he folds the sheet back, exposing the body of an older male from the waist up.

The room sinks into utter quiet . . . then both Jimmy and I begin a frantic and noisy scramble through our various notes on the case, looking for the physical description and photo of Jason Norris, the info that Diane so diligently provided before we departed Hangar 7.

I find mine first and thrust the image in front of Jimmy. He takes it in hand and studies the picture, glances briefly at the body, then back at the paper.

"He's white," I observe.

Ben grins. "I know, right! It's my first autopsy where a Black man turned white. I mean, you hear about people's hair turning white after a good scare, but this is some next-level metamorphosis."

A well-refined sense of gallows humor is always something to be admired, but I can barely return his grin before something else occurs to me. It occurs to Jimmy at the same moment because he blurts, "This guy is old—at least thirty years older than Norris."

"This is Mr. William Johansson, a longtime native of Bakersfield and an avid gardener, particularly when it comes to plants of the cannabis variety." Ben points to the stitching on the chest. "This well-executed *Y* incision is from his *last* autopsy, performed by my colleague just six days ago in this very room."

Stepping back from the table, Ben pauses, as if to contemplate the corpse. "When he died—the first time—detectives initially suspected foul play because Mr. Johansson was found stuffed headfirst into an open-topped fifty-five-gallon drum filled with some variety of *fertilizing* tea—whatever that is.

"The deputy coroner assigned to the investigation determined that poor William was reaching into the barrel, possibly to unclog the back side of the external faucet, when he somehow slipped and managed to kick over his step stool. He went into the barrel headfirst and went deep enough that he couldn't reach a hand up and grasp the edge of the barrel.

"A thinking man who wasn't addled by use of his own product might have thought to push off from the bottom of the barrel, but not William. Instead, he bobbed around a bit in the water, kicking and thrashing, and finally expired. His *business partner*"—Ben frames the words in air quotes—"found him the next afternoon, half-waterlogged and fully dead. Case closed."

"I guess that's one way to go," I mutter.

"Oh, with the amount of THC in his system, he probably barely noticed. We should all be so lucky."

Jimmy's fingers begin to strum against the cold steel of the autopsy table—never a good sign. "So, where's Jason Norris?" he asks, trying to hide his growing frustration.

"That I can't answer," Ben replies. "I'm guessing Johansson was misidentified because Norris's wallet was found in his pocket. He was also wearing Norris's watch on his wrist; some fancy thing with a personalized inscription to Norris on the back. I'm guessing they were stolen from the real Norris, but you'd know that better than me."

"How?" Jimmy asks, directing the question at himself as much as to Ben. The word is both a challenge and a plea. "Jason Norris is from San Jose. He met his friends at the airport on Thursday, and they headed straight to their campsite on the Upper Kern. There was no report of a crime, nor was there opportunity."

"Maybe they were stolen from the campsite . . . or the vehicle?" I suggest.

Jimmy's not buying it. "A guy like Jason Norris doesn't leave his wallet lying around unattended. I guarantee he took it to the river with him; probably had it sealed in a Ziploc bag just in case he fell in."

"So how did his wallet end up in the pocket of a guy who was dead and buried last week? And the watch . . . ?" A sudden grimace of disgust clouds my face. "What kind of sick bastard digs up a corpse and puts him on display on a park bench?"

Ben nods his understanding. "I don't know if this part matters, but he wasn't exactly dressed for burial. He had on a pair of jeans that were too short by about three inches, a T-shirt, and a fishing vest—one of those with all the pockets. He also had on a ball cap with the logo from some accounting firm. It's all in his personal effects if you want to take a look."

Jimmy glances at me and in an incredulous voice says, "He was wearing Norris's clothes."

"I wouldn't necessarily jump to that conclusion," Ben replies quickly, holding up a cautioning hand as if to slow down the thought train before it jumps the track. "Some people just have odd requests when it comes to how they want to be buried. Maybe Johansson was a fisherman; maybe that's what he envisioned himself doing in the afterlife. You never know."

Snapping his fingers, Ben says, "There was this lady a couple of years ago who insisted on being buried dressed as Dorothy from *The Wizard of Oz*. She even had a pair of custom-made ruby slippers, if you can believe that."

Jimmy asks, "Did anyone check Johansson's grave?"

"Why?"

Pointing at the corpse, Jimmy says, "He's not in it."

Ben grins as if it were a joke and shakes his head.

"As I said, we only figured this out shortly before you arrived. Last time we saw this guy was earlier in the week when we released his body back to the funeral home. I couldn't tell you where they buried him."

"But the funeral home would have picked him up after the autopsy, right?"

"Sure."

"And you have the name and address of the funeral home in your records?"

"Yeah, we track everything. The public tends to get upset when we misplace a body."

The irony is too rich for Jimmy. He looks Ben in the eye and then slowly casts a downward glance at the remains of William Johansson.

Ben smirks and shakes his head. "Uh-uh. This one's not on us. We passed him off to the funeral home; whatever happened after that is on them."

"I guess I better talk to them, then," Jimmy says. "How about that name and address?"

"Sure," the pathologist replies. "Let's check with the receptionist." He motions for us to follow and leads the way from the autopsy room.

As we exit, I cast a final backward glance at William Johansson, the old man who somehow managed to stir up a storm of trouble, even in death. He doesn't look back, but I swear there's a smile on his face.

# 6

Riggs Funeral Home is quick to insist that they buried William Johansson in Greenmont Cemetery, a relatively small and isolated graveyard several miles southwest of the Bakersfield city limits.

Ralph Riggs, the owner and chief body-slinger at the funeral home, is sure that we must be mistaken about the corpse at the coroner's office. He's sure that the recently deceased don't just crawl out of their fresh graves, and he's damn sure they don't walk their dead ass to town and park themselves on a city bench.

He's sure of a lot.

"So, you're a hundred percent certain that William Johansson was in that casket when it went into the ground?" Jimmy presses.

"Certain as I'm standing here." Ralph spreads his arms as if to emphasize his presence.

There's an air about the guy that I can't quite peg. He dresses like a banker, talks like a preacher, and presents like a salesman. My image of an undertaker has always strayed toward that depicted in westerns: some lanky plainsman in a dark wool frock coat and some version of a black felt hat. Ralph doesn't fit the image.

"Can you describe Mr. Johansson?" Jimmy asks.

Ralph thinks a moment, eyes drifting up.

"White gentleman in his seventies, bald head, maybe six foot tall, though it's hard to be certain." Ralph winks. "By the time we get them, they're usually horizontal"—he waves his open hand back and forth in a flat line—"if you get my meaning."

"And you saw him in the coffin?"

"I did. His son wanted him buried in a sky-blue tuxedo, which is something we don't get a lot of requests for. Navy blue, black pinstripe, even jeans and a T-shirt, but not sky blue." Ralph rocks his head from side to side with one corner of his mouth pinched up. "That shade in particular. It's kind of hopeful, like robin eggs in the spring, and I find that people aren't generally that optimistic at a funeral."

"Imagine that," I say.

He grins and shrugs. "I know; go figure. In any case, it was an open-casket ceremony and we didn't close the lid until right before we loaded him into the hearse. After that, two of my guys were with him until he was lowered into the ground."

"Did they stay until the grave was closed?" Jimmy asks.

"No need. By the time they get around to putting the dirt back in the hole, the mourners are almost always gone. Besides, our job is to deliver the deceased; the cemetery handles the rest. Grave digging is no longer about backs and shovels, gentlemen. These days it's about backhoes."

Somehow backs and shovels sound more respectful.

Greenmont Cemetery is maybe ten minutes outside Bakersfield, and Jimmy wants to swing by and make sure nothing's out of place. As a courtesy, he calls Diane and asks her to locate a cemetery official and advise him of our visit.

Ending the call, Jimmy drives in silence for several minutes, but I notice he keeps checking his watch, despite the clock on the dash. Soon, he's drumming his fingers on the steering wheel, a neurotic tic of his that surfaces when he's either nervous, thinking, or antsy.

"What's going on with you?" I finally ask.

"What?" He acts like he doesn't know what I'm talking about.

"No." I wag a finger at him. "*I* said what? You don't get to answer a what with a what." His fingers start up again on the steering wheel—*da da da dum, da da da dum*—so I point at them and exclaim, "See! That's what I'm talking about. That, and you've checked your watch six times in six minutes."

"It's nothing."

"Really." I raise my eyebrows. "Look, I know it's been a long day, but you need to either stop checking your watch and lay off the drumming, or you need to level with your partner." I draw out the word *partner,* to drive home the point.

The drumming stops and he's quiet for a full minute. Then, with a sigh, he asks, "What do you think we're going to find at the cemetery?"

I shrug. "Lots of graves . . . hopefully closed."

"But you already know that William Johansson—"

"There might be an explanation," I interrupt, not wanting to hear it.

"A man, dead and buried, shows up on a city bench. That in itself is unusual, but how do you explain the fact that he's wearing Jason Norris's clothes and has his wallet—the very man we've been searching for, I might add; the man who's *still* missing, along with three of his friends. That's a little too much *coincidence,* don't you think?"

He's right, of course. I just don't want to admit it.

"You know why I'm in a hurry?" Jimmy's suddenly all talkative. "Because I'm afraid of what we might find."

"If someone dug up that grave, it would have been reported by now."

"Not necessarily," Jimmy shoots backs. "You heard Riggs.

The place is isolated. Maybe it's the kind of place people don't visit often. And if they do, maybe they'll see a pile of dirt and just assume it's for an upcoming funeral."

I want to argue with him but can't. The one thing I learned about Jimmy a long time ago is that when he's got something on his mind, it's best to just let things play out.

Greenmont Cemetery reveals itself as a flat, uninspiring rectangular oasis of neutered green, something akin to the color of watered-down guacamole. The lawn is well tended but looks anything but robust. Any virility the grass once held has long since passed, much like the residents of this out-of-the-way spot. The headstones are flush with the ground, and the only structure on the property is a diminutive toolshed.

Following the directions provided by Ralph Riggs, we park at the back and find William Johansson's grave a short walk off the narrow road that dissects the cemetery in half. From all appearances, it seems to be undisturbed. There's no marker, but we have little doubt it's the correct plot because it's the only grave in the small cemetery with rectangles of freshly cut turf resting over recently turned soil.

The flowers are another giveaway, though not by much. A small wreath of red and yellow roses, carnations, and chrysanthemums is on a wire stand resting solemnly at the head of the unmarked grave. It looks like the type of generic wreath equally suited to funerals or weddings and was most likely the weekly special at a discount florist. Gathered around it are a half dozen other arrangements, and several individual flowers.

"Looks like a grave," I observe dryly.

Jimmy seems more at ease, as if the sight of the intact grave has settled something in his gut, but rather than replying directly to my observation, he makes this weird noise at the back of his throat that falls somewhere between *hmm* and *harrumph*.

"So maybe it's a hoax after all?" I say, pressing the point. "Maybe someone snatched Johansson's body in transit and sat him on the bench as some kind of elaborate prank. Probably filmed it too. It's stupid what people will do for YouTube clicks these days."

I snap my fingers as another thought occurs to me. "What if it's a competitor? You know, someone trying to undermine the funeral home?"

Jimmy laughs and gives me a look. "Not everything is a reality show."

I shrug. "Just a thought."

Jimmy doesn't reply but instead begins a slow walk around the gravesite as daylight begins to fail. I can see his eyes roaming over the replaced turf, examining every cut and gap. He does the same with the flower arrangements and the spot where a headstone will soon rest.

"It still doesn't explain why Johansson was wearing Norris's clothes—" He suddenly stops and cocks his head to the side. He's not looking at the fresh grave, but at the marker two spaces over. Moving closer, he kneels and brushes his hand across the bronze face of the gravestone, which identifies the interred as another Johansson, no doubt a relative.

Glancing at the grass around the marker for a moment, he rolls back onto his haunches and shuffles backward, taking in a wider view of the area. Seconds tick by in utter silence, each one seeming to be an eternity unto itself. He barely moves, and I can tell he's trying to make sense of whatever he's seeing. It's a bit unsettling watching him, mostly because when he's done this sort of thing in the past, it hasn't ended well.

When the truth finally finds him, it rocks his world like thunder before a storm.

With a roar, he leaps to his feet.

The sound and commotion are so startling that I give an involuntary yelp and stumble over my own feet, nearly falling backward onto Johansson's grave. I don't have time to think or analyze because Jimmy's running away from me at a frightening clip, making a beeline for the Mustang.

I have rules about cemeteries.

Well . . . *now* I have rules about cemeteries. I may have just made them up, but they still apply. The main rule, the most important rule, is that if someone starts to run, you follow. You don't pause to assess the situation; you don't worry about looking silly or scared, you just run. At a minimum, you need to run as fast as the person you're following; that way you don't get left behind. Getting left behind is bad.

If you can run faster, that's even better.

I've seen some odd things that I can't explain during my time with the Special Tracking Unit, things revealed by shine that convince me there's something beyond death. This should be comforting news, and it usually is, but not when I'm standing in a graveyard on the cusp of night.

As we near the yellow Ford, I expect Jimmy to slow and fumble for his keys, but instead he runs right past the car. Confused, I follow and watch as Jimmy slams full force into the latched door of the lone toolshed.

The flimsy door explodes inward, carrying him with it.

I arrive a moment later to the sound of tools being tossed around, then Jimmy appears in the doorway with two shovels in hand. He shoves one in my direction and starts back toward the grave at a half run without a single word of explanation.

I can't take it anymore.

When we reach the grave site, I bark, "Jimmy!"

But he just squats and starts frantically ripping loose clumps of turf from the top of Johansson's grave, tossing them to the side. I raise my voice an octave and demand, "What are you doing?"

"Help me!" He doesn't look up. "Get this turf off so we can dig."

"Uh-uh!" I snap. "It's illegal, and that cemetery official is on his way. If he finds you digging—"

Jimmy drops the shovel with a suddenness that's shocking. Motioning for me to follow, he directs me to the nearby gravestone that so captivated him just before he ran off to the shed. "See that?" He points.

I have no idea what he's talking about and say as much.

"Look at the dirt," he replies in frustration. "When the backhoe dug Johansson's grave for the ceremony, they dumped the dirt on a tarp over there." He points to a spot on the opposite side of the burial site, well away from where we stand. "I know they dumped it over there because you can still see the impression where they laid down the tarp."

He points to the ground, adamant. "There shouldn't be any dirt here."

"I still don't—"

"It means the grave was dug up sometime after the ceremony. Whoever dug it up also used a tarp or some type of plastic sheeting, but unlike the cemetery workers they got sloppy and some of the dirt ended up spilling off the edge."

I've been to my share of funerals, so I know that a covering is placed over the ground where the attendees are seated. This is done for ambience, but also to cover the graves in that area so they can't be seen. People don't like walking on graves. Call it taboo, or superstition, but it's just not something one does if it can be avoided.

I've never thought about what they do with the dirt.

"What are you saying?"

Jimmy points forcefully. "I think Jason Norris is in that grave."

Without another word, he hurries back to the burial mound and continues removing sod.

"That's crazy." I'm still not convinced, but am alarmed at the prospect. As Jimmy's shovel tears into the earth, I suggest a backhoe. "It could take hours digging by hand."

"Do you see a backhoe?" His words are terse, and he lifts his hands in frustration, saying, "Because I don't. I'm sure they just haul one in when it's needed, and I'm not waiting around."

"Six feet, Jimmy!" I plead. "This is a big grave, and if we have to go down six feet it's going to take half the night."

"The dirt is soft; we can do it in an hour. Besides"—he throws a shovelful of dirt—"six feet is a myth. In most places, a couple of feet of soil over the top of the casket is all that's required. A couple of feet is easy."

He pauses to toss more sod from the grave, then leans on the shovel a moment to catch his breath. "Give me another option, Steps, and I'll listen, but don't tell me to stop. Everything we know tells us that Johansson was in this grave when it was closed. Whoever dug him up went to a lot of trouble to make the grave look undisturbed."

Jimmy straightens and then pushes the shovel into the loose soil with a quick thrust. Before tossing the dirt to the side, he pauses and looks up at me. "Someone dug up this grave. They took Johansson's body and then filled the hole up and carefully replaced the sod. Why would they do that? Think about it."

He's right, and the truth of it slaps me in the face.

Picking up my shovel, I approach the head of the grave and quickly move the flowers off to the side, careful not to disturb or dislodge any of the petals. As I prepare to plunge the steel blade into the twice-fresh grave, I imagine for the briefest of moments that I hear the muffled cry of something deep in the ground, something broken and unintelligible. I cast the thought aside and try to forget, but it's too late.

The haunt of the graveyard has me in its grip, and as I dig, the sweat of my exertion rises to dampen my shirt. A chill soon settles in my bones and I shiver, not from the cold but from the prospect of what might await us.

# 7

Dusk.

I've always assumed it was just that gray period after the sun goes down, a word synonymous with *twilight*, albeit less mystical. As it turns out, there's a bit more to it than that. Dusk, it seems, is the latter stage of twilight, the darkest part, which sounds easy enough until you learn that there are three twilights: civil twilight, nautical twilight, and astronomical twilight. Each comes with its own version of dusk so that civil dusk comes right before the transition between civil twilight and nautical twilight, and nautical dusk casts its shadow right before it steps across the threshold into astronomical twilight. Finally, there's astronomical dusk, which is the darkest and final part of the three twilights, the lonesome umbra that's eventually consumed by night.

Twilight, dusk.

Deeper twilight, deeper dusk.

Deepest twilight, deepest dusk.

Who knew it could be so complicated?

It's about an hour after sunset, well into astronomical twilight, when two sets of headlights turn off the road and into the cemetery. By this time, we're working by the light of two portable lamps that Jimmy retrieved from his kit, which is in the trunk with our luggage and the small collection of tools and equipment we haul around everywhere we go—all the things one might need for murder and mayhem.

As the vehicles make their way toward us and then park, I lift one of the lamps and wave it in the air, feeling for a moment like some old railroader signaling a conductor with a kerosene lantern.

It's not like they don't see us, so I'm not exactly sure *why* I wave the lantern, only that it seems like the polite and helpful thing to do. Jimmy looks up at me from the hole, sighs as if he knows what's coming, then stretches up a hand so I can help him climb free of the thrice-dug grave.

By this time, we're two feet down, and the feel of the soil, which has grown firm and dense, suggests that we're getting close. It'll have to wait a few minutes while we explain to a cemetery bureaucrat why we're digging up a grave without a court order under the cover of astronomical twilight.

*I wonder what the penalty is in California for grave robbing?*

As Jimmy takes his place beside me, I set the lamp back down and wait.

One of the vehicles is an unmarked, the type a detective would drive. The other, a Prius, is strictly civilian. No cop, not even an undercover, is going to be caught driving a Prius—at least not on duty. What they do on their own time is up to them. It's kind of one of those don't-ask, don't-tell situations, only for cars.

I'm assuming the lime-colored Prius belongs to Thomas Postlewait, an official with the Southern Kern Cemetery District. Thomas is here because we came to the cemetery with the best of intentions. Diane had located him shortly after Jimmy's call, and he was more than happy to meet at the cemetery and answer any questions we might have. Efficient as Diane is, I'm sure she also contacted Bakersfield PD and asked for a detective—again, just in case—and then paired up the two of them.

Thomas Postlewait is tall and lanky, and though I can only see his silhouette, he reminds me a bit of Abe Lincoln, but in skinny pants and without a beard. I half expect him to retrieve a top hat from the passenger seat and plunk it down on his head. The guy stepping out of the unmarked patrol car is his opposite. He's about five-five and considerably chunkier than Abe, but not fat—well, not obese.

The two men confer momentarily on the side of the road and then start toward us. Mr. Short-and-Stout has a flashlight and leads the way. They reach us a minute later, and after an awkward standoff, introductions are made all the way around. Postlewait's opposite turns out to be Detective Chen Feng of Bakersfield PD. I like him immediately. He seems to have a permanent smile on his face, and I imagine he's one of those cops with a wicked sense of humor.

"Call me Ross," the detective says, extending a hand. "Only my grandfather still calls me Chen."

Normally, this is the part where we'd make small talk for a few minutes, get to know our counterparts, and maybe build a little rapport, but Tom Postlewait is immediately agitated when he catches sight of the open grave behind us and storms over for closer inspection. As he walks, his footsteps seem to pound the earth, and his arms fling about, both of which are meant to convey his displeasure at what he sees.

"What are you doing?" he demands, aghast at the sight of the excavated hole and the stacked dirt. "No one said anything about digging up a grave! Where's your court order or your authorization from the Health Department?" He ends the statement with a slight wheeze in his voice, as if he forgot to breathe during the diatribe.

Gulping down a fresh lungful of air, he continues, and this time it's the practiced bureaucrat that shows through. "I'm sure that you're aware that once a body has been buried, it's considered to be in the custody of the law." He glances from Jimmy to me, then back to Jimmy. "According to California code, no remains of any deceased person shall be removed from any cemetery, except upon written order of the health department having jurisdiction, or of the superior court of the county in which the cemetery is situated." He recites the statute word for word as if he'd memorized it for just this occasion. "FBI or not, you're breaking California laws."

At that, he folds his arms across his chest and glares at us.

"You said California law prohibits the removal of a body from a cemetery," I paraphrase. "We're not removing anyone; we're just digging up a grave to see who's there."

Postlewait pauses and you can tell he's thinking, no doubt reciting the statute in his head, checking to see if I'm right.

"It doesn't matter," Jimmy says impatiently. "We have exigent circumstances."

In a rapid-fire recitation, he explains about the missing men on the Upper Kern, the discovery of Johansson's body on the park bench in Bakersfield, and his belief that—alive or dead—Jason Norris lies in Johansson's coffin.

"You're saying the man buried here was found in town?" Tom says, still processing.

"This morning," Jimmy repeats with a nod.

"Then there must be some mistake." A confused, somewhat amused smile is on the bureaucrat's face. "Are you sure he was in the casket when they buried him?"

"We've already been through all that." Jimmy's voice is now terse. "I've already talked to the funeral home and they confirmed seeing him right before they closed the lid and brought him to the cemetery."

"This Johansson," Ross says, "is he a white male in his late sixties, early seventies?"

"Yeah," I say with a nod.

"Bald?"

"Yeah—how'd you know?"

Ross shakes his head. "I thought his cheeks were a bit rosy for a dead guy." He suddenly grins at me, as if he'd made a joke. "I heard dispatch requesting a death investigation at Tell Park this morning. Patrol responded because it looked like it was probably natural causes, but I was in the area doing a follow-up on another case, so I swung by to see if they needed anything."

Ross shrugs. "Looked like the guy might have been out for a walk and felt a stroke or heart attack coming on, so he sat down on the bench."

"So, you're saying this is true?" Postlewait exclaims.

"Yeah, seems to match up."

"Then that means . . ." Postlewait stares at the open grave, horrified.

"Yeah, that part too," Ross says. Then, shedding his jacket, he extends a hand. "Give me that shovel." Without hesitation, he jumps down into the grave and digs hard and fast for ten minutes, until his breathing becomes labored and Jimmy insists that he climb out and take a break.

Tom Postlewait seems to have collected himself by this point and asks to take a turn. Hopping down into the open grave, he mutters something about digging up coffins in the middle of the night, then goes to work.

He's barely started when the blade of his shovel hits something solid.

# 8

Jimmy and I had failed to consider a rather significant point when we first started digging. Not being well versed in funerary details, we just assumed that we'd dig down, wipe the dirt off the lid of the casket, and tip it open for a peek inside.

When the blade of the shovel resounds with a hollow thud, it's Postlewait who brings this oversight to our attention. "That'll be the vault."

Jimmy and I look at each other and simultaneously ask, "What vault?"

It's not that I've never heard of grave vaults, I just thought they were for Knights Templars, kings, and famous explorers, not for William Johansson of Bakersfield, California.

"It's not concrete," Postlewait says as he taps the tip of the shovel repeatedly into the soil and listens to the low thud of impact. "That's good news, at least. Probably not even a vault; might just be a grave liner. If it was concrete, we'd have a problem. They require special equipment due to the weight of the lid."

"So, we have to get past the vault lid before we get to the actual casket?" Jimmy asks.

"Yes, but once you open the vault—or liner—the casket is

right there, in pristine condition. Some vaults are even waterproof."

"Good to know," I mutter under my breath.

When Postlewait begins to dig again, his fatigue starts to show. I reach down and tap him on the shoulder, motioning for the shovel. He seems relieved and readily takes my hand. With a heave, I haul him out of the hole and then hop down and take his place.

Meanwhile, Jimmy has the second shovel, and because there's no longer room in the grave for two diggers, and because he's incapable of standing around and doing nothing, he starts tidying up the growing pile of dirt. His efforts are mostly in vain, but I'm not going to tell him. It's a good distraction and keeps him from checking his watch every few minutes.

No longer able to dig straight down, I begin working horizontally, removing the dirt shovelful by shovelful. A closed-loop hook soon appears at the head of what Postlewait now confirms is a grave liner, a budget model, no less. Upon seeing the hook, Jimmy runs off toward the Mustang to get a rope from his kit. By the time he returns, I've brushed the remaining dirt off to the side with my hands.

The lid of the two-piece liner is polyurethane, as Postlewait suspected, and comes loose on the first pull. After a little maneuvering and repositioning, we lift it free of the grave and set it off to the side.

Johansson's casket waits below.

Its presence is disquieting, made more so because I'm now straddling it, feet wedged into the dirt lip on either side of the liner. As if the moment weren't surreal enough, a pack of distant coyotes takes up a boisterous dialogue of howls and yips from somewhere in the darkness.

Then I notice the shine.

The top surface of the coffin is host to a plethora of shine and not just those of the funeral-home attendants and mourners. There are older traces from the men and women who manufactured the casket, and those who crated, shipped, and uncrated it.

Among all these, one stands out.

Like the others, this special shine populates the lid of the casket, adding to the abundant wash of color and texture where hands, bodies, and forearms touched and rested. This one radiates a distinct dark green, like polished malachite, and seems no more important than any of the others but for one difference: it radiates as a footprint on the lid of the casket, right in the spot where I might have stepped if I'd lost my balance.

It's the kind of footprint you leave when you're digging up a coffin.

No funeral worker, mourner, or manufacturer would step on the lid of a casket. It's simply unthinkable, sacrilegious even. That kind of disrespectful behavior is reserved for the likes of grave robbers and FBI trackers too stupid to know when they're in over their head.

Staring at the glowing green footprint as it shimmers up from the depths of the grave, I give a curt nod—as if acknowledging it. The action fixes something in my mind, sets it there, and locks it in place.

*Polished malachite* is our suspect; I'm certain of it.

The casket has a split lid for viewings, and I realize, since I'm the only one in the hole, that everyone is going to expect me to open it. I look around for better footing, not so I can lift the lid, but so I can crawl out of the hole before anyone else comes to the same conclusion. As I shift my weight, however, my left foot slips free of its earthen perch and falls six inches to the casket below. This dislodges my right foot, and I lose my balance completely.

When I land on the casket, it's with a disquieting thud and a low groan of pain. For the briefest of moments, I swear I feel something shift inside. It brings to mind scenes from too many horror shows; shows where the actor's next move is usually to put his ear to the casket and listen for that quiet shuffle within. The mere thought is enough to get me on my feet again.

"What are you doing?" Jimmy asks disapprovingly like *I'm* the one who wanted to desecrate a grave tonight.

"I slipped."

"Anything broken?"

"On me or the coffin?"

"Both."

"We're fine; thanks for asking."

He waits a polite moment, then asks, "So . . . you going to open it?"

"No."

"Steps!" he hisses softly—like the others can't hear. Scolding me with his eyes, he says, "Seriously?"

I grumble some words best not heard, then nod my head in defeat. Kneeling, I shift my weight to the left edge of the coffin because, frankly, the lid doesn't seem all that solid.

Shimmying forward, I grasp the edge of the metal viewing lid and whisper, "Please be empty," as I give a little tug. It begins to lift, and I make a spontaneous deal with myself that I won't peek until it's fully open and secure. That way if I die or pass out, the lid won't land on my head.

With little effort, it moves freely on its hinges until the upper part of the casket stands open and exposed. Only then do my eyes drift down.

"Uhhh," I say, to no one in particular.

Then the coyotes start up again.

# 9

The only thing worse than digging up a grave in the middle of the night and finding it empty is digging it up and finding that the poor bastard inside was buried alive. As I stand at the edge of the coffin staring down, trying to make sense of what I'm seeing, it takes a moment for this fact to register. The shredded fabric, pulverized stuffing, and bloodied fingertips leave no doubt: it's the stuff of nightmares.

Blood stains the satin lining in dozens of places, leaving behind the overlapping impressions of fingers and palms from now-still hands. The corpse lies before me, its eyes—the portals to the soul—showing nothing.

Any spark of the divine has long since departed.

Anyone who has ever paused to contemplate his or her earthly surroundings knows that life is filled with the unseen, the greatest of these being God, love, and oxygen.

One might be able to live without God or love—at least for a time—but the big O is a different story. The air we breathe contains about 21 percent oxygen, and it doesn't take much of a drop in this level before impairment begins to show. At 10 percent most lose consciousness, and at 8 percent or below, death can occur. The time it takes one to die at these levels varies, but once oxygen levels drop between 4 and 6 percent, death comes within minutes.

This is called asphyxia, and it can manifest in dozens of ways. There's drowning, choking, hanging, chemical exposure, chronic obstructive pulmonary disease, smothering, strangulation, and crushing, to name a few. On the stranger end of this scale is autoerotic asphyxiation, a rather embarrassing way to go . . . but who am I to judge?

Crushing people under stones was once a common means of eliciting a confession in the Old World, a practice known as *peine forte et dure*, a fancy French way of saying "forceful and hard punishment."

I imagine Giles Corey found it forceful and hard.

In 1692, he was pressed to death during the Salem witch trials as his accusers placed a board over him and then continued to stack stones on top as he refused to confess his guilt. Though such practice was common in Europe for hundreds of years, Corey's death is the only known instance of *peine forte et dure* in American history.

In the end, it wasn't his ribs snapping and his spleen rupturing that killed him, but rather his inability to gasp a single life-sustaining breath. The weight of the stones became too great and his compressed lungs simply didn't have the strength to inflate—even a little.

The dead man in the coffin didn't die from crushing asphyxia like Giles Corey, but he's dead just the same. His terrible demise is made worse by the indignity of occupying another man's coffin—though I suppose the dead don't care about such things. Still, it's the type of thing that Stephen King might come up with during breakfast while nibbling on a toasted English muffin.

The body and its recent tribulations seem to conjure up a macabre sense of gloom. It settles over the cemetery like a fog, bringing silence and fear. When I look up from the dead man to the three darkened silhouettes at the edge of the grave, I can tell they feel it too: something has changed.

The once-friendly light from the portable lamps seems suddenly eerie and inadequate; a weak, dead light that's ill-suited to the task of pushing back the darkness. It tries, nonetheless, but at the end of its tethered rays, shadows abound, lurking behind every obstacle as they hide from the light.

Some cosmic switch has been flipped.

In an instant, the wayward body has changed our mood and stepped everything up to the next level of creepy—Boris Karloff creepy. Creepy like Nosferatu couldn't make it home before daybreak, so he crashed at a friend's pad. I half expect the deceased to suddenly bare his teeth and go for my throat.

It's not like I haven't seen the dead before; I once collected their pictures in a scrapbook to punish myself for failing them. They're stacked like cordwood in my memory. Yet I still feel the sudden urge to flee the grave, to get as far away from the body as possible.

Stumbling backward in the grave, I turn and beat a hasty retreat, scrambling up the three-foot wall of dirt at the foot of the coffin before Jimmy or anyone else can offer a hand. Standing, I begin frantically slapping and brushing the dirt and imaginary spiders from my body. It's a spasmodic, creeped-out, shivery sort of dance that carries on for a good twenty seconds—right up to the point when I notice everyone staring at me.

"I . . . had something crawling . . . ," I start to explain, but then decide it's not worth the effort and wave their eyes away.

Ross doesn't seem as fazed by the body—either that or he's putting on a good show. Slipping off his jacket, he crouches at the edge of the hole and uses his flashlight to get a better look at the footing. Easing himself down, he works his way to the head of the coffin and goes through the motions of checking for a pulse. Next, he shines the light into the still eyes and sadly declares the obvious: "He's gone."

Yet the beam of his light lingers.

"The eyes are hazed over," he says a moment later. "That means he's been dead at least three hours." Ross tries to move the forearm, but it's stiff and locked in place. "Rigor has set."

Standing on the edge of the coffin, Ross retrieves his cell phone and speed-dials dispatch, requesting deputies and a coroner. When he finishes the call, Jimmy extends a hand and hoists him from the hole.

"Do you think that's Jason Norris?" Ross asks, lifting his chin toward the body.

"Black male," Jimmy says, studying the corpse. "Age is right. I don't remember anything about him being bald, though I suppose that's a minor point. People change their hair all the time."

"What about the suit?"

"Sky blue with ruffles? That can only be the suit that Riggs described, the one that Johansson's son insisted on burying him in." Jimmy shakes his head. "Remind me to update my will and specify my preferred attire for the afterlife."

"All I want is pajamas and slippers," I say, having regained some of my composure.

Three sets of eyes turn my way.

I shrug. "If I'm gonna go, I might as well be comfortable."

# 10

It's a slow process dealing with the dead.

Each case is different, but the flow often begins with deputies. They trickle onto the scene and make the initial determination as to whether the decedent passed from natural causes or something more sinister. If it's the latter, detectives are notified, and if they're lucky, the call comes during the middle of the workday and not at 3:00 A.M.

Detectives are rarely so lucky.

Usually, by the time the coroner arrives, a disheveled parade of vehicles is in attendance, sparkling in the reflection of their emergency lights. These include marked and unmarked patrol units, a command vehicle to coordinate the investigation, and perhaps an ambulance or fire engine.

Tractors are rarely part of the murder parade.

Despite this, a broken-down backhoe chugs into the cemetery an hour after we crack open the twice-buried coffin. It's not the prettiest tractor, nor the quietest, but it seems to be in harmony with the cemetery caretaker, who's perched on its springy seat.

After Ross's initial series of calls, we'd decided that it would be better for evidentiary reasons if we lifted the entire coffin out of the grave, rather than trying to manhandle Mr. Norris up and over four feet of dirt.

The coffin may still yield latent prints, DNA, or hair follicles that could play into the investigation as we move forward, forensic evidence that we're going to need if we hope to identify the suspect and rescue the three remaining fishermen.

What began yesterday morning as a straight-up search and rescue has rounded a bend.

This is now a homicide.

Finding a body in a cemetery is a bit like finding a doughnut in a doughnut shop: it's just not all that surprising. But finding a body in someone else's coffin, particularly the body of a man who was alive and well the day before . . . well, that's three levels beyond doughnuts and grave markers.

No one contests that Jason Norris was buried alive.

His worn and bloody fingertips are silent witnesses to the deed and the aftermath, as is the shredded lining of the coffin. There's no other explanation. Buried alive equals murder—terrible murder—no matter how you look at it. I only hope that his air gave out quickly and spared him the horrors of the tomb.

As the tractor clatters to a stop twenty feet away, the rail-thin caretaker in dark coveralls shuts it down and then steps from his perch with an awkward hop. He looks to be in his midtwenties and walks toward us with a pronounced limp. Introducing himself as Johnny Hart, he speaks with a stutter and a bit of Midwest twang.

"B-b-best I could do on short notice," Johnny says, thumbing at the tractor. "Someone said something about d-d-digging up a grave, so I also g-g-grabbed some lifting straps; figured we could run them through the lifting handles on the sides of the coffin."

"Will that work?" Jimmy asks.

"Sure, it'll work. The handles are d-d-designed to take the weight." Stepping over to the hole, Johnny glances down. "Looks like you already got the d-d-digging part out of the way." He turns to Jimmy. "You want me to hop d-d-d—" Johnny sighs heavily and starts over. "You want me to hop into the hole and rig it up?"

"That would be great. Need a hand?"

"No, I g-g-got this. G-g-gonna have to close the lid, though, if that's okay."

"That's perfect," Jimmy replies. "We need to protect the inside as much as possible. For that matter, the less you touch while you're down there, the better."

"*CSI* stuff, right? Yeah, I saw the show. Well, d-d-don't you worry; I'll b-b-be like one of them tightrope walkers and pretend there's nothing to g-g-grab onto."

Limping back to the bucket of the tractor, he drags out four heavy-duty yellow straps and slings them over his shoulder. As he lowers himself into the grave, the cuff of his left leg hangs up and exposes a few inches of his prosthetic leg. It must just be the lower leg since he seems to be able to bend at the knee easily enough.

He catches me looking and pauses, lifting the leg into the air. "Industrial accident three years ago. I could b-blame it on my stutter, but I should have b-b-been paying closer attention. After they fitted me with this, I figured I should g-g-get a job that involves less machinery." A grin fills his face again, and without elaborating on the accident he moves forward over the coffin and closes the lid, easing it down gently so it doesn't slam.

It takes Johnny a couple of minutes, but he soon has the four lifting straps threaded through the pallbearer handles as close to each corner as possible. Handing the ends of the straps to me, he pulls himself out of the hole and fires up the tractor. With the kind of finesse that only comes with practice, he moves the tractor up to the left side of the grave, centers the bucket over the hole, and then lowers it until it's almost flush with the ground.

I'm trying to figure out what he's going to do with the straps since I don't see any tie-down points on the bucket, but he quickly produces two lengths of chain, one of which he loops over the left side of the bucket, the other over the right. He then threads one of these chains through the two straps at the foot of the coffin, and the other through the remaining straps at the head.

Raising the bucket until there's a little tension on the chains and straps, he lets them settle and then backs the pressure off. Hopping down from his seat, he spends a moment making some adjustments so the coffin comes up level and Norris doesn't pour out one end or the other.

"Looking g-g-good." Johnny gives a thumbs-up. Hauling himself back onto the tractor, he stands rather than sits, looking for a moment like a bull rider in the chute just before he settles on his mount. Working the lift on the bucket, he puts tension back on the straps, then slowly begins to lift the coffin from the grave.

I hear a small pop and a groan as the coffin rises flush with the top of the hole. Then, with an explosion of noise, the left lifting handle at the head of the coffin shears off, followed almost immediately by the left handle at the rear. With nothing to hold the left side of the coffin aloft, it pitches violently onto its side and I watch in horror as Jason Norris spills out. I don't see him land at the bottom of the grave, but I hear it: a sickening thud that sounds all the louder because of the darkness.

Leaping from the tractor—an impressive trick considering his leg—Johnny rushes to the edge of the grave and looks down. "It's not my fault!" he brays, his words distraught.

As the rest of us press forward and gather around, I can see Norris in an awkward heap four feet below. Thomas Postlewait is holding his head with both hands and repeating

"Oh, God," as if it were a mantra. Jimmy, it seems, is unfazed by the spilled contents of the coffin, and I notice he's leaning in close and studying one of the sheared-off handles intently, though he's careful not to touch it.

"Oh, God!" Thomas says.

"It's not my fault," Johnny cries again.

Ross says nothing. He's watching Jimmy and finally asks, "Whatcha got?"

Jimmy shakes his head. "Odd that only the handles on the left side broke off, don't you think?" Donning a pair of latex gloves, he loosens the dangling handle from its strap and holds it out for Ross, tipping it in the light. "Notice anything?"

It takes Ross only a moment. "Smart bastard," he says in a hushed voice. "You think he's just toying with us, or is this supposed to mean something?"

"Probably just messing with us," Jimmy says.

By this time my curiosity is spilling over. "What is it?"

Rather than tell me, Jimmy waves me over and again tilts the handle this way and that in the wash of light.

It takes me longer than Ross—possibly because I have Johnny the caretaker breathing over my shoulder—but I finally see it. "Hacksaw marks?"

"Yeah," Jimmy replies slowly. "But notice how he didn't go all the way through? He wanted them to break off when the coffin was in the air."

"Okay, that's sick."

"It's not my fault?" Johnny says again, this time as a question.

"No, this was sabotage."

"So, he wanted this to happen?" I ask. "Why?"

Jimmy shrugs. "Slows us down, for one. It might also contaminate any evidence he left, though if he took the time to do this"—Jimmy hoists up the handle—"I doubt he left fingerprints or DNA behind."

For a moment, we take turns staring at the handle, the coffin, and the body of Jason Norris at the bottom of the hole. Eventually, Johnny asks the obvious: "Wh-what now?"

Jimmy rocks his head to the left, then straightens it as if working out a kink. "Somebody's going to have to go down there, I suppose."

*Who* that somebody might be isn't readily apparent, and nobody seems eager to volunteer. Pretty soon we're all pretending to stare at the hole while sneaking furtive looks at one another, waiting for someone to offer up.

As the impromptu selection process continues, and the frequency and duration of the glances increases, Johnny stands out as an odds-on favorite. He's the logical choice, and most eyes start to gravitate his way, enough so that he soon picks up on it.

"I can't touch no dead g-g-guy," he practically yelps. "I only dig the holes and lower them down; I don't touch them. That's b-b-bad luck, touching a dead g-g-g—a dead g-g-g—" He sighs. "A corpse." He sets his chin and waves both hands dismissively, making it clear that there's nothing further to discuss.

Imagining that he's next, Thomas stiffens and calmly says, "I didn't come dressed for grave robbing."

It's a weak argument considering he was pitching out dirt with the rest of us not an hour ago and only became squeamish when we found a dead guy at the bottom of the hole. As if reading my thoughts, Thomas motions toward his already-soiled shirt and tie, evidence to suggest he'd done his part.

That leaves just me, Jimmy, and Ross.

After eyeballing each other for a full minute, I finally say, "Oh, for Pete's sake!" Peeling off my jacket and tossing it aside, I motion toward the cockeyed coffin suspended over the grave. "Someone get that thing out of the way," I bark. "I don't want it falling on me."

Just as I'm about to jump into the hole with the blue-ruffled stiff, headlights slow on the road and then turn into the cemetery. A white panel van materializes out of the darkness as it draws near, the kind of van used by electricians, plumbers, and locksmiths. As it parks behind Ross's unmarked, I suddenly realize what I'm looking at.

With a sigh of relief, I utter perhaps the rarest statement in the English language: "Thank God! It's the coroner's office."

# 11

*Monday, March 9*

Jimmy has this annoying habit of phoning my room to make sure I'm awake.

It's become more consistent over the years as if he were my personal, self-appointed wake-up concierge. He's so annoyingly dependable that I rarely bother setting an alarm. I mean, what's the point?

When the phone rings at 7:00 A.M., I don't have to wonder who it is or what the person wants. I just roll over, press the handset to my face, grunt some semblance of acknowledgment, then hang up while Jimmy's still speaking—something about meeting him near the breakfast bar at seven thirty.

Lying on my back, I stare at the ceiling and rub the sleep from my eyes. Do I feel like getting up? No. Because getting up is the first step toward a long day, and last night was long enough to last the rest of the week.

How many times have I woken like this? Another city, another day, another motel—the motel part being the worst of it.

Most people don't think about motel rooms the way I do. That's because they're on a rare business trip or a vacation, and sleeping away from home when you're not accustomed to it has an air of adventure. They don't pause to wonder how many other adventurers have slept in the same bed, sneezed onto the same nightstand, had sex in the same shower. They don't see it, so it doesn't exist; and if it doesn't exist, no one need run around like a madman spraying disinfectant on every surface.

Me? I see everything.

There's not enough disinfectant for what I see.

If I were CSI, I wouldn't need fluorescents and alternative light sources to see the fifty-five-gallon barrel's worth of blood, semen, sweat, saliva, and body oil that has passed through this room. All I'd have to do is open my eyes and witness the glowing shine on every surface and in every configuration. When I shower, I keep my eyes closed so I don't have to look at the thousand people that were here before me.

If I were normal, I'd probably like some of the places we've stayed at over the years, but as things stand, I tend to keep my glasses on while I'm in the room. A little ignorant bliss never hurt anyone . . . for the most part.

It's with this lingering thought that I push myself upright on the pristine stained sheets, step onto the immaculate soiled carpet, and make my way to the defiled shower.

When I arrive downstairs at exactly 7:33 A.M., I see Jimmy working on one of his crossword puzzles at a small round table just off the motel lobby. He doesn't look up, so I make for the breakfast bar and scoop up a poppy-seed muffin and a small bottle of orange juice. Plopping down across from him, I crack open the orange juice, drink half of it in one tip, then peel down the moist paper sides of the muffin liner.

"What's the plan, boss?"

Jimmy holds up a finger, asking for a moment as he tries to unwrap his mind from the puzzle. It's a typical response for him when he's stuck on a word.

"Which one?"

He points to eleven across, which reads CZAR'S GIFT. Studying it a moment, I note that it's seven letters across with a *b* in the third space.

"Fabergé," I say almost immediately, then take a bite of muffin.

His pencil pauses over the empty boxes, counting out the letters. "Fabergé, as in the eggs?"

I just nod, still chewing, then realize he's looking for a little more depth in the answer. I hurry and swallow, washing it down with a quick shot of orange juice. "The House of Fabergé was based in Saint Petersburg and made sixty or seventy jeweled eggs over about thirty years. Most of these were made for the czars, first for Alexander the Third, and then Nicholas the Second, who gave them as Easter gifts to their wives and mothers. That's how they became known as Imperial eggs.

"The last two were supposed to be delivered in 1917, but that was a bad year for Russia. First, the February Revolution removed the czar from power, and then the October Revolution overthrew the provisional government and the Communists swept into power. The following summer, the Bolsheviks executed the Romanov family and Fabergé eggs became a part of history."

"I suppose you just memorized that from one of your books?"

"You don't have to memorize when it's interesting."

Jimmy smirks at me and shakes his head. Pulling the paper close, he writes Fabergé in eleven across, then folds the crossword puzzle and stuffs it into his Fossil briefcase.

I give him a moment, then ask, "What's the plan?"

He glances at his watch quickly. "We have an eight o'clock meeting with Canela Perez, the congressman's sister and chief of staff."

"Any word on when they're going to do the autopsy on Norris?"

"Already started. Dr. Herrera said he'll call with the results when he's finished, but everything points to asphyxia. Oh, here's something interesting. Ross had San Jose do the death notification with Norris's wife and learned that when he left on the fishing trip he had a full head of hair."

"So, he shaved it off?"

"Or someone shaved it for him."

The two-story office complex on Rosedale Highway in northwest Bakersfield is a modern building hewn from concrete, steel, and glass. The subdued landscaping merges perfectly with the building and its many small details, resulting in a classy and mentally stimulating vision of architecture that anyone would be pleased to call his or her office.

The only thing out of place is the pair of media vans parked at the curb.

They add a discordant feel to the place, clashing with the building from every angle: there's no symmetry, no rhythm, no feng shui. One van has its antennae raised thirty feet into the air in an obnoxious display of entitlement and self-importance. A female reporter hovers nearby with a mic in hand as she addresses a camera, no doubt pontificating on the disappearance of the congressman as she details his many controversial statements and positions.

The discovery of Norris's body hasn't made it out to the press yet, but it's only a matter of time. That's when the real feeding frenzy will begin. I've seen it before. As word spreads, the press will swarm the area, circling like sharks around a bloated whale carcass, and turning the office complex into a three-ring circus of biblical proportion.

Jimmy drives by the front of the building slowly. He ignores the dozen empty parking spots and turns at the corner.

"There's one." I point to an empty spot in the back lot, well shielded from the prying eyes out front. Parking the Mustang, we find an equally convenient set of glass doors at the rear of the building that lead to the lobby. Taking the stairs, we look for room 207 and find it at the end of the hall on the left.

The congressional office of Marco Perez occupies sixteen hundred square feet on the second floor of the building. It's a corner office, so the windows face both south and east. With such a configuration, one might expect a sweeping view of the Bakersfield skyline, but such a skyline doesn't exist.

Bakersfield is a rather flat city filled with low, flat buildings. The three tallest structures are the Stockdale Tower, the Plaza Towers—both twelve stories—and the ten-story Bank of America Building. Everything after that is nine floors or less, with most under six stories.

The receptionist greets us with a harried look and quickly ushers us into a modest adjoining office. Detective Ross Feng is standing in the center of the room and greets us with his contagious smile, though the upturned corners of his mouth seem subdued this morning. Turning, he introduces us to a slight yet strikingly beautiful woman standing beside him.

"Steps, Jimmy, this is Canela Perez, the congressman's sister."

"Call me Ella," she says quickly, extending a hand. Her voice is steady and calm, but you can sense the tension haunting her words. "Ross tells me you're part of an FBI tracking unit?"

Jimmy nods. "That's correct, ma'am—"

"Ella," she insists.

"Ella," Jimmy confirms with a tip of his head. His face is warm and kind, one of the fifty-faces-of-Jimmy that I've come to know over the years. This one is reserved for victims and their families, and there's nothing contrived about it because he genuinely feels for them.

Ella cuts straight to the point: "Can you find my brother?"

Jimmy glances over at me, then nods his head slowly and

firmly. "We can. We're pretty good at both tracking and investigating, and the intelligence analyst that assists us is one of the best in the Bureau."

"And what about Jason? The detective tells me you found him dead last night?" As she finishes, a single tear scuttles down the side of her nose, and she brushes it away impatiently.

"I'm afraid that's true. We don't know the cause of death yet, but it was likely due to lack of oxygen."

"How?" she asks incredulously.

Jimmy hesitates.

"Please," she presses, the word coming out desperate.

Jimmy glances at me, then nods. "I'm going to tell you something, but I need you to understand that it's confidential case information, at least for the present. Can you assure me that your office won't share it with anyone, even the congressman's colleagues?"

"Of course. You have my word."

As he unfolds the events of the previous night—our dark foray in the graveyard—her lower jaw begins to quiver. Her eyes grow hollow, as if bereft of happiness or even the hope of happiness. When Jimmy finishes, her knees are shaky, and Ross helps her to a chair.

It takes Canela a moment to compose herself, first staring at her hands, then at the arm of the chair, and finally at us. Glancing from face to face, her mouth opens wide and I half expect a great wailing moan to issue forth. Instead, three whispered words walk across her tongue and spill upon the carpet: "Jason was claustrophobic." Her whole body gives a convulsive shake.

It's the kind of shiver you give when a cold, invisible finger runs down your spine.

Jimmy and Ross fill her in on the less horrifying details of the investigation, emphasizing the considerable resources that California, Bakersfield, and the US government were prepared to throw at this case until the men were found.

"Did you know the others well?" Jimmy asks as he finishes.

"Enough to call them friends. I've known them since Marco was in college; since they were all making fly-fishing lures together for Caddisco."

"Caddisco?"

"Marco's company, named for the caddis insects that most lures are modeled after." Looking from face to face, Ella takes in our confusion. "I'm so sorry. Of course, you don't know how this annual fishing trip began, or the company that gave them all their start."

She shakes her open hands next to her ears, the type of gesture one might make when not thinking clearly. "My mind just won't stop," she says in a low voice. "It keeps dragging me down to the worst conclusions, the worst possible ending. The only time I can even focus is when I think of those earlier times."

"Tell us about them," Jimmy says in a soothing tone. "Tell us about the fly-fishing and the company they started."

"You don't want to hear—"

Jimmy cuts her off gently. "We do. The only thing we know about the congressman is what's in this file." He holds up Diane's hurriedly gathered notes. "We'd love to know more."

She almost smiles at that, then her whole body seems to relax as she pushes back in her chair, a storyteller preparing her words.

"Marco began tying lures when he was sixteen. He was awful at it and must have lost a pint of blood that first month. But the one thing about Marco"—she smiles—"is he just doesn't know when to quit. The more times he got poked, the more determined he became, and it wasn't long before he was turning out some nice-looking flies. After that, they just kept getting better and better.

"Other fishermen soon started offering him money for his flies, and once he figured out there might be a profit in his new hobby . . . well, the businessman in him blossomed. A year later, he paid cash for a little red Pontiac Fiero—drove my mother crazy with that thing."

Ella looks up at me—deduces that I don't know the first thing about cars—then turns to Ross. "You remember the Fiero? The little two-seater sports car?"

"Sure." Ross smiles. "I pulled over a few in my day, and it was always some crazy teenager behind the wheel."

Ella nods. "Then you know what I'm talking about. In any case, Marco was hooked on lures"—she gives an apologetic shrug—"no pun intended. By the time he got to college, he was able to pay for his courses, books, and a nice off-campus apartment. The only problem was that the orders were starting to come in faster than he could fill them. That's when he brought on Noah Long."

"Were they friends, or was Noah just an employee at that point?" I ask.

"Oh, friends! Noah was Marco's first friend at college. They were tight, those two, even talked about getting an apartment together, but Marco likes his privacy. This was around the time the business really started to take off. Some fishing magazine heard about Marco, and aside from being impressed with the lures, they liked the human-interest side of the story. You know, a kid putting himself through college on a kitchen-table business.

"When the article ran, the orders started pouring in. Wade and Jason were hired, and Marco started focusing more on marketing. There were other employees who came and went, but it was the four of them who were the constant: they *were* the business."

She takes a drink from her water bottle and reflects a moment.

"As it turned out, spring break that first year came in March. That was the first time the boys made a trip together to the Upper Kern. Marco wrote the whole thing off as research and development—which it was! They had a bunch of new designs they wanted to test out. Still, it was so much more than just testing lures. They came back different men; better men. It was a bonding experience that they turned into an annual pilgrimage, one that continues to this . . ." Her voice trails off.

After taking another drink, this time gulping, she sets the bottle down, and I see her hand tremble ever so slightly. This seems to bother her, and she pulls it into her other hand and clenches it, determined to be brave.

"By their senior year," she continues in a softer voice, "Caddisco had grown into a trusted brand with a reputation for quality—the kind of quality that makes a brand valuable. So, when one of the big-box sporting establishments came around offering to write a big check, the boys talked it over and decided to sell. Marco insisted on splitting the proceeds four ways, and each of them walked away with a high six-figure payout, and that was after taxes." She tries to smile. "I think that was when Marco decided he didn't like high taxes."

She looks up and makes eye contact with each of us in turn.

"That's what started it all. It was the sale of Caddisco that launched them on their careers. All except Wade, I suppose. He just wanted to be a cop or a lawyer and ended up being both. And since it doesn't take seed money to be a cop, he bought himself a house instead."

She pauses for a long moment, her eyes intent on the far wall as if seeing things there that were hidden from the world, visions among shadows.

"Marco went off to UC Davis School of Medicine; Jason got hired by an accounting firm in San Francisco and later relocated to San Jose, and Noah"—she pauses and lets out a great sigh—"he packed his car and spent the next month driving to Wall Street, seeing the sights on the way.

"I had a thing for him back in those days," she adds with a matter-of-fact shrug. "Just a schoolgirl crush, I suppose, but the kind that hurts for years."

A knock at the door disturbs them and the receptionist pokes her head in, meekly advising Ella that she has another visitor.

Rising, Ella moves to the door as a man enters and extends a hand toward her. He's about Jimmy's age—early-to-midthirties—but without the energy and bounce. And where Jimmy has a full head of black hair, this guy is starting to thin out on top and there's already a touch of gray at his temples. He's wearing a black suit, a white shirt, and a red power tie. His shoes look like they've been dipped in shellac and buffed with the Golden Fleece out of Greek mythology. I swear you need sunglasses to look at them. But then, Jimmy says I tend to be hyperbolic—a nice way of saying I exaggerate. In any case, it doesn't take me more than a split second to peg the newcomer as a Fed.

"Special Agent Kip Weir, FBI," the suit says as he gently shakes Ella's hand, speaking as if he were an undertaker consoling family rather than a federal agent. His eyes cast about and find me, Jimmy, and Ross staring back at him. Dismissing me and Jimmy immediately, probably because we're wearing jeans and polo shirts, he focuses on Ross, who at least has a tie that complements his shirt and slacks.

Closing the eight-foot gap in a few strides, Special Agent Kip Weir extends a hand to the detective, who takes it and introduces himself. Then, gesturing at Jimmy, he says, "This is Special Agent James Donovan and his partner, Magnus Craig. They're with the Special Tracking Unit."

"Call me Jimmy," my partner says as he shakes hands.

"I'm Steps," I say when it's my turn.

With introductions complete, Kip glances around, as if unsure of the situation. "So, Special Tracking Unit . . . ?"

"We were asked to come down and see if we could help," Jimmy clarifies. "Are you out of Bakersfield or the Sacramento Field Office?"

"Sacramento," Kip replies dismissively, obviously still sorting out the pecking order in his head. "Sorry, it's just . . . I wasn't told we'd asked for any help."

"We got a call from DC."

Jimmy could've said that the director of the FBI called the previous morning and asked us to come down, but he doesn't operate that way. Referencing DC without getting specific is an easier route. Kip will assume that his boss's boss made the call, which makes it their idea. That makes it more palatable. It's a diplomatic move on Jimmy's part, and a good way to avoid stepping on toes. We learned a long time ago that a low profile is the best profile.

Jimmy and I give Kip the rundown on our visit to the river the previous day, throwing in copious amounts of tracking lingo. Then we work our way forward to the perplexing discovery in the morgue and the unfortunate exhumation of Jason Norris.

"Damn," Kip whispers when we finish.

It's a fitting word.

*Damned* might be a better one . . . or maybe that just applies to me.

# 12

Every cop has a rhythm and flavor when it comes to conducting interviews. The basics are instilled at the academy, but many go on to more advanced training, such as the Reid technique or something based on the PEACE model. In the end, a good interview is just a conversation, and everyone converses differently.

For most, it's not just the questions, but the order of the questions. It's not just the intonations, but the body movements that accompany them.

My lovely fiancée, Heather, can pull truth from me with the ease and skill of a pickpocket. It's not just her honed interview style, but her ability to reach beyond the words to find meaning in posture, ear tugs, and eye movement. She's a necromancer when it comes to body language and uses her magic to mercilessly separate the truth from the lie.

The point is, while training gives you the tools, everyone develops a process based on the person's specific skill set and experience. Some like to focus more on building rapport first, while others dive right in. The best interviewers change their technique depending on the situation.

In the end, the true measure of an interviewer is results.

Kevin, one of my buddies back home, once told a suspect

that in addition to being able to get DNA from epidermal cells, science had advanced to the point where a lab could identify *specifically* where those skin cells came from.

None of this is true. Not yet, anyway.

Kevin went on to tell the suspect that *epipenial* cells come from the penis and nowhere else, and so he found it odd that the suspect's epipenial cells were in the victim's underwear. This, despite the suspect's adamant and frequent denials regarding sexual contact.

"That's kind of weird, right?" Kevin said as he finished . . . and then he just leaned back and waited for an explanation.

The guy confessed almost immediately.

Kip Weir is *not* a good interviewer—no disrespect to the guy.

He seems nice enough, but he's obviously more of a just-the-facts-ma'am type of investigator. Warmth does not exude from him, it hides from him, despite his funerary tone. As he explains to Ella that he's been assigned the case and that this is the FBI's highest priority, his words are lukewarm, mechanical, rote, as if he were reading them from a flash card he carries around in his starched shirt pocket.

Jimmy glances at me on the sly and gives a subtle what-the! grimace.

Glad I'm not the only one who noticed.

"Does your brother have any enemies?" Kip asks a few minutes into his questioning.

"He's a politician," Ella replies.

"So that's a yes?"

"Yes."

"Do you have anyone specific in mind?"

"One or two, plus half the country." She crosses her arms. "It's a polarized environment if you haven't noticed. My brother is a pin in a world of balloons, which means he either avoids some issues entirely, or he constantly hears little explosions going off all around him. Those little explosions being people losing their minds. You should see some of the mail he gets."

She meant the last rhetorically, but I jump on it.

"*I'd* like to see the mail."

She glances my way, perhaps wondering if I'm serious, then holds up a finger as she walks from the office. A moment later she returns and places in my hands a bundle of perhaps fifty letters with a fat rubber band holding them together.

"Those are the worst of the worst. We stopped giving them to the Secret Service because Marco was worried that he was being overly sensitive, or even paranoid. I kept them anyway—just in case."

"This is all of them?" I ask.

"Yeah, for this month."

"It's only the ninth."

She nods.

"You get this much hate mail every nine days?"

"No." She gives a small shake of her head. "As I said, I only keep the worst of the worst."

While Special Agent Weir continues his soul-crushing interview, Jimmy and I retreat to the chairs in the reception area and start going through the stack of seething mail. If you believed the letters and their conflicting impressions, one might believe that Marco Perez was the evilest, most twisted man to walk the earth since Cain brought a rock down on his brother's head and introduced humanity to that fresh new thing called murder.

"Recognize any shine from the river?" Jimmy asks quietly after we've had time to peruse the stack and examine each letter.

"You mean the river with a million different shines spread out over hundreds of acres and stacked one on top of the other?" I ask, perhaps a bit too sarcastically.

"No, the other river." When I look up, he just smiles. "So that's a *no*?"

"That's a no."

His demeanor tells me he expected as much. Holding up a letter, he says, "This Abel Moya guy seems to be particularly upset with the congressman. I counted seven letters from him. That's almost one a day."

"Maybe he has mental health issues?"

"Why? Because he writes a lot of letters? *You* write a lot of letters and you're"—Jimmy pauses to eyeball me—"mostly stable."

"Thank you," I reply snidely. "But, for the record, I only mail one or two a week, and those are only to Heather."

"Yeah, but you're scribbling on them all the time. Seems every time I turn my back, you're hunched over with a pen in hand. I'm surprised you don't have carpal tunnel syndrome."

I stare at him a moment. "Abel Moya?" I ask pointedly.

Jimmy grins and holds up a small stack of Abel's letters. "Did you read any of these?"

"I skimmed them."

"He's pretty pissed at Marco over the whole border-security issue. Doesn't make any direct threats, but he comes close."

"Seems like a lot of people are pissed at Marco," I observe.

"Goes with the territory."

Glancing at the receptionist, who's now fielding phone calls, I reach out and tap the letters in Jimmy's hand, whispering, "I don't recognize that yellow," indicating the Moya letters.

During my years with the STU, I've seen a lot of yellows: dandelion yellow, custard yellow, piss yellow, and minion yellow among them, but never one quite so dull and uninspiring. The shine on the letters looks like it was left to bleach in the sun and got dusty along the way. And the scratchy texture looks like the once-shiny surface of a compact disc after an annoyed cat had a go at it.

My head tips toward the envelopes and pulsing shine. "It wasn't at the cemetery and I'm pretty sure it wasn't at the river . . . but as I said, the river was a mess."

"You still think the green shine from the cemetery is the key?" It comes off as a statement, but his words carry a hint of question.

"I do."

"How can you be sure?"

"A footprint on the lid of a buried coffin is a pretty good clue. And while I can't guarantee it, I'm pretty sure I saw the same shine at the river, near the spot of blood on the rock."

"Pretty sure?"

"I'm as close to certain," I say patiently, "as a flame is to paper right before combustion." With the fingers of my right hand, I give my best impression of paper being consumed by fire.

Jimmy considers this a moment. "What if he's working with someone?"

"Someone like Abel Moya?"

Jimmy shrugs and cocks his head, as if to say, *Sure, that's a good example.*

"To what end?"

"I don't know, but our suspect *did* manage to abduct four grown men; something like that's a lot easier if you have help."

"That's . . . possible," I concede. "I *did* see a couple of references to Aztlán in those letters."

"Yeah, I saw those too," Jimmy says briskly, contempt defiling every word as if his mouth has a vendetta against his vocabulary.

Three years ago, Jimmy and I crossed paths with a killer named Pablo Ramirez, who believed himself a champion for Aztlán, the mythical home of the Aztecs. He killed three people in his war to claim the entire Southwest for the Mexican people and then shot himself in the head like a coward when he was cornered. The press had a field day with the murders before moving on to the next blood-soaked orgy.

At the time, I remember thinking that if *anyone* had a claim to the Southwest, it would be the Hopi, Comanche, Apache, Navajo, and other tribes who were well established on those lands long before the Aztec Empire existed.

But it's a moot point.

Human history is about expansion, contraction, conquest, and migration. The lands that the Comanche and Apache took from the previous occupants were likewise taken from them, just as Aztlán was taken from the Aztecs—if it ever existed in the first place.

Jimmy hits speed dial on his phone, and I hear the faint static of a human voice picking up on the other end. "Diane," Jimmy says, "I need the horsepower on a guy named Abel Moya, everything you can find. I'm assuming he lives here in Bakersfield, and he might be associated with Mexican nationalists."

Static crackles briefly on the other end.

"No date of birth, but if you can't find him, I can ask Bakersfield PD."

That sets the static into high arcs, like a Tesla coil mainlining a nuclear reactor.

"Fine." Jimmy chuckles. "Get back to me when you have something."

"How's Diane?" I ask in a singsong voice after he disconnects.

"She sends hugs and kisses."

We let Special Agent Weir finish his just-the-facts-ma'am interview with Canela Perez, then ask about Abel Moya.

Ella immediately stiffens. "I told Marco that one was different," she says as if somehow vindicated by the question.

"He said it was nothing, just another guy blowing off steam, but he scared me. I reported him to the Secret Service four or five times over the last six months, but they said they can only interview him and pressure him to stop. Unless he makes a direct threat, they can't arrest him." She looks at me, then back at Jimmy. "Is he the one who did this?"

"Probably not." Jimmy holds up a soothing hand. "He seems to know the law and how to skirt the edges so that he doesn't get in trouble. A guy like that doesn't generally go postal. It's the ones who come right out and *say* how they're going to kill you that worry me. They've got no impulse control, so you're never quite sure if they'll follow through on the threats."

"And the quiet ones," I add in the lull that follows.

"Excuse me?" Ella says.

"The quiet ones," I repeat. "Those are the ones *I* worry about because the first time you hear from them they've usually already done the deed."

Ella visibly trembles as I finish, and I immediately regret the words. "Sorry. I didn't mean for it to come out—"

"Don't apologize," she says quickly. "I want the truth, nothing less." Looking back and forth between me and Jimmy, then throwing a sideways glance at Kip and Ross, she says, "Promise you'll be straight with me, no matter what."

It's an odd world when you can be proud of someone you've just met, but that's exactly what I feel as Ella makes us promise, each in turn. It wasn't the battlefield of politics that made her this way, I realize, but something else, something familial and deep-rooted. I can't help wondering if Marco is of the same caliber.

"Can I see those?" Kip points at the letters still in Jimmy's hand. He spends a few minutes reading through them as Ella explains that the Secret Service has an extensive file on Abel, including notes related to his lucrative business as a human smuggler.

"He thinks if the Hispanic population in the US grows large enough, he can achieve Aztlán through the ballot box rather than through bloodshed. That's how he justifies his smuggling operation—he says it's for the cause: more votes and all that. Of course, that doesn't stop him from charging for his services or exploiting his customers."

"America needs entrepreneurs," I reply enthusiastically.

Ross chuckles, but Ella looks for a moment like she's going to reach into my mouth and yank out my tonsils. That changes when she notices the upturned corner of my mouth. Making eye contact with curious hesitation, she peers into my soul and softens almost immediately, letting out a long, pent-up sigh. For the first time, I see the hint of a smile on her face as she gives me a touché tip of her head.

The moment proves to be an icebreaker, and I find that Ella and I suddenly have an unspoken understanding, even a rapport. It wasn't there a moment ago.

When Kip finishes scanning through the letters, you can tell by the slight change in his posture and tone that he thinks there might be something to Abel Moya, something worth pursuing. I can't fault him for his instincts. If not for shine, I might be barking up that same tree. Besides, it's not like we have any other leads to go on.

As years of FBI training and experience take over, driving him forward, Kip begins to interview Ella more aggressively, by which I mean he leans toward her at a five-degree slant and enunciates every tenth or twelfth word with an honest-to-God inflection. The more answers he gets, the more he seems to think that Abel Moya is the guy.

When I give Jimmy a surreptitious glance, he returns a barely noticeable shrug, as if to say, *It's his show,* conceding the interview to Kip.

Jimmy and I have worked together long enough to know each other's minds, kind of like old married couples who can hold entire conversations and never say more than seven words. In my glance and Jimmy's shrug, a mutual understanding is reached. We'll let Kip run with the Abel Moya angle, mostly because it'll keep him out of our hair, but also because it'll close out a lead that needs to be run down regardless.

As for Ross, I'm pretty sure he's going to ask to tag along with Jimmy and me. My hunch is drawn from how he keeps looking at Kip as if he's some automaton from Planet X.

I'm just about to intervene on Ella's behalf when Jimmy's phone rings. Just a regular ring, not one of the special ringtones he has for his inner circle. He doesn't put it on speaker, so I'm relegated to listening to half a conversation and trying to extrapolate the other half.

"Donovan," he answers. He listens a moment. "We're at the congressman's office. . . . Sure. Why? What's wrong? . . . No, that's fine." He glances at his watch. "We'll leave now. Give us ten minutes."

"Where are we going?" I ask as he disconnects.

"Coroner's office."

"I thought you said we didn't have to attend the autopsy?"

"I did, but that was before Dr. Herrera found something."

"Like what?"

Jimmy just shakes his head. "He wouldn't say."

The body of Jason Norris looked relatively unmolested when we dug him up last night . . . I mean aside from the obvious lack of oxygen and his being dead. Other than that, he looked great. So, unless the good doctor found the creature from *Alien* tucked inside Jason's rib cage, I can't imagine what would have Dr. Herrera so keyed up, or why an office visit is necessary.

As it turns out, he has a good reason.

I can tell that Jimmy's digging the Mustang because when he comes screaming out of the parking complex and whips the wheel to the left, he keeps his foot mashed into the gas pedal and puts the car into a controlled slide. The rear wheels spin furiously, buffing the asphalt and exhaling a long, pungent breath of black smoke. Some might call it reckless driving, but I like to think of it as urgent law enforcement business.

Besides, the car's a beast.

I'm starting to think about upgrading from my Mini Cooper.

# 13

Dr. Ben Herrera's voice booms through the large autopsy room as soon as we enter, the copious amounts of stainless steel seeming to pick up the words and throw them at us in waves.

"You know, I'm busy enough around here without you guys digging up more work," he quips.

I look at his face to see if he's kidding, and the Botox veneer he reserves for families of the bereaved gives way to an impish smile.

"Digging in a graveyard in the middle of the night," he says with a tsk-tsk shake of his head. "Do you know that in the nineteenth century body snatchers were called *resurrectionists*? They were so busy, it seems, meeting the demands of the medical schools that some cemeteries were later found to be nearly empty." He studies us with morbid glee. "Can you imagine?"

Jimmy smirks at him. "I've been called a lot of things in my time with the FBI, but *body snatcher* is a first."

*"Resurrectionist,"* Ben corrects with a grin.

The autopsy room looks the same as it did yesterday, but with one significant difference: Instead of finding the elderly corpse of William Johansson on the table, we see that of Jason Norris. The sky-blue burial suit that briefly belonged to William has been removed from Jason, and his body lies naked and exposed, though not yet dissected.

For murder victims, death is only the first indignity.

I've grown accustomed to bodies over the years—accustomed, but not comfortable. It's unsettling looking down at someone who was so recently filled with life, and who now lies unmoving, forever stilled by time or trauma. Even if I'd just stepped into this world from another dimension and had no sense of life or death, I think I'd look upon the body of Jason Norris and recognize that something is missing, that the spark that was him has somehow fled.

Jimmy would tell me this is our innate sense of God and the soul.

I respect Jimmy and his views, just as I respect all who seek such answers. I've never been what most would call religious, at least not like Jimmy, but I've seen things I can't explain. If that makes me "spiritual," then I'm okay with that, though I'm not entirely sure what the word means in the bigger sense of things. Maybe no one knows. Maybe *spiritual* is just one of those terms people use when they want to believe in something, but just don't want to call it God.

I *do* believe in something.

I believe because I must believe. I've seen that missing spark leave the body on several occasions and go . . . somewhere.

What the spark is remains unclear, but I've seen signs of intelligence in its movements and actions, a sense of purpose. For years I've sought answers to this mystery in books about near-death experiences, reincarnation, and even historical accounts of famous mediums, but the questions continue to outweigh the answers.

I suppose some knowledge is not meant for this world.

Maybe that's why they call it faith.

Retrieving a plastic evidence bag from the stainless-steel counter before him, Dr. Ben Herrera checks the seal and waves the bag in the air, a serious look now on his face. "Sorry to drag you down here like this, but I knew you'd want this right away." He steps toward Jimmy and hands over the envelope.

Turning it over in his hands, Jimmy stares at it for a moment but says nothing. Ross and I instinctively move in and peer over his shoulder. What I see takes a moment to process, but when it settles into place, I nearly gasp.

"We found that stuffed into his left pocket," Ben explains after giving us time to digest the discovery. "Your suspect wanted it found during the autopsy and placed it there with that in mind." Ben shakes his head.

Through the clear plastic of the evidence bag, I study the developed Polaroid picture. Filling the exposed rectangle is the close-up of a man's face. He has a gag ball in his mouth and a nasty contusion over his right eye. His features are overexposed as if a flash had been used at close range in the dark.

"Wade Winchell," I mutter.

The deputy district attorney has looked better. His two-dimensional eyes peer into mine as if trying to convey something; as if he knows the purpose of such a picture and how all this might play out. Despite his predicament, a stern, controlled look is on Wade's face. His eyes are cold steel.

I admire him for it.

I wonder if I would be so composed.

"What about the others?" Jimmy asks. "Any Polaroids of Noah or Marco?"

"No, just the one."

"Maybe Wade was the target all along," Ross suggests.

"From what I hear, he's made some powerful enemies over the years, and to be honest, this feels more local." Ross rubs his stomach as if contemplating lunch rather than homicide. "Jason was probably killed because he's baggage, a loose end. He's also from out of town, same as Noah Long. If you think about it, it's unlikely that someone targeting Jason or Noah would follow them to Bakersfield to do the deed. It would be a lot easier to hit Jason in San Jose or Noah in New York."

It's a good argument.

Killers tend to be more comfortable around the familiar: county roads, remote woods, lonely bridges. Places they know. Places they can ply their hate or lust with less fear of being caught or cornered. On the other hand, if this is a professional hit—which it feels like—then all bets are off.

Waving the Polaroid in the air, Ross says, "This might be—I don't know—like when a hunter bags a big-ass moose. Most hunters like to preserve the moment, so they snap a couple of pics." He shrugs. "Maybe that's what we're seeing here."

"This is more than preserving the moment," I observe quietly. "He's sending a message. It's like bagging that moose and mounting its head on a pike as a warning to the others. He's telling them, 'Watch your step or you're next.'"

Jimmy looks up sharply when I say this.

"What?" I say.

He's silent a moment, but takes the picture back from Ross, vetting the thought as he stares at the image on the Polaroid. "Not *you're* next," Jimmy finally says, holding the picture out and pointing at the face staring out at us, "but *he's* next. He's telling us that he's going to kill Wade next if we don't stop him."

The air seems to suddenly be sucked from the room.

"Jeez," Ross mutters, swallowing the word hard.

Ben clears his throat behind us, the kind of throat clearing you do when you want someone's attention, but don't want to be indelicate. "I'm afraid there's something else," he says when we turn his way.

Holding out a second clear plastic evidence bag, he waits for Jimmy to take it. Unlike the first bag, this one isn't flat. It has a pronounced bulge caused by a black mass about the size of a softball.

Jimmy holds the bag a moment . . . then squeezes.

The mass gives, suggesting something soft and pliable. When Jimmy hands the bag to me, he already knows what it is and its significance, though not its meaning. Flipping the bag over in my hands several times, I pull it up close to my eyes and squint through the clear plastic. Jimmy leaves me to it, walking over to the body of Jason Norris. Crouching, he examines the man's bald head without touching. When he's satisfied with his assessment, he stands and glances at the doctor, who just shrugs and gives a slow shake of his head.

That's when I understand.

"Hair," I say, more to myself than those around me. The sudden urge to get rid of the envelope overwhelms me, and I hand it off to Ross as quickly as I can, trying not to look distressed.

"We found it in the jacket pocket," Ben says flatly.

"Why shave his head?" Jimmy wonders aloud.

"William Johansson was bald," I say, leaving an unspoken question in the words.

"Makes sense," Ross says. "He swapped Johansson for Norris. Might as well do it right and shave his head to match?"

"Johansson is white; Norris is Black," Jimmy points out. "One was close to eighty, the other is in his forties. If he did it for uniformity, I think he picked the wrong grave."

"No one said criminals are smart," Ross replies.

"Yeah, but they're not always stupid either." Jimmy studies the corpse of Jason Norris another moment before looking up and meeting Dr. Herrera's gaze. "Anything else?"

"Isn't that enough?"

Jimmy finds a bench along the sidewalk in front of the coroner's office and plops down as he pulls Special Agent Kip Weir's card from his shirt pocket. He dials the number and spends a moment with our FBI counterpart recounting our findings. Weir, it seems, has become fixated on Abel Moya. I can hear his voice on the other end, and though I can't make out every word, I get the gist.

My partner's rolling eyes fill in the gaps.

Jimmy finishes the call and slips his phone back into his pocket. He glances at Ross, who's talking jovially with a colleague he ran into on our way out.

"Weir's calling in resources from the field office: ten agents, an analyst, and a mobile command center," Jimmy says quietly. "Says he's going to run Abel Moya to the ground." Jimmy raises his eyebrows slightly, as if skeptical.

"Moya's not the guy."

"I know, but we can't exactly tell him, can we?"

Rocking my head, I use it to gesture toward the coroner's office and whisper, "The dark green shine from the cemetery? It was all over the photo. No one else touched it other than Dr. Herrera. This *malachite* is who we need to be hunting, not"—I wave the name away impatiently—"Abel Moya."

Jimmy nods his agreement.

"Marco may be the target—or maybe not," I continue. "Either way, it would be sloppy on our part if we make that assumption without checking the others. Someone needs to get on the phone with New York and see who Noah was in bed with; see if any threats were made, or if he pissed off any nefarious investors. You can't run a multibillion-dollar hedge fund and not make some enemies."

"Agreed," Jimmy murmurs. "I'll contact Diane and have her make some calls." Tipping his head toward Ross, who's still yakking with the other detective, Jimmy asks, "What about him?"

"Eventually we might have to ditch him," I say softly, "but right now there's nothing to track, so no harm in keeping him around. Besides, he's kind of cool." Ross starts doing his belly-rub thing again, which I point out to Jimmy with a telling flick of my finger. "Reminds me of a Teletubby when he does that," I whisper.

"A Teletubby?" Jimmy says with a suppressed chuckle.

"Well . . . look at him! He's either a Teletubby or he's kneading twenty pounds of dough, and I don't see any baking pans lying around."

Doing his best to be inconspicuous, Jimmy watches the detective out of the corner of his eye, but Ross seems oblivious to the attention and equally oblivious to the actions of his left hand and fingers as they massage his belly in a slow, counterclockwise direction.

"Jane did that with Pete during the last three or four months of her pregnancy," Jimmy notes. "Always rubbing her belly, like that was going to speed things along." He tips his head toward Ross. "Maybe he was pregnant in a former life?"

Jimmy says this in a voice that's too loud and arrives with unfortunate timing. Ross is just waving goodbye to the detective and moving our way when the words rise and fade, leaving enough residue from their passing that Ross manages to glom on to a few words.

"You have a pregnant wife?" he asks, mishearing the word *life*.

"No . . . yes—she *was* pregnant," Jimmy stammers. "She's not anymore. She gave birth. We have a son."

As I'm trying not to laugh, Ross thumbs at himself. "Two girls and a boy."

He has pictures on his phone, which he's more than glad to share as he explains that the boy, Allan, is starting high school in the fall, and the girls are a few years behind. Like a good father, Jimmy produces several recent pictures of Petey, and Ross proclaims that he's the spitting image of his dad—which must be the UPS driver, because, if anything, Petey favors his mom. He even has her vivid green eyes.

"What about you, Steps?" Ross asks. "Any kids?"

"I have books," I reply, refusing to get sucked into this conversation.

The first musical notes from *The Pink Panther* spill from Jimmy's phone and he answers before the song can take shape.

"What have you got, Diane?"

Instead of putting the phone on speaker, which would have been the polite thing to do, Jimmy wanders away from us, and it quickly becomes clear that he's looking for a flat surface. Fishing one of his precious pens from an open shirt pocket, he snaps his finger at me and motions for something to write on.

My pockets are empty. "You got any paper?" I ask Ross.

He empties his pockets and hands me a neatly folded gum wrapper. It's better than nothing, so I hold it up for Jimmy and give him a how-about-this? shrug. He just glares at me. I wasn't trying to be a smart-ass; it's just when you demand paper, you should be satisfied with what you get.

Jimmy's *not* satisfied, so I jog two parking spaces to the left and motion for him to unlock the Mustang door with the fob. When I hear the click, I open the door, retrieve his Fossil briefcase, rifle through it, and emerge triumphantly with a half-used notepad.

By this time, Jimmy has caught up, and I hand the paper off to him—along with the gum wrapper. After discarding the wrapper with disgust, he leans over the hood of the Mustang and uses it as an impromptu desk. It's not ideal, but it'll do.

"Give it to me again," he says to Diane.

After a hurried writing session, he thanks Diane and ends the call. Turning, he pauses to read his handwriting, perhaps making sure it's legible. "Diane called her contact at Homeland Security, and it seems they have a special interest in Abel Moya. They've had an open investigation on him for the past three or four months."

"What kind of investigation?" Ross asks.

"Human smuggling. He's been operating out of a warehouse near the intersection of Allen Road and Hagerman Road—"

"Hageman Road," Ross corrects. "That's about ten miles west of here."

"Yeah, well, Homeland Security Investigations has had the place under off-and-on surveillance for a couple of weeks now."

"Anything we can work with?" I ask.

"They don't have a warrant for his arrest, but Diane says they have enough for probable cause. They were hoping to build a stronger case before arresting him, maybe scoop up some of the others involved in the operation, but they understand the urgency. They're putting the PC statement together as we speak and said they'll email a copy in thirty or forty minutes." Jimmy glances at Ross. "I gave them your email address. Hope that's okay."

Ross grins. "Sure. I'll make a call and get my guys working on the search warrant."

"We should probably give Weir a heads-up," I suggest.

Jimmy nods. "Yeah, I'm sure he'll want to take lead."

"Let him."

Jimmy starts to scowl at me but then thinks better of it and nods. This is, after all, another distraction. Abel's not the guy, but we've got nothing else to go on, so we may as well vet him and get him off the list.

Jimmy's call to Weir is brief.

When Jimmy disconnects, he stares at the phone a moment before speaking. "Kip wants to move on the warehouse as soon as the warrant's in hand. He's convinced that Marco and the others are inside."

"His circus, his monkeys," I mutter under my breath.

# 14

The no-frills tan warehouse off Allen Road rests within a network of dozens of similar warehouses, all linked by six crisscrossing roads. Some warehouses serve a single client, while others are divided into two, three, or even four spaces and leased to businesses with smaller requirements. It's what some might call an industrial complex, and thus a modest stream of vehicles comes and goes throughout the day, everything from UPS and FedEx trucks delivering individual packages to tractor trailers delivering pallets and containers.

Jimmy's choice of a surveillance position is spot-on.

A hundred yards north, straight through the windshield, is the front of Abel Moya's rented space. Unlike the other businesses in the complex, it's unadorned except for a small sign next to the office door that reads CLOSED—a permanent statement from the look of things.

The entry door and accompanying sign are up a short flight of stairs to the left of the space. To the right of the door, two large windows are cut into the otherwise solid wall, their glossy black holes hinting at a dark interior. Finally, all the way to the right, a heavy steel roll-up door marks a loading dock.

Sorting through his go bag, Jimmy retrieves a pair of Steiner tactical binoculars and sets his sights on Abel Moya's distant warehouse. He sweeps left and right, then lingers on the windows for a full minute before lowering the German nocs to his lap.

"Looks deserted," he mutters, handing off the binoculars. "Take a look."

Letting the lenses draw the warehouse in for closer inspection, I focus on the windows first, noting the partially closed blinds. There's no movement inside, but I do find something encouraging. "Abel Moya's been here."

To anyone else, the statement might sound like wishful thinking, but Jimmy understands. Abel's faded-yellow shine is all around the building. I can even see smears of dusty yellow where he tried to wash the windows. The one thing I can't tell Jimmy, even in our practiced code, is that the dark green shine from the cemetery—the polished malachite—is nowhere to be seen.

If Abel is responsible for the abductions of the four men and the murder of Jason Norris, there's nothing here to hint at it. And if Mr. Malachite is an accomplice, I would have expected to find signs of his passing—at least a random visit.

There's nothing.

We're wasting our time.

Though this is as clear to me as the vast emptiness of our universe, there's nothing to be done about it. A lever has been pulled and there's nothing to do for it but ride this cart to the end. Perhaps if we get Abel in custody and Special Agent Weir can be convinced that he's not involved, we can better focus his attention elsewhere.

Perhaps.

The layout of the building suggests a mix of warehouse and office space, occupying about three thousand square feet in total. Probably half of that is warehouse space, but we won't know for certain until we're inside.

And though the building looks empty, a blue nineties-era Acura parked out front suggests otherwise. A thermal scope indicates the engine is still warm—warm but not hot.

It's not long before the op starts to breathe life.

We may not be in the command vehicle or sitting with the SWAT team members for the final brief, but when you've done enough of those, you can tell when things are about to get real. The texts increase, the radio traffic picks up, and the cell-to-cell comms increase.

More important, you can *feel* it.

Something buried deep in the lizard-brain part of the skull screams, *Danger, danger, danger.* Adrenaline dumps into the bloodstream at increasing levels, coursing through a hundred thousand miles of arteries, veins, and capillaries.

Skin tingles and hair rises.

When Ross finally gets the text we've been waiting for, he scans it. "We're good to go. The BearCat is prepositioned two blocks away." He presses an earbud into place and adjusts the volume on his portable radio, which is set to the tactical frequency picked for this operation.

"Two-man advance team moving along the front," Ross narrates, giving us a play-by-play. In the distance, as if on cue, we see two crouched figures working their way along the front of the building and pausing just right of the nearest window.

"They're using a pole camera to get a look inside," Ross mutters. His perpetual smile is still in place, though it's now tight and drawn as if he were wearing a mask of transparent latex.

"Movement confirmed," he says in a near monotone, sounding for a moment like Kip Weir. "At least one . . . correction, at least two subjects inside . . . no weapons visible. . . . Undercover units are in position behind the warehouse. . . . No movement . . . the back door is closed, and the outside is blocked by wooden pallets."

Ross leans forward in the backseat, his head now between Jimmy and me with a forearm on the upper back of each front seat. "SWAT is advising that one of the subjects is walking toward the front door. . . . Hold . . . negative, negative, subject turned around and went into a side room."

After another minute of observation, the pole-camera team withdraws and takes position at the right front corner of the building, out of sight but ready to move.

"BearCat rolling," Ross calls briskly. An odd vibration begins to emanate from my seat, and it takes me a moment to realize the detective is tapping his foot and thrusting his knee into the back of the seat at the same time.

Vigorous tapping.

A nervous tic.

He's practically in the front seat with us.

Moments later, a murdered-out armored vehicle the size of a large SUV powers into view from the left. Its sides are festooned with black-clad figures, and as it screeches to a halt in front of the warehouse, the men and women of Bakersfield SWAT leap from their perches and flow toward the front door like black mercury.

The hodgepodge of tactically clad bodies quickly forms a neat and ordered stack. They converge on the entry and barely seem to pause as the lead, a mountain of a man, shatters the door with a single whack of his ram and steps to the side.

SWAT officers pour in, shouting commands and clearing rooms one by one.

"Go, go, go!" Ross suddenly yells, waving a bladed hand toward the warehouse.

This wasn't part of the plan.

Strictly speaking, Jimmy and I are here to observe the

operation and do a walk-through after the dust has settled. This minor detail doesn't seem to faze Jimmy. Bringing the Mustang to life with a decided roar, he pounds the gas pedal to the floor. Ross flies back, laughing almost maniacally as the beast of a car accelerates and pins him to the backseat.

As the Mustang's raw horsepower devours the distance to the warehouse, biting yards off in chunks, Ross finds his balance and points to a spot twenty feet back from the mean-looking BearCat. "There!"

Jimmy lights up the brakes and noses the car to the left, parking at a forty-five-degree angle to the building so that the driver's side faces away and the passenger side—my side—is exposed to any hostility that might pour from the warehouse.

As I'm contemplating this, Jimmy and Ross bail from the vehicle. Ross doesn't bother waiting for Jimmy to exit the door, but leaps over the side of the car from the backseat. It reminds me of a scene from so many movies, but with less grace.

Drawing their weapons as their feet hit the pavement, the two of them scoot up the side of the Mustang and take position along the nose, covering the front door with their Glocks.

Meanwhile, I'm still scrunched down in the front passenger seat.

The primal part of my brain is screaming a flashing red warning that this might be a bad idea, but the only other options are to drag myself across the center console and out the driver's door or jump out the passenger door and run around the back of the car without getting shot.

I don't like either choice.

Besides, I've got a clear view of the action from here, and a good amount of glass and steel is between me and any shooters. What could go wrong?

A moment later, I see Jimmy's head peek up over the front

fender as he watches the warehouse. His eyes come my way and then flare when he sees me hunkered down with just my eyes peeking over the dash. "Steps!" he barks.

Ross thinks it's funny.

Making a big show of huffing and sighing, I drag myself across the center console—which is just as awkward and uncomfortable as I imagined—and over Jimmy's seat. The steering wheel presses uncomfortably into my ribs until, at last, I pour myself out the driver's door using nothing but biceps, triceps, and a little forearm action. I find the asphalt without too much difficulty. Dragging my legs free, I use my left sneaker to ease the door closed and then push myself upright. Ross grins and motions for me to take up position behind him.

The view sucks, but I keep the thought to myself.

I'm just catching my breath when Ross presses his finger to the earbud, listens intently, and says, "Uh-oh!" He repeats it a second time, more urgently this time, as if the meaning of the transmission is starting to sink in.

Then he finds his inertia. Swearing majestically, he leaps to his feet.

For a moment he looks like he's going to run, but then he screams, "Get in the car; get in the car!" Without waiting to explain, he throws himself into the backseat, landing with all the finesse of a humpback whale, minus the enormous splash.

"Get us out of here, Jimmy!" he yells, his face still planted on the seat.

At that moment, black-clad SWAT members begin to pour from the warehouse, running for all they're worth. Some of them make for the BearCat, while others run right past and keep going. Some take cover behind nearby warehouses.

"Get us out of here," I say in a remarkably calm voice.

The Mustang barely roars to life before Jimmy jams it into gear and smashes the gas pedal. The tires spew black smoke as the yellow monster tears at the ground, clawing itself into a full sprint. The acceleration throws me against the back of my seat and holds me there. I don't know what we're running from, and I don't care.

In some circumstances, only the dead stop to ask why.

# 15

Blast radiuses are a tricky thing.

They depend on the type of explosive, the quantity, and the placement, among other factors. Small devices are generally only a threat to the immediate area and can usually be detonated in place or removed to a safe location for destruction.

Larger devices are more problematic.

Twenty-five to thirty barrels of ammonium nitrate fuel oil (ANFO) or ammonium nitrate and nitromethane (ANNM) is another story entirely. Such a quantity could leave a crater where the warehouse stands and level every building around it.

As SWAT swept through Abel Moya's office and warehouse, that's exactly what they appear to have found stored on wooden pallets just inside the big roll-up door. Initially unsure what they were dealing with, they removed the tarp covering the collection and triggered a countdown clock. As the device hummed to life, the word ARMED glared at them in neon-red letters.

Hence, the hasty exit.

In 1947, the freighter *Grandcamp* was docked at a pier in Texas City, Texas, when a fire broke out in one of its holds, most likely caused by a cigarette. Twenty-three hundred tons of ammonium nitrate had already been loaded onto the ship, and when the flames reached the explosive cargo at about 9:00 A.M., the ship was blown to pieces in an explosion that was heard 150 miles away. The blast left carnage in its wake: five hundred homes leveled, almost six hundred dead, and another thirty-five hundred injured.

They found the ship's three-thousand-pound anchor two miles away.

Assuming all twenty-five to thirty barrels in Abel Moya's warehouse contain ANFO or ANNM, the resulting blast would be equivalent to the Oklahoma City bombing in 1995. Centered at the Alfred P. Murrah Federal Building, the explosion destroyed or damaged over three hundred buildings in a sixteen-block radius.

Perhaps because of this, SWAT commander Keith Baker gets no arguments when he orders the command vehicle to a fallback position a half mile from the warehouse and then dispatches patrol units to the surrounding neighborhoods and business parks announcing a mandatory evacuation. The call and echo from the car-mounted speakers can be heard coming from every quarter, the voices cascading over one another, projecting urgency and demanding compliance.

Allen Road is shut down completely, as is Hageman Road.

The whole thing is a colossal mess, and the evacuation eats up more than an hour. Even then, we can't be sure everyone got out. The only thing lending balance to the operation is the knowledge that the bomb only read ARMED. No countdown was triggered. After reviewing body-camera footage from SWAT members, the team is satisfied that no explosion is imminent.

Going frame by frame, they note the exact moment that the red LEDs come to life—come to life and just . . . wait. Their sudden flare is a bit like a bull pawing the ground and kicking up dirt before the charge. It's a warning. The footage also shows what looks like a battery pack and wires going into the barrel directly under the display panel.

Somebody knew what they were doing.

Three hours after first arriving at the industrial park, the armored BearCat once again screeches to a stop in front of the warehouse, but instead of disgorging black-clad men with nasty weapons, two officers exit briefly and haul out a black rectangle that they set on the ground.

They leave just as quickly as they arrived.

The rectangle rests on the ground, unmoving. It's perhaps a yard long by maybe ten inches high and twenty wide, and the only thing particularly unusual about it is the manner of its delivery.

Then it moves.

As if waking from slumber, it seems to stretch and then rises, pausing to take in its surroundings. The small head turns left and right on its long, thin neck until it finds the front door and fixes its sights. With a mechanical lurch, the body swivels and starts forward, moving at the tortoise pace of perhaps two miles per hour.

Watching the remote-controlled robot through Jimmy's Steiner 10x42 tactical binoculars, I'm impressed when it reaches the outside steps and barely pauses before climbing to the upper platform. The SuperDroid HD2 tactical robot is a favorite of SWAT teams because it can be used for a variety of purposes. In addition to overcoming obstacles, its tanklike construction features cameras and a six-axis arm that can open doors and lift objects both light and heavy.

It's perfect for retrieving explosives and removing them to a safe disposal location. Unless, of course, those explosives are accumulated in a couple dozen fifty-five-gallon drums wired to a detonator that's ready to *tick-tick-tick* on its way to *boom*.

Even the mighty SuperDroid has its limitations.

Nicknamed Johnny 5 by the team—after the robot from the 1986 film *Short Circuit*—the SuperDroid will be called on for something a bit more specialized today. The next twenty minutes will tell whether the unit's life comes to a sudden, violent end among the scorched ruins of a hundred buildings, or whether the robot will live to fight another day.

For Johnny 5, the outcome will not be dictated by the superior artificial intelligence displayed by his mechanical brother in the movie, but by the dexterity and skill of the explosive ordnance disposal (EOD) specialist now manipulating the controls from a half mile away in the command vehicle. I didn't catch the EOD operator's name, but one of his teammates called him Stick, which, if you ask me, is a pretty stupid moniker for a moderately overweight EOD guy.

But who am I to judge?

I've only ever met a handful of EOD types, two of whom were nicknamed Lefty on account of the missing or partially missing digits on their right hand. Lefty's a cool name, but that's a club not worth the admission price. Jimmy has a former Air Force buddy nicknamed Boomer, whom I met in Kansas City three years ago. When I asked why they called him Boomer, Jimmy said it was because he'd shout out, "Boom," every time he detonated something.

A world of pressure bears down on Stick from behind as a dozen sets of determined eyes stand fixed to the screen that displays the camera feed from Johnny 5. When the robot makes entry through the shattered front door, every breath is held. The crowd presses closer, and the lookie-loos undulate in a constantly shifting mass, each vying for a better vantage point. The weight of their presence—even if imagined—is almost palpable.

My presence adds to the gravity.

Guided by Stick, Johnny 5 makes straight for the warehouse and its frightful collection of drums and pallets. The heavy-gauge door is closed when the SuperDroid reaches it. The jagged wound in the Sheetrock looks ominous through the camera feed, like a hungry mouth. It's the kind of hole you don't stick your hand into if you want to pull it back out in one piece.

Maneuvering the joystick with the patience of a monk, Stick raises the robot's articulating arm and lines it up with the door handle. From the subtle manipulation of the controls, bordering on a caress, the robot grasps the handle and gives a gentle counterclockwise turn. We don't hear the latch release from the striker plate, but the door opens into the cavernous warehouse nonetheless.

The light is still on, so Stick wheels Johnny 5 over to the barrels and spends several minutes looking for trip wires or booby traps. Finding none, he raises the arm until the camera is looking down on the digital display and the disquieting letters that suggest a real potential for calamity.

One wrong move might carve a jagged crater into the ground where the warehouse now stands. In such an eventuality, the fate of Johnny 5 might be the least of our worries. I don't know a lot about explosives, but I'm starting to wonder if a half mile is enough distance from such a collection of barrels.

"Battery pack," Stick says, pointing to a bundle the size of a six-inch sub sandwich. It's wrapped in duct tape, but you can see wires attached to both ends, and the rough outline of perhaps a dozen D batteries in three stacks.

"Can you cut it?" Ross asks. "Or is that just in movies?" It's the same question I had, but I didn't want to look stupid.

"Yes and no," Stick replies in a cool, even tone. "We need to make sure it's not a decoy and then check for backups." He taps the screen as if to indicate the display module. "This isn't a complicated setup, which makes me think it's a decoy." He points out various wires connecting the battery pack to the display and the display to a small black box resting in the gap between barrels.

"If that's your detonator," Stick says, indicating the black box, "what are these?" He drags his finger along some barely visible lines on the screen, and I realize they're additional wires, perhaps a dozen of them. They disappear under the tarp and away from the detonator, begging questions—questions to which we need answers.

"Can you remove the rest of the tarp?" Keith Baker asks from his perch behind Stick's right shoulder.

"I can try, but didn't you say that's what activated the display?"

"Yeah, pretty sure it was a thread tied to the corner of the tarp. The flashlight on the arm should light it up if the other corners are rigged." The statement borders on wishful thinking.

"I'll give it a go. I'm just saying that if one thread arms it, another might start the countdown."

"Or light it off immediately," I mutter.

Several heads turn my way, as if weighing the possibilities, but most either don't hear or don't pay attention.

Maneuvering the robot to the left corner of the palleted collection, Stick zooms the camera and does a thorough scan for threads or other triggering devices. Satisfied, he gently clamps onto a fold in the blue tarp and prepares to lift. "Grab your butts," he suggests to the room, and in one smooth motion, the robot's metal arm lifts the cover and folds it back onto the barrels, exposing the left corner.

No threads snap, no red letters blaze defiantly, no thunderous explosion rocks the command vehicle.

"So far so good," Stick says in a voice two pitches too high.

He repeats the process on the rear corners, which proves more difficult due to their proximity to the wall, but it's nothing that can't be solved with minimal violence and maximum patience.

Folding the loosened tarp into a four-foot-wide strip running down the center of the barrels, Stick directs Johnny 5 to the left side of the pallets to grasp the end of the tarp. Engaging the tanklike tracks of the robot, Stick has the robot pull the covering clear of the drums and drag it across the concrete floor until it's well away from the work area.

The air-conditioning in the command vehicle is blowing cold from the front and rear overhead units, but I still feel a trickle of sweat running down the center of my back. I'm not the only one feeling wet and sticky. Just about everyone else in the RV is either pitted out, damp around the neck, or in desperate need of a circa-1970s sweatband.

The only guy who seems to be taking it in stride is Detective Ross Feng. When he catches me glancing his way, he grins in his goofy way and nods, as if to say, *Good times, eh, Steps?* I smile back, not because I agree with the sentiment, but because the guy's too likable to ignore.

Examining the naked barrels for additional battery packs or detonators, Stick begins to mutter incoherently to himself. I can't tell if he's puzzled or pissed. This continues as he traces out each wire, then he makes a rather surprising announcement.

"They're decoys."

"Decoys?" someone asks skeptically.

"I've got six wires dropping down between the barrels at six different locations, every one of them ending at nothing. They're just hanging there."

"Does that mean the detonator *is* the detonator?" I ask.

"Seems so."

Turning his attention back to the display panel with its connected battery pack and detonator, Stick grows quiet as he manipulates the robot camera this way and that. The only sound in the command vehicle is the overhead AC unit and a low rumble from someone's stomach.

Minutes slow as time turns to molasses.

The crypt-like quiet lingers as Stick studies the device from every angle, even tipping the display gently up on edge to examine the underside. Then, with the suddenness of lightning, he slaps the countertop with such force that the sound makes the whole room jump. Issuing a guttural, animalistic roar—as if losing his mind—he does the unthinkable.

Clamping the robot arm onto the detonator, Stick rips it from the side of the barrel with an exaggerated, fatalistic yank of the joystick. I duck instinctively, expecting a blast, but none comes. A confused round of gasps and hisses fills the confines of the RV as Stick next turns his attention to the battery pack, jerking it so hard it rips the wires free and sends them flopping across the nearest barrel.

To those of us watching helplessly, his reckless actions seem born of desperation, of sanity surrendering to delirium . . . but it only seems so.

With a shout the size of Texas, Stick slaps the countertop again and then jumps to his feet. "It's a fake!" He gestures at the monitor and glances from face to face. "The whole thing. The bastard's playing with us." Stick exudes confidence as he goes on to explain his findings to the brass, but I notice a tremor in his right hand as it hangs at his side.

I've seen the effect before.

It's the aftermath of too much adrenaline and cortisol pouring into the circulatory system and then finding itself out of a job. Shaking is just one of the possible physical effects of such a hormone dump. There's also increased heart rate, constricted blood vessels, a pale or flushed face, tunnel vision, dilated pupils, hearing loss, and more.

A relaxed bladder is probably the worst of the possible side effects, at least as far as I'm concerned. Not that I'm speaking from personal experience. A few random drops scared out of the urinary tract hardly qualifies.

The body's fight-or-flight mechanism is a marvel of genetics, but its kill switch is a little slow on the uptake. As the adrenaline slowly drains from Stick's system, the shakes will settle and then vanish altogether. I've been down that road more times than I care to recall.

When the EOD tech sees me looking, he just smiles, gives a small nod, and tucks the hand into his pocket.

# 16

It takes EOD another forty-five minutes to conclude that all twenty-seven barrels in the warehouse are filled with nothing more than water—brownish, murky water, but water nonetheless. Ross gets the all clear from SWAT and leads the way through the office door, down the hall, and into the troublesome warehouse. Shine abounds, but none that matches the polished malachite from the cemetery.

We find ourselves standing next to the collection of unmasked fifty-five-gallon drums, the wires, display, and fake detonator stacked neatly on top of the nearest barrel. Crossing his arms, Ross takes in the sight and snorts.

"People and explosives," he mutters. The words should simply be a statement, but the way Ross says them you just know they're a prelude to something more.

He doesn't disappoint.

"Last year, we had this little asswipe twenty-year-old cop wannabe working security at an industrial park on the south side of town. In his infinite wisdom, he decided to make his own flash-bangs. Blew off half his hand in the process."

Ross looks at me, dumbfounded. "They found his index finger impaled on a roofing nail that was poking through the shed ceiling, if you can believe that. Never saw anything—"

Ross's phone rings and he holds up a finger; an index finger, ironically.

As he slowly drifts away in conversation, Jimmy just chuckles. We leave Ross to his call and make our way back to the office spaces, and I motion Jimmy into what looks like a makeshift conference room. Its purpose is unimportant; the only thing I care about is that it's empty at the moment.

"We're wasting our time on Abel Moya," I say bluntly.

He nods, as if expecting this, but nonetheless says, "You're sure?"

"I'm positive. Hundreds of people have passed through here in the last few months, including a lot with green shine, but none are remotely similar to our gravedigger."

Jimmy suspected as much but is disappointed nonetheless. "Good luck convincing Kip."

"We need to have another talk with Ella. There's something in the congressman's history that we're missing . . . either that or he's not the target."

Jimmy nods. "Meaning we've allowed ourselves to get tunnel vision, ignoring other possibilities."

"We started with the most logical—"

Jimmy holds up a hand to stop me. "I know, and you're right. We focused on Marco because he's a congressman and because Secret Service is breathing down the director's neck. This could just as easily be about Jason, Wade, or Noah." Giving me a hard look, Jimmy adds, "Are we sure that photo of Wade means he's the next to die? Couldn't it just as easily mean that he's the reason for all this—for Jason's death and any others that follow?"

"Wade's next," I say unequivocally. "You know it as well as I do. We've seen this type of signaling on other cases, though never this obvious."

Jimmy meets my gaze, his face grim and set.

I'm about to speak again when something catches my eye. A partial syllable—a meaningless guttural not meant to stand on its own—has already escaped my lips, but the rest of the word dies in my throat. My eyes fix upon the floor behind Jimmy with such intensity that he turns to look but sees nothing.

Aside from the conference table and a handful of chairs, the room is Spartan. A fridge sits in the corner next to a particleboard stand that holds an antiquated printer covered in dust. The only other item is an unused four-by-eight whiteboard that rests on the ground and leans into the back wall. Its face is mostly clear of marks, save for a few dates, some minor notations, and a phone number for a pizza-delivery service.

"What is it?"

"The whiteboard," I say in a low voice.

He makes a gesture as if to say, *What about it?*

Slowly and in a clear but quiet voice, I say, "Some of the footprints that lead up to it don't come back."

It takes a moment for the enormity of this to register, but when it does, Jimmy's hand flies to his Glock and he motions me back. Moving flush up against the wall on the left side of the board, he holds his handgun at the ready as he tips the panel forward a few inches at a time.

"What is it?" I hiss.

Jimmy shakes his head briskly but doesn't look at me or answer, intent on what lies concealed behind the whiteboard. At last, and without warning, he pulls the top corner away from the wall and lets the whiteboard fall forward. It strikes a chair and knocks it onto its back with a loud crash before striking the edge of the conference room table with a calamitous crash. An open box of office supplies skids across the table surface and plunges to the floor on the other side, adding to the cacophony.

The wall behind the whiteboard now stands exposed.

Where one would expect Sheetrock and paint stands a jagged three-foot-by-three-foot hole that opens into darkness.

It's as if some enormous rat chewed its way through the wall and then hid its misdeed behind the innocuous board. I half expect a gray-whiskered nose to poke through, followed by sharp teeth and beady black eyes.

It's a *different* animal I should be concerned with.

For all we know, armed men could be watching us at this moment, perhaps with fingers on triggers as they decide whether to blast away and rain hell down on us or to escape. The thought chills me and I angle away from the gloomy opening.

That's when the voice rings in my ear.

It's so close and startling that I utter an involuntary noise that I'd just as soon forget.

"What's this?" Ross repeats as I turn to find him standing three feet behind me. Seeing the flustered look on my face, he chuckles. "Someone's a bit jumpy." Clapping me on the shoulder, he looks to the wall. "You found a hole." He says it the way one might acknowledge finding a lost sock or a misplaced comb.

Retrieving his flashlight, Ross shines it into the hole and sweeps from right to left. Distant shapes stand silhouetted in the murky background, but he finds nothing of note until he sweeps the beam to the left. There, perhaps seven feet away, a face looks back at him, blinking in the light.

Opening its mouth, the face begins to speak.

# 17

"We found twenty-three of them," Keith Baker informs us as SWAT finishes their sweep of the second warehouse. "There are two groups, one made up of Hondurans heading to Oregon, and the other is a smaller group of Mexicans going to Northern California. We ran a six-pack past a couple of the leaders"—Keith's referring to a six-image photo lineup—"and they all identified Abel as their coyote."

Keith hands three sheets of paper to Ross, each depicting the same lineup of six subjects displayed in two rows of three each. The sheets are signed, and the third image—that of Abel Moya—is circled in the upper-right corner.

"Abel was the one who brought them across?" I ask.

"Yeah, plus one other. We haven't identified him yet. They used two vehicles."

"When?"

"Two days ago."

Turning to Ross and Jimmy, I say, "Two days ago was Saturday." I pause to let the significance sink in.

Ross eventually nods. "Hard to imagine Abel sneaking people across the border on the same day he kidnapped four men on the Upper Kern." His tone is thoughtful and somewhat distant.

I say nothing; better to let his own words convince him.

Abel Moya may be a first-rate criminal, but he's not *our* criminal.

The inside of the second warehouse looks different with the lights on, though still Spartan. In the center of the concrete floor, seated in two rows facing each other, the immigrants barely raise their heads to look around, staring instead at the floor, at their hands, and, occasionally, at one another.

Three children are among the six women and fourteen men.

If flowers wilt under too much sun and not enough water, these children are the most delicate type of daffodil. Their heads hang heavily from their thin necks, as if too cumbersome to hold aloft; as if the mere thought of lifting such a weight might snap it right off. Their arms dangle at their sides like sun-scorched leaves. Even the mildest of winds might lay waste to them, leaving them prone and scattered upon the ground.

I've always been a strong advocate for border security—and still am; but now, seeing the dirty and disheveled children, something bends in my chest, threatening to break. I can't help but wonder if there isn't a better way.

I excuse myself a moment and run back outside to the Mustang. Snatching up my backpack, and Jimmy's as well, I hurry back inside. Dumping the contents onto a table, I sort through and extract anything edible—even the granola bars.

Jimmy starts to protest, but then realizes what I'm doing and comes over to help. All told, we have twenty-one granola bars, two containers of Pringles—one full, one nearly empty—a sleeve of Ritz crackers, a jar of lightly salted peanuts, some beef jerky, a bag of trail mix, and five bottles of water.

With Ross's help, we start distributing the food, beginning with the children, who each get a full bottle of water. They're ravenous; no telling when Abel last fed them. Maybe their ticket north didn't include meals. The thought stirs an ember in my gut, a hot glow I recognize as anger, a stirring that borders on hate.

I want Abel Moya.

He had nothing to do with the disappearance of Marco and his friends, I'm sure of that now, but I want him just the same. Priorities being what they are, the congressman comes first, but I vow to come back when this is all over and help Ross find this guy. Find him and put him away for a long time.

A modicum of justice for starving, withered children.

Aside from the chained door at the front of the building and the roll-up door next to it, SWAT found a door on the west wall that leads out to a raised, porch-like structure. Weathered cardboard and old pallets fill most of the porch, some heaped in misshapen piles and others placed vertically, like old books and magazines on an overlarge shelf.

It's through this door that Abel and his confederates made their escape; I can see his worn yellow shine on the floor and the door handle. Following the track with Jimmy and Ross close behind, I step outside and see where his stride lengthens into a run as he makes for the corner of the next building over. Even from here, I can see where the steps disappear abruptly at a now-empty parking spot.

Turning, I'm just starting to put my glasses on when something catches my eye: a flash of neon color that shouldn't be here. Looking closer, I see a single foot protruding from underneath several layers of cardboard on the right side of the porch. The shine is warm and pulsing, so I know the owner of the foot is still alive, I'm just not sure if he's still attached to the foot.

Moving in for a closer look, I see that the foot is clad in a battered sneaker and attached to a dirty ankle that disappears under the pile.

"Jimmy!" I hiss.

It would have been easy to miss the foot without the iridescence of shine, but as things stand, it glows like the embers of a bonfire. I glance at Jimmy and tip my head in a take-a-look manner. He follows the gesture, and as the wayward appendage registers, he unholsters his Glock with a slow, whisper-quiet pull.

Ross follows suit, though he doesn't yet see what we're looking at.

Moving forward, I hold a finger up for Jimmy, then indicate that I'm going to throw the pieces of cardboard off while he keeps locked on the subject. On the silent count of three, I lift the four large sheets of cardboard straight up and flip them in a 180-degree arc, exposing the man below.

"FBI!" Jimmy shouts. "Keep your hands where I can see them."

The man lays motionless, eyes closed and mouth agape, as if dead.

He looks to be in his fifties or sixties, though life on the street tends to wear more deeply at the lines of both face and body, so he may be in his forties. His lack of movement makes me wonder if he might be near death, but then he gives a single snort, rolls onto his side, and begins to snore prodigiously.

Slightly perturbed, Jimmy kicks gently at the man's sneaker. "Rise and shine, partner." When there's no reaction, Jimmy kicks the shoe again, a little harder this time. "Hey, buddy!" he yells. "Wake up!"

No reaction.

The man may as well be in a coma.

Ross moves up and does a quick pat-down for weapons, finding a pocketknife in the guy's right front pocket and a two-foot section of rebar tucked up tight against his body. Removing these items, Jimmy gives the fellow a vigorous shake. If his clothes, unkempt appearance, and makeshift bed weren't ample evidence that he's homeless, the odor that wafts off him settles the argument in a rather odious manner.

After several more minutes and a considerable amount of shaking and shouting, the man stirs and looks up at us through pupils the size of BBs. His irises are huge by comparison, circling the dots like space matter being pulled into a black hole. His flushed skin and the dark circles under his eyes suggest he's a heroin addict, but he also smells like a brewery.

"Sir, didn't you notice we have a police emergency?" Ross asks sharply.

"I made a police emergency?"

"No, we *have* a police emergency. It's going on all around you."

"Is that why the cops were here?"

"Sir, how much have you had to drink today?"

The man holds up four filthy fingers and says, "Three beers."

"Wonderful," Ross mutters. Reaching out, he takes the man by the elbow. "Let's get you clear of here before something happens."

"Something already happened," the homeless man says briskly as if just remembering. "I was attacked by some fifty-foot woman. Just came barreling out the door like I wasn't even here. Cracked my spine right in half like it was nothing, like I was one of them Mexican piñatas; I'm probably going to be a paracollegiate." He gives a confused look. "A para . . . what do you call them?" He tries to snap his finger.

"A paraplegic?" Ross suggests.

"Yeah, one of them. With the wheelchair and the robot voice. I can feel my invertebrates snapping as I move." He twists unsteadily at the hip from left to right and then performs a couple of stretches to show the extent of his injuries.

"Your invertebrates are fine," I assure him. "Same with your vertebrae."

His gaze is withering. "You don't know that! That's 'cause you never had your spine cracked in half."

"Fair enough." I hold up my hands in surrender. Then, in my most calming voice, I ask, "What was that you were saying about a woman . . . ?"

"A fifty-foot woman."

"She was tall?"

"No, dumbass, she was a fifty-foot woman." He looks at me like I'm an imbecile. "The kind that looks good at fifty feet but gets uglier the closer she gets: fifty-foot woman. It's pretty simple if you pay attention." He taps his index finger hard against his skull, apparently suggesting I use the brain that God gave me.

"Was she alone?"

"No, these two guys was following her. They drove away in the car parked over there." He points to a parking spot by the next building, apparently unaware that it's empty.

"There's no car there."

He looks, hesitates. "Didn't I just say they drove away? That means they took the car with them."

"Do you remember what kind of car it was?" Jimmy asks.

"One of them Japanese numbers—a Nissan Accord or something."

"A Honda Accord?"

"Nissan!" He spits the word at Jimmy. "Didn't I say Nissan? Or are you as stupid as the other one?" He glances at me tellingly, as if there were any doubt as to who *the other one* was.

Jimmy perseveres. "What color was it?"

"Gray."

"Dark gray, light gray?"

"Primer gray, like they did it with a rattle can." The man huffs and pats his pockets for a cigarette. "How many more questions do I have to ask before I can leave?"

Jimmy and Ross exchange a look and motion a young cop forward. "This officer is going to take a statement from you," Ross explains. "After that, you'll be free to go."

"Just don't leave town, right?" the man quips.

"Yeah," I shoot back, "you might want to cancel those vacation plans."

Before he can reply, the young officer moves in and hustles him away. The old man manages to shoot an evil look my way as he goes.

# 18

*Monday, March 9—8:43 P.M.*

The bark that issues from Congressman Marco Perez's office as we enter surprises me, though not as much as the happy bundle of fur that rolls my way. I say *rolls* because the young boxer's hindquarters are parked on a classy two-wheeled sling, his back legs propped up and immobile. He reminds me of a harness racer, only without the jockey.

"That's Roller," says Canela—Ella—as she comes around the desk to greet us. Roller is already on us when she adds, "Don't worry, he's harmless. Marco went to Guadalajara last year to visit our cousin and came back with this guy." She kneels next to the dog and scratches him behind the ears.

When she looks up, I can see the glassy redness of her eyes, the signs of sorrow. She'd been crying before we arrived, but you wouldn't know it by her steady voice or the resolute lift of her chin. The woman is a rock, and her courage is all the more heartbreaking because of it.

As I look at her, at the sorrow she hides, I feel something firm up in my gut, in my mind. Call it determination or drive, all I know is that we have to get her brother back. His worth is not in his being a congressman, but in that he has a sister like Ella and a heart that bleeds for handicapped dogs.

If the others notice Ella's eyes, they don't say.

If they notice *my* eyes, they don't say.

"What happened to him?" Ross asks, running a hand over Roller's head.

"We don't know. He was probably hit by a car, but it could have just as easily been a thug with a two-by-four. Alejandro—that's my cousin—he owns a restaurant in Guadalajara, and his wife runs a rescue. They always seem to have a few sorry cases they can't adopt out"—Ella smiles—"including this fella."

"Good thing for him your brother likes dogs," Ross suggests.

"Oh, he doesn't—or he didn't. Roller took a fancy to him from the moment he arrived and wouldn't leave him alone. If Marco was standing, he'd be there right next to him, leaning against his leg. If he sat down, Roller came up and rested his chin on his leg. By the end of the week, Marco couldn't bear the thought of leaving him behind."

I can sympathize with Marco: I don't like dogs either.

I suppose they grow on you.

My brother's little Yorkie, Ruby, pulls the same stunt on me all the time, coming up and insisting on sitting next to me on the couch, laying her head on my leg. It's pathetic. I tell her to have some dignity, but she just ignores me and demands a pat.

Ross and Jimmy are busy pouring love on Roller. I'm surprised Jimmy isn't on all fours. After a moment, the boxer looks up at me as if to say, *What about you?* But I just nod, and the dog and I understand each other. When the dogfest finally concludes, Ella leads us to an alcove surrounded by bookcases on three sides.

Now *here's* something I can appreciate.

It's set up almost as a cozy reading nook, with four chairs huddled together around a large coffee table. The shelves are filled not with law books, but with the works of literary greats, both new and old. There are books by Shakespeare, Dickens, Hemingway, Twain, Joyce, Orwell, and Austen, right alongside Stephen King, J. K. Rowling, Ray Bradbury, and Toni Morrison.

I could spend hours just reading the titles.

Before we get down to business, Ella makes a call to a Thai restaurant one block over and orders some fried rice, pad thai, spring rolls, and gai pad med mamuang, which I've never heard of, but she assures me it's delicious.

"Marco was always pragmatic," Ella says slowly, the words filtering out from the dark recess of her high-back chair. With the sun now settled beyond the horizon, and the windows faded to black, the only remaining light comes from a floor lamp at the side of our gathering. The night brings with it a quiet melancholy.

"He took problems head-on," Ella continues, "and was forever confused by those who didn't. Politics, it seems, is filled with grand ideas and impractical notions—the more absurd the better. Marco agreed to a lot of things he wasn't thrilled about and opposed a lot of things others were too willing to concede. This earned him a reputation as a bit of a troublemaker among his peers, not to mention a lot of hate mail . . . but"—she shakes her head—"I still can't imagine why anyone would want to kill him for it."

She speaks of Marco in the past tense: the *was* as opposed to the *is*; the done and not the doing. It's as if she's preparing herself for a truth she cannot bear; as if his body is all but found, his spirit fled.

It's pitiful when someone loses hope and surrenders to bad news that has yet to arrive. I'd correct her, remind her that Marco is still out there, still alive, but I've learned from the sharp edge of experience that a dull blade is sometimes best. If she's already half convinced that Marco is dead, the truth—if it turns out so—will be more bearable. And if by some fortune presently beyond my sight we recover her brother alive, her joy and relief will wash away these present thoughts as if they never existed.

As the conversation continues and we slowly find the bottoms of the Thai take-out containers, Ross makes an innocuous statement that flings him into a conversation he wasn't prepared for.

"We are either a nation of laws or we are nothing," Ella says with a sting in her voice. "One party calls them undocumented, the other calls them illegal. One wants them for the votes they bring, the other for the labor they provide. Both parties play games, and nothing is ever resolved."

"Our agency's policy is to refer to them as undocumented," Ross explains apologetically.

"I know." Ella gives a dismal shake of her head. "I apologize if my tone seems directed at you, Detective, it's just this whole immigration issue . . . it's been a bitter pill for many years. No one seems to want to solve it.

"When Marco was first elected, the Hispanic community loved him. Finally, it seemed, they had one of their own to cheer and hold up." She raises an eyebrow. "That honeymoon lasted less than a year. When Marco openly supported a border-security bill, the tide quickly turned, and he found himself booed by the same people who previously embraced him. Some of them called him an Uncle Tom, apparently confused about the origins of the term.

"Others took his support as a sign that he was in their camp—until five months later when he supported an amnesty bill. There were some—a small few—who appreciated him sticking to his principles, respecting the pragmatism of his seemingly opposed positions. Most just chose to hate."

"No one ever said people are rational," Jimmy offers,

"especially when they've made up their mind about something."

"Right, but they don't even try. If my opinion differs from theirs, and they hear me say that we need to increase security along the border and crack down on sanctuary cities, they'll hear only the first few words and then ignore the rest. With a few words, they've already decided that I'm wrong and they're right. Worse than that, that I'm evil! Simply for having a different opinion on how to solve a problem. How are we supposed to run a country that way?"

She leans forward. "When logic and reason are treated as anachronisms, what becomes of justice and rule of law? Are we no better than the many corrupt and lawless countries around the world, places where favor is courted and purchased at the expense of freedom and justice?"

"I saw some kids at that warehouse today, three of them," I say soberly. "They couldn't have been more than seven or eight years old. How do we tell them no?" I pet Roller, who had parked himself next to me as soon as I sat, and whose head now rests affectionately on my lap, his eyes looking up at me.

Ella looks down and sighs resignedly. "That's the problem, isn't it? I see them too, and I ask myself why we can't make room for just three more, or three hundred more, or three thousand more. Surely it can't make a difference. But there are seven billion people on this planet, and six billion of them would do just about anything to come here. If we were to take just a tenth of them, the population would triple, and America would cease to be America. It's a matter of balance and survival as much as it is law and order."

Ella lets the room lie in silence a moment, then adds, "As much as we may want to help, the fact remains they entered a country that is not theirs and from which they have no claim or expectation, and they did so illegally. If I slipped across the Mexican border illegally, I'd find myself in an unpleasant prison for several years. Where are their outstretched arms?"

"What about our moral obligation?" I press.

"If someone breaks into your home, are you obliged to give them a room?"

"Of course not, but that's—"

"Different? How?"

I don't have an answer for her. "That's not the point—"

Ella cuts me off. I expect her to be incensed by now, but she's suddenly as calm as a glassy lake. No doubt she's had this same conversation a hundred times, maybe a thousand.

"It's exactly the point, and because my brother says what he believes, he's a traitor to his race. And now, someone's gone and—" She cuts the words off before her mouth can utter them.

When she speaks again, her voice once more comes from the depths of the high-back chair, where her face lies in shadow. "What are we all, really?"

"How do you mean?" Ross asks.

She leans forward and looks the detective in the eye, her face striking and beautiful under the single light and the directional shadows. "Did you know that our last name—Marco's and mine—has Hebrew origins? Perez, a name so Spanish and Mexican that it could be nothing else, yet it had its origins in the Hebrew language and means 'son of Peter.'

"Garcia is Basque and pre-Roman in origin. Cantu is Italian, and Fernandez is Germanic. It's the same with Gonzalez, Gomez, and Rodriguez, all of which are Germanic, a family of languages that includes not just German, but English, Dutch, Danish, Norwegian"—she pauses as if referring to a list in her head—"Swedish, Icelandic, Gothic, Burgundian, and some others."

She looks at us, her question genuine and sincere: "So what are we?"

"Bunch of mutts," Jimmy says with a half smile.

Ella returns the smile grudgingly.

"My mom was first-generation," Jimmy explains. "Came over with her parents when she was ten—legally," he quickly adds. "I still have relatives in Sonora."

"Was?"

Jimmy gives her a quizzical look.

"You said your mom *was* first-generation?"

He holds her gaze. "She died when I was five."

Ella nods in understanding. "I'm sorry. What about your dad?"

"Alive and obstinate as ever."

"Irish," I say with a nod as if that explains everything.

"So, we're a bunch of mutts, then," Ella says with a note of satisfaction. If she had a drink in her hand, she'd have raised it at that moment in a toast to consensus and solidarity.

"I suppose it doesn't matter," Jimmy says. "In a few more years, DNA is going to rewrite what we think of ethnicity, for better or worse."

"Let's pray it's for the better," Ella says.

As we leave the congressman's office, Ross texts a former colleague, now a member of the NYPD Intelligence Division. He asks for anything they have on Noah Long, leaving the request intentionally broad. Better too much information than not enough.

Marco may be the most likely target, but Noah and Wade are still contenders.

# 19

*Tuesday, March 10—1:00 A.M.*

The BMW's distinct Long Beach Blue paint job is a wonder even in the pale light of the witching hour. With its deeper shadows and sharper reflections, it's a razzle-dazzle of cobalt and metallic. It rolls silently into an empty parking lot, finds a secluded spot, and the lights go out.

Long it sits.

If one were to watch the SUV long enough, eyes adjusting back to the dark, one would soon notice that shadow also lies within the vehicle. Something ominous wrapped in black.

It occupies the driver's seat as if overflowing, a freakishly large mass that can't be real. Any thought that it's an illusion, however, a trick of light or night, vanishes when a match is struck and a cigarette is lit. As the shadow inhales, the angry orange flare of the tip is high in the side window, placing the shadow's head near the ceiling.

He takes his time smoking the cigarette.

When the SUV's door finally opens, a monster of a man steps out and stretches in the weak luminescence of the dome light. He shows little concern as he walks to the back of the vehicle and opens the rear hatch, once again bathed in yellow light. Effortlessly, he drags a body close and then lifts an unconscious man free of the vehicle, slinging him over his shoulder like a thirty-pound bag of beans. As he walks toward the dark office complex, he pauses to thumb the key fob and is rewarded by a small chirp from the BMW.

He whistles while he jimmies the front door.

It only takes a moment and then he's through the entry. His hulking figure fades to nothing as he strides into the gloom, a shadow within shadow.

# 20

*Tuesday, March 10—7:20 A.M.*

The coffee shop buzzes with morning noise: the hiss of steam, the *tink* of stainless-steel pitchers, the bark of baristas calling out drinks. Underscoring this impromptu performance is the desperate shuffle and murmur of those seeking a much-needed fix, something to get them through the morning without the unpleasant consequences of murdering a coworker with the removable armrest from their office chair.

Coffee saves lives.

Based on Jimmy's mood during the drive over, he's my lead suspect for any spontaneous homicides we might happen upon. As we clear the door, he makes a beeline for the counter, and I half expect him to push the waiting customers out of the way and muscle his way to the front. He doesn't, of course. He's too polite and proper for that.

Then again, the Nazis were occasionally polite and proper.

When the Third Reich took power in Germany, the Nazis made decaffeinated coffee a part of state policy, believing caffeine to be a poison. They were determined to keep the Aryan population healthy, and because the party knew what was best, they had no problem forcing their will on the German people.

Turns out their understanding of caffeine was just as flawed as all the other things they knew for certain. The Mormons abstain from caffeine and you don't see them invading neighboring churches or subjugating Presbyterians.

Maybe the old saying is right: everything in moderation. If that's the case, I still have a problem, because Jimmy left moderation behind six months ago.

Most mornings Jimmy would have tanked up at the motel's breakfast bar, but not today; he's cutting back. It's a laudable goal considering how off the chart his caffeine consumption has become in recent months. In this case, however, *cutting back* means waiting a whole seven minutes while we drive from the motel to the coffee shop halfway between us and the police station.

When Jimmy reaches the cash register and orders a twenty-ounce dark roast, you can almost see the tension fall from his shoulders. At the same time, I feel a hand at my elbow and turn to find Detective Ross Feng grinning at me.

"Morning, Steps," he says cheerfully, that big, contagious smile wrapped across his face like a caricature. You'd think we had a day of golfing planned.

"Morning, Ross."

"How's our boy?" He tips his head toward Jimmy.

"He'll be better when he gets some coffee into his system."

Ross chuckles. "Reminds me of myself when I was with the task force." Extending a hand, he presents a manila folder with a quarter inch of paper peeking out.

"What's this?"

"Intel on Noah Long out of NYPD."

"Already?"

"They work twenty-four-hour shifts these days. One of their analysts put it together for us while we slept. It was waiting in my email this morning." Ross rears back on his heels and stretches, chest out almost as far as his gut. "It'll cost me an expensive bottle of Scotch next time Portman's in town," he says through a yawn, "but I always pick up the tab, so it's no great sacrifice."

"Well, thank God for little miracles. Have you looked at it yet?"

"Cursory glance. Nothing jumped out, but we can divide it up and go through it while we drink our breakfast." He looks at my empty hands. "You're not getting anything?"

"I'm not much of a coffee person. I sometimes get a watered-down mocha, but I had some orange juice at the motel, so I'm good."

Nodding, as if he doesn't understand, he leaves me where I stand and queues up at the register with the other lemmings.

"I'll just . . . find a table," I call after him.

A spot in the corner is just clearing, so I hover nearby and swoop in as the departing customers gather their empty cups and head for the door. When the pistol-packing caffeine fiends work their way through the line and join me a few minutes later, Ross sets a bottle of orange juice and an orange-and-cranberry scone in front of me.

"Thank you. You didn't have to do that."

"Can't have you succumbing to hypoglycemia while we're chasing down bad guys. Besides, I used the department credit card."

Dividing up the Noah Long report, we read and eat and sip in silence for perhaps ten minutes. Jimmy is well into his clump of pages when his cell phone breaks into song. It's the theme from *The Pink Panther*, and he answers before the second *da dum*, putting the phone on speaker.

"Morning, Diane."

"I've been going over the time line," our matron replies

without preamble as if continuing a conversation already in progress. "There's no doubt that Marco is the target, as I suspected from the beginning."

"It's a little premature—"

"I've been staring at the whiteboard for hours," Diane blazes on, "and it just hit me."

"Hours? Diane, it's like"—Jimmy glances at the time on his phone—"seven thirty in the morning. How long have you been in the office?"

"Since three. Couldn't sleep. Marco is the target," she again insists. "He's the only local. The only one actually living in Bakersfield, even if he spends half the year in DC."

"What does local—"

"Because the killer is local."

"And you know that how?"

"Think about it, genius: William Johansson was buried six days before they found him on that park bench; that's a week ago Monday."

"So?"

"So, on the day he was buried, Jason Norris was at a conference in Atlanta, Wade Winchell was in his office in Los Angeles, and Noah Long was in New York signing the papers for the acquisition of a forty-million-dollar software company."

"So?" Jimmy repeats.

Diane sighs. "William Johansson's obituary didn't print until Sunday. His grave is unmarked, and the only people who knew where he was buried were family and a few friends. If the suspect was looking for a fresh body, how'd he know about Johansson?"

"Are you saying it's a friend or relative of Johansson?"

"No! Well . . . maybe. What I'm saying is that anyone stalking Noah or Jason would have been on the other side of the country. If it was Wade, the suspect would have been staked out in Los Angeles, though I suppose he could have driven to Bakersfield on the off chance of finding a funeral service in progress."

Jimmy's quiet a moment, then he exchanges a look with Ross. The two men raise their eyebrows in unison as if agreeing that Diane's theory has merit.

"Okay," Jimmy finally says, "you're usually right on these things—"

"*Usually?*" Diane scoffs.

"Let's see what we can find out about Johansson," Jimmy continues, ignoring the remark. "We've kind of ignored him in all of this, thinking he was just a prop—and I'm still not convinced he's anything other than that," he adds quickly. "It can't be that hard finding a fresh grave and a convenient body; all you have to do is drive through a few cemeteries and look for the stack of flowers and wreaths."

"I'll get started right away," Diane replies in a sugary-sweet voice, which probably means she's already working on it. With Diane, it's hard to tell. "By the way, I have an update on Abel Moya for you."

Jimmy glances at me, an odd look on his face.

"I found two new addresses in Bakersfield," Diane drones on. "He's not directly linked to either of them, and I'll spare you the brilliance that led to their discovery since I know you don't have the patience for such things. Suffice it to say that he has a girlfriend, and what he lacks in paper trail, she makes up for. I'll send the addresses to your cell."

Jimmy's reaction perplexes me, but then I realize we never told Diane that Abel was no longer our prime suspect.

"Thanks, Diane," Jimmy replies hurriedly. "Special Agent Weir is heading up the hunt for Moya. I'll make sure he gets the addresses."

There's silence for a moment. "Why aren't you heading up the hunt?"

"We . . . we are," Jimmy replies—a drowning man gasping for air. "We're just working a different angle . . . for now. A new angle."

"Mm-hmm."

"Thanks, Diane." Disconnecting the phone before she can reply, Jimmy lets out a long breath and looks at me. "Think she knows?"

"Nah," I say with a shake of my head. "You were very subtle, particularly the new-angle part." I give him an okay sign with my thumb and index finger.

Ross chuckles at us like we're a couple of knuckleheads and says, "I like her."

# 21

After the conversation with Diane, it seems pointless to continue through the Noah Long dossier, but we do anyway. When Jimmy turns over his last page and Ross pushes his unfinished stack to the center of the table, the feeling seems to be mutual.

"There's nothing in here worth killing for," Jimmy says, and Ross gives an accompanying nod. The table grows quiet, and then their eyes turn my way, looking for consensus.

Stacking my papers neatly together, I stand them on end and tap them against the table to align the tops and bottoms, then I hand the stack to Ross. "Looks like we're back to Marco."

"Marco," Jimmy concurs.

"The big question, then—"

Ross is interrupted by his phone. He answers before it chirps a second time, pressing it to his ear and covering the opposite ear with his left hand to block the noise and bustle of the busy coffee shop. The cacophony is too great, however, and he soon rises and gives us the one-moment signal with his index finger. Stepping quickly left and then right, he works his way around tables and chairs and out the front door. We watch him a moment as he paces back and forth on the sidewalk, his conversation animated, his belly jiggling with laughter at one point.

When the detective returns, he's decidedly more cheerful. "I had some of our guys do a neighborhood canvas of the area around the cemetery yesterday afternoon—"

"What neighborhood?" I interrupt. "It's in the middle of nowhere."

"True, but a mile north there's a housing community that includes an old strip mall and a half dozen small businesses. With burglaries on the rise in the area, I thought we might catch a break and find some surveillance cameras pointing toward the road."

Jimmy leans forward in his seat, suddenly attentive.

"They found four cameras, but only two of them were pointing at the road—and only one of those works."

"Typical," I mutter.

"The owner was happy to provide a copy of Saturday night's recording, and my guys stayed late last night and watched six hours of mostly stagnant video."

"But?" I say expectantly.

*"But,"* Ross says with considerable gusto, "a white work van got their attention, maybe a mid-2000s Ford. They first spotted it heading south about one A.M."

"There must have been dozens, even scores of vehicles that went down that road Saturday night and into Sunday morning," Jimmy says, less than impressed. "What makes this one special?"

"Because four hours later the same van passes by heading north."

Silence settles over the table.

"How do they know it's the same van?" I ask.

"It's got some logo on the side, faded, but they say it looks like a tree."

"A tree?"

Ross shrugs. "They're detectives; I'm sure if they say it's a tree, it's a tree."

"Do you have a lot of businesses around here with tree logos?" I ask. "Maybe tree toppers, tree-service companies, things like that?"

"Can't be that many," Jimmy says before Ross can answer.

"The logo was old," Ross reminds us. "Whatever business originally owned the van, it's doubtful they still hold the title. From what little they could see, it sounds like a typical doper vehicle, the type of rig you find parked out front of a drug house, or up on blocks in the yard."

Jimmy shrugs. "It's some place to start."

"Agreed." Ross nods. "I just don't want you to get too hopeful. I've got a CI, a reliable guy I recruited when I was with the drug task force. I'll give him a call and see if he knows of any nasty characters driving a white van with a tree on the side. I'll also throw Johansson's name past him, see if it rings any bells." Ross takes a long pull from his coffee, sets it down, and gives Jimmy a wink. "Looks like we finally have something real to work with."

"I guess so," Jimmy agrees.

We watch Ross for a long moment, expectant. When the moment grows long, Ross fidgets a bit in his seat. "I got something on my chin?" He wipes at his face.

"No—"

Jimmy cuts me off. "When you said you were going to call your CI, we thought you meant . . . now."

Ross laughs. "Brother, it's"—he glances at his watch—"barely seven forty-five in the morning. I don't know what kind of CIs you're used to working with, but mine never rise before noon. If I call him too early, I'll just piss him off."

"So, we wait?"

"We wait." The detective hoists his cup aloft. "Isn't that why God made coffee?"

# 22

By nine thirty the morning crowd has mostly cleared from the coffee shop, and what remains is a spattering of heads curled over keyboards or textbooks. For me, Ross, and Jimmy, what was intended as a quick stopover to get ready for the day has turned into a two-hour research session.

Between the three of us, we have two laptops. The Wi-Fi at the shop is strong and steady, and it's as good a place as any to do what we need to do.

"Harmony Lawns, Harmonious YardScapes, Helwig Landscaping," I read aloud as I write the business names one by one on a sheet of paper. We've been tracking down every business in the county even remotely involved with trees, trying to match up the logo from the surveillance video.

Ross and Jimmy are checking individual websites using their laptops, while I use my smartphone to identify the targets and feed them names. So far, we've checked all the arborists, nurseries, urban foresters, tree-service companies, and tree-related nonprofit foundations. I didn't know there was such a thing as a tree-related nonprofit, but I suppose it makes sense. I found two of them in Kern County.

We must have run through a hundred companies by now, and still no luck.

Right now, we're working on landscapers—and there's a lot of them. I've already bet Jimmy that when we finally sort all this out, we'll find that the logo belongs to some company that's not even remotely connected to trees: Herb's Pressure Washing, or something like that.

Jimmy's a true believer in the process, though, so we continue to slug through the endless list. Diane would normally do this for us, but she's doing the workup on William Johansson. That and Jimmy feels guilty about forgetting to tell her about Abel Moya. I know him; he figures that by putting in some extra work he can make up for the oversight.

For Jimmy, guilt is like compound interest: it grows with time.

Not only does he feel guilty about the Abel Moya snafu, but that we didn't come clean is starting to fester and itch at the back of his mind. I try to tell him that's what happens with cases like this. Things slip. Stuff's forgotten. It happens all the time.

He thinks it would have been better all the way around if we just confessed to the mistake when we talked to Diane this morning. She would have lectured us a few minutes and held it over our heads a few days, but in the end, all would have been forgiven.

That's what Jimmy thinks.

I'm not so sure.

"Millstone Aqua Gardens," I drone, scratching the name onto paper and noting that my handwriting has degraded significantly in the last hour. While this registers in my mind, I find that I don't care. My brain, it seems, is almost as glazed over as my eyes.

Whatever we pay Diane, it's not enough.

Ross's phone rings and he seems relieved to push away from the laptop. He answers and the coffee shop is quiet enough that he doesn't have to cover his ear or evacuate to the parking lot. Whatever the news, there's no laugh this time, no cheerful banter. Ross's face goes slack, the perpetual smile gone.

He looks like he's going to be sick.

When he ends the call, he sets the phone on the table and stares at it for a moment. His eyes tell me he wants to smash it or hurl it across the room, but the phone is only the messenger. You don't kill the messenger.

Ross speaks with deliberation as if drawing each word up from his gut. "An employee at Nelson Dental arrived at work this morning to find Wade Winchell duct-taped facedown on a dental chair."

"Alive?" Jimmy practically whispers, as if the quieter he asks the more hope there is of it being true.

Ross shakes his head.

The three of us sit frozen for perhaps a full minute, each staring off into our own personal hell, not daring to make eye contact. Then, slowly, I pocket my phone while Jimmy and Ross close their laptops and gather their notes. They stuff the material into their respective briefcases, and we rise from our chairs as one. Collecting the empty coffee cups, scone wrappers, and napkins, we dump them into the trash and walk out into the world.

No more words are necessary.

# 23

*People march toward hell one step at a time.*
*Sometimes they commit murder the same way.*

—JIMMY DONOVAN, FBI

The flat-roofed, single-story building on Seventeenth Street stands as a monument to 1960s architecture. The walkways are clean and the windows have been washed, but the place brings to mind an out-of-fashion dress that, upon closer inspection, is threadbare and smells of mothballs.

A dry fountain adorns a corner of the desolate flower bed out front, its basin now filled with an assortment of supposedly decorative rocks, topped by a green ceramic frog that appears to be a recent addition. The faded brown and tan paint clinging to the walls of the complex reminds passersby that the structure has yet to enjoy the slow gentrification sweeping through the neighborhood.

Despite its sturdy bones and still useful spaces, the building looks forlorn.

The yellow police tape doesn't help.

"Hey, Ross. It's pretty bad in there," the patrol sergeant cautions as we approach.

His eyes dart to Jimmy and then to me, lingering a moment as if to weigh our purpose. Dismissing us just as quickly, the sergeant returns his gaze to the detective. "I've never"—the words falter—"I've never seen anything like this. What the hell's the world coming to?" The sergeant looks for a moment as if he might lose his breakfast.

Ross says nothing. He puts his hand on the sergeant's shoulder, as if to say, *I know*, and then moves on by. We follow.

A perimeter of yellow police tape surrounds the entire building and parking lot, pushing back the media vans and gawkers who have already gathered. The responding officer's call for assistance had been brief but unhinged, almost panicked. Even if the veteran reporters hadn't known the code for homicide, they would have heard the urgency in his voice, felt it in the choked words that spilled out over the police band.

Pointing a cautioning finger at the broken glass scattered at the base of the entrance door, Ross leads the way into the office. What strikes me first is an all-too-familiar smell. Not decomp, but the metallic taint of violence that proceeds it. Somewhere in the building a significant quantity of blood is festering, turning.

The second thing that strikes me about the office is that the interior in no way matches the bland exterior. The walls are fresh and marked by few blemishes, the carpet is full and shows little wear, even the reception counter, a magnificent piece of live-edge cedar, glows with new resin.

If buildings can be schizophrenic, this one is Dr. Jekyll and Mr. Hyde.

We hear the voices before we see their source.

They emanate from someplace around the corner at the end of the main hall, a garbled mess of words falling over one another, indistinguishable save for an occasional string of syllables.

As we draw near, the world becomes surreal: a waking dream. I pause at the edge of hell itself as my eyes absorb the thing that gathered us here, and which now demands our attention.

I say *thing* because what lies in the dental chair is not Wade Winchell.

Once upon a time, it may have been the tough district attorney. But that was yesterday, yesteryear, a lifetime ago. Today something different occupies the vinyl, something . . . not human.

"We save the ones we can," I hear Jimmy croak. It's our mantra, our steadying words. His hand clasps my elbow briefly and then falls away, reminding me that we have work to do, despite the horror before us.

Slipping my glasses off, I feel them tremble in my hand.

On the ground before me, in dark neon green, is the polished, pulsing malachite from the cemetery. The disturbing shine traces through the macabre room. It covers the floor in those places not awash in blood. It's on the strips of black plastic that hang like curtains from the ceiling, walling off the small work space from prying eyes.

It's on Wade.

It's *in* Wade.

A full set of dental instruments rests on the counter. Even these, though unused, show impressions of malachite where they were handled and examined. The handler may have admired them, enjoyed their feel, but it was no dental instrument or combination of instruments that flayed and cut Wade Winchell. This was the work of a butcher, and it took a butcher's tools.

Despite the presence of green shine, it's Wade's pewter shine that dominates the room, splattered, pooled, and omnipresent, as if the killer went out of his way to fling the body fluids at the walls, the ceiling, the floor. A bloodfest of intentional cruelty.

Stepping back from this horror, I glance down the hall. The malachite footprints stand apart, heavy on the carpet as the butcher carried his victim like a side of beef to the back of the office. Of Marco and Noah, there is no trace. Wade, like Jason, went to his death alone.

It was probably better that way.

Dr. Ben Herrera beat us to the crime scene and now crouches next to the body laid out facedown in the fully reclined dental chair. The good doctor is unfazed by the horror that lies before him. His calm is an illusion, I suppose, a professional necessity. Occasionally, he directs a CSI to take a close-up of one thing or another, variables and discrepancies that may or may not prove useful in the coming investigation.

Most of the work will be completed back at the coroner's office, but some things need to be recorded before the body can be removed.

When Ben notices us, he quickly waves us forward. In a low voice, he begins to unravel the *true* nightmare that lies before us.

"He was alive until almost the end," the pathologist begins as if continuing a thought interrupted. "There are marks drawn on his back like those a surgeon would make." Ben turns a flap of loose skin over in his hand so we can see. "The marks are amateur and don't match the cuts, so they were probably used to terrorize the victim before the real horror show began."

"He was conscious during this?" I ask.

"Probably not at first. I imagine he was sedated when he was brought in and strapped down, otherwise he would have put up a fight, and there's no evidence of that."

"So, he waits until Wade is secured," Jimmy says, "then he wakes him. It's not good enough to simply kill him, he wants to see the terror in his eyes as he does it."

An ominous silence settles between us, punctuated by the grisly scene.

Ben is still holding the flayed flap of skin and, as if suddenly aware of it, returns it to its folded-back position. With a gloved hand, he gives us a tour of the carnage wrought upon Wade's opened upper torso.

"I've found a combination of hatchet, chisel, and saw marks," the pathologist continues, clearly rattled by what he's seen. "This wasn't surgery, it was brute force versus flesh and bone. Why he didn't just use a Sawzall or jigsaw I don't know, but I think he liked it. There's no other explanation."

Ben swallows hard but continues in a clean, clinical voice.

"He separated the ribs from the spine one by one, and . . . and yanked them up and away." Ben runs his finger along a row of spikes rising from the right side of Wade's back. They point away from the body at a forty-five-degree angle, like the plates of a stegosaurus, but dagger thin and white.

A similar row runs down the other side of the mutilated back.

Ben stares at the mess and then speaks again, but in a small, still voice, as if the words are meant for him alone. "The lungs were pulled from the chest cavity, still attached, and laid out, as if on display. He was probably still breathing at the time . . . still using them."

The words and the image jar me.

"There are some superficial lacerations on both lungs, as well as some deeper cuts, likely caused as the ribs were being separated." The pathologist wipes his forehead with the back of his wrist, careful not to touch the bloodied gloves.

"How many ribs are in the human body?" I ask after counting nine broken and upturned bones on each side of the spine.

"There are twenty-four," Ben replies. "Twelve on each side."

I nod my understanding. The killer didn't break them all, just the nine on each side required to expose the lungs, to pull the spongy organs from their cavity, and lay them out for the world to see. Something clicks in my head as if a light switch were suddenly thrown or a revealing match were lit.

"He *was* alive," I say with uncommon certainty. "That was the whole point."

Jimmy turns to me, and Ben looks up, waiting for more.

"He was still alive because to do the ritual properly the lungs had to breathe in and out, at least a couple of times. They would flutter where they lay as if flapping in some small way, like wings."

"What *ritual*?" Jimmy asks, a horrified look on his face.

"It's called the Blood Eagle." I glance at each of the men in turn. "It was supposedly devised by the Vikings, a particularly nasty method of execution reserved for only the worst offenders or traitors. It was so bad that some historians doubt it was ever used."

"They might want to rethink that," Ross says, glancing tellingly at the body.

Jimmy turns. "Where'd you hear about this?"

"The History Channel."

The hum of the investigation consumes the dental complex. Voices overlap and mingle with the steady shuffle of bodies and equipment, creating a low resonance that, at a distance, sounds more like the vibration of subterranean machinery, a song of death from the pit of the world.

Jimmy and I find a place to tuck out of the way, while Ross joins his fellow detectives in the hunt for latent prints, DNA, hairs, or clothing fibers.

A half hour later, they're just discussing how best to cut Wade's mangled body free of its restraints when Ross's phone rings. He waves us closer, then covers the mic and whispers, "They found Marco's BMW."

The conversation lasts less than a minute, and Ross promises to "get out there" as soon as we finish at the dental office. Ending the call, he stuffs the phone back into his pocket.

"They found it?" Jimmy asks as if to confirm Ross's words.

"Yeah, some telecom employee was working on a cell tower on Round Mountain this morning and spotted something that looked out of place tucked away in a draw on the other side of the ridge. When he went to investigate, he found the still-smoldering hulk of a torched BMW X5. The sheriff's office was just up there and pulled a VIN off the engine block. It's Marco's, all right."

"What about—"

Sensing my question, Ross shakes his head. "No bodies inside."

"At least that's something," Jimmy says with obvious relief.

Ross glances over his shoulder as an empty gurney wheels by. "We'll be here at least another half hour, so if you want to head up there, I can meet you when I finish. It's about eight miles as the crow flies, but the switchbacks will add some time to the drive."

"They've secured the scene?" Jimmy asks.

"A couple of deputies are sitting on it. Special Agent Weir is on the way and has requested CSI. Fortunately, that's outside the city limits, so the county will handle it, otherwise . . ." Ross motions around at the flurry of activity and the many personnel wearing shirts with either CSI or CRIME SCENE INVESTIGATOR marked across the back.

"Yeah," Jimmy acknowledges, "busy day."

"Nothing we can't handle."

Jimmy nods as if coming to a decision. "Finish your work here. We'll wait." He looks past Ross as the tempo around Wade's mangled body suddenly changes. "Anything we can help with?"

Ross shakes his head. "No. We're getting ready to transport the remains. Ben's worried that the cut ribs might turn Wade into two hundred pounds of potatoes stuffed into a half-full bag." Ross shrugs. "Without the stability provided by the spine and ribs working together, things might get . . . sloppy."

"How sloppy?"

The detective sighs. "I'd stay out of splash range."

After recruiting two wide-eyed uniforms to help him, Ben unfolds a body bag and lays it out atop the gurney, smoothing the wrinkles. With some back-and-forth shuffling, he moves the gurney alongside the dental chair so that only the smallest gap separates them, then lowers the gurney height until the two surfaces are on an even plain.

"We're just going to slide him across," Ben explains to the uniforms. "No fast movements, just slow and steady."

The transfer is a four-person job, and with Ben's team short one person, Jimmy steps up and dons a pair of latex gloves. Taking the empty place near the exposed lungs, he grips Wade's right arm and shoulder and guides him across the crack between the chair and the gurney.

Something flutters to the ground, the flash catching my eye.

I'm not sure where it came from, but it looks for a moment like an index card, only the shape's not quite right. Perhaps it was underneath Wade or fell from his shirt or pant pocket. It may have been placed there before Wade. For all I know, it could be a manufacturer's label that worked its way loose from the underside of the gurney.

I seem to be the only one who notices the fluttering specimen.

The presence of the item at the crime scene—regardless of origin or pedigree—means that it's evidence. If it fell from the gurney, it's just a distraction; but if it fell from Wade, it could be important.

It lands facedown on the floor, settling into a pool of blood that's well under the gurney and the dental chair. It couldn't have picked a worse spot. Even now, the blood may be soaking into the item, ruining it. There's no time to lose.

Quickly donning a pair of latex gloves, I squat next to the mangled body, one hand on the edge of the gurney for balance. I lean into the space underneath—not exactly something I'm keen to do. When I can't reach, I wave a hand at Jimmy, but he and Ross are busy talking to Ben.

Extending my fingers, they play at the edge of the item, touching it but unable to grip. Then, with a desperate thrust, I reach farther, as if my shoulder, elbow, and wrist bones suddenly collaborated and stretched themselves out as far as tendons would allow.

With a grunting gasp, I snatch up the item from its bloody resting place.

It's not paper, but a Polaroid.

As I set it on a napkin next to the sink and dab away the blood, I already know that only two possible images can be hidden under the gore: it's either Noah Long or Marco Perez.

It takes but a moment to uncover the truth of it.

"Uh, Jimmy?"

The image on the Polaroid is a close-up of Noah Long's face, no doubt much more haggard than when he arrived at Meadows Field Airport last week. After placing the Polaroid in a clear evidence bag and sealing it to maintain the integrity of the evidence and the chain of custody, we lay it on the counter at the reception station where the overhead lights are brightest.

Jimmy points behind Noah's head. "Is that a mattress he's lying on?"

"A *bare* mattress," I note.

"Better than a coffin," Ross mutters, then looks apologetic.

The only other item in the picture worth noting is a copy of the *Bakersfield Tribune* resting next to Noah's head, and not by accident. The date is too small to read, but the images and articles match Sunday's paper.

Handing off the packaged and sealed Polaroid to the detective sergeant so it can be booked into evidence, we exit the hellhole that was formerly Nelson Dental and find the welcoming comfort of the Mustang convertible. The rumble of the engine as it fires to life seems a ward against evil deeds and evil men as if nothing can touch us while we're inside.

I wish it were so.

# 24

Ross says he doesn't get carsick. Ever.

But the detective is looking a bit green around the edges by the time we reach the dirt spur running off Round Mountain Road. The long, stretched-out Slinky of twisting road leads us at last to the gutted remains of Marco's BMW. Most of the mountain roads back home would have been dirt and gravel, accented by an endless string of potholes from the logging trucks.

On Round Mountain, the roads are paved. Thank God for small favors.

The ruined BMW is tucked neatly into a carved-out draw on the north side of the road, the ground around it coated in black as if the fire had cast a permanent shadow upon the land, an umbra fading out from the center.

Logic dictates that the arson was carried out sometime overnight.

Vehicles burn black, filling the sky with the billowing stain of burnt tires, incinerated plastics, and consumed fabrics. Such a fire during daylight hours would have been visible throughout Bakersfield, drawing unwanted attention from those already hypervigilant to the dangers of wildfire.

By night, however, this scar in the sky would be nothing

more than a shadow upon a shadow. The night would conceal the spreading plume and tuck it away. Even the smell of it would dissipate with distance and time, its source undetectable.

As for the fire itself, the sharp dip of the draw was chosen well. Here, even twenty-foot flames would be hidden from all but the closest prying eyes.

Parking the Mustang two car lengths from the scorched hulk, Jimmy shuts it down. Kip is already on scene and wanders our way, a piece of charred wood in his hand. He tosses it away before reaching us.

"How are things at the dental office?"

"Ross's people seem to have it well in hand." Jimmy hesitates a moment. "I thought we'd see you there?"

"I had to go to Sacramento last night." Kip glances around—glances at nothing—as if the very act were a distraction. "The ASAC wanted a briefing first thing this morning."

Jimmy's face sours. "You told him we're in the middle of an investigation, right?"

"He's my superior," Kip replies stiffly. "Some of us don't have the luxury of running autonomous units; we take orders."

"We take orders too," Jimmy replies defensively. "That's why we're here."

Kip drops his head and raises a consoling hand. "Cheap shot. I didn't mean it to come off that way." He meets Jimmy's eyes, then glances at Ross and me. "For what it's worth, I told the ASAC your theory on Abel Moya. He . . . doesn't agree. He's still our number one suspect, and I've been ordered to continue the hunt."

"You're hunting the wrong person," I say, biting back some of the rebuke in my voice.

"Look, I've got no problem going toe-to-toe with the ASAC,

but I need something a bit more solid than your analysis. No offense."

I'm about to reply, but Jimmy shoots me a cautioning look, and I close my lips. The four of us stand in a circle for a half minute. The air seems electric with tension as if a storm cloud had descended and swept its static-filled tentacles around us.

"Well, you FBI types are just loads of fun, aren't you?" Ross finally says.

That seems to break the static, and even Kip manages a half smile.

As we make our way around the SUV, I note that the only thing left of the tires is the mess of steel wire once embedded in the rubber: they don't call them steel-belted radials for nothing. The windows are all gone, and since I don't see much evidence of shattered glass, I assume most of it melted. There's nothing left of the vehicle that isn't metal, and even some of that looks to have barely survived.

Kip throws a thumb at one of the deputies standing by his patrol car. "Andy says the fire marshal is on the way, though considering the circumstances, there's little doubt this was arson."

"And we're sure no one was inside?" Jimmy asks. "It looks like the fire was pretty intense, maybe enough to cremate a body or two."

"Even cremations leave some bone fragments," Kip reminds him. "Still, it's not my area of expertise. We'll have to let the fire marshal make that call."

"What's your theory?"

"On how it ended up here, and why?"

"Yeah."

Kip pauses before answering. "I'd say he used the car to transport Wade to the dental office, and when he finished there, he drove straight up the mountain and torched it, destroying any evidence."

"Why didn't he hang on to it? He's still got Noah and Marco to deal with."

"Maybe he figured the BMW was too much of a liability." The FBI agent shrugs. "Maybe he arranged other transportation. Or maybe Noah and Marco are already where he wants them."

"I doubt it," Jimmy replies quietly.

"Why?"

"Because this guy likes putting on a show." Jimmy frowns and shakes his head. "He's got something planned for each of them. He's telling a story, we just have to figure out the ending before . . ."

"Before the end," I say.

"Exactly."

Ross is looking around as we speak, a perplexed look on his face, as if trying to work something out in his head that just doesn't make sense. Pretty soon it gets serious, and he starts rubbing his belly in a slow, contemplative revolution. "Any chance this guy has a partner?" he finally asks.

Kip and Jimmy exchange a look, leaving it to me to ask the obvious.

"Why?"

"Well, it's eight or nine miles back to civilization as the crow flies, which means it might be closer to fifteen or twenty miles if you go by road. He either had a partner come pick him up or he walked out of here in the dark."

Continuing to knead his belly, Ross waits for an answer that doesn't come.

"I'm guessing Uber doesn't pick up from dark, remote mountain sites?" I say with intentional sarcasm. Kip doesn't pick up on my tone and whips out his cell phone. After clicking the Uber app and punching some keys, he shakes his head.

"They don't come out this far." He points south, his eyes still on the screen. "They *do* pick up at the base of the mountain, though."

"I guess we can cross Uber off our list," I say.

"Why don't you have a look around," Jimmy tells me, probably sensing that I'm about to say something I might regret. He's intuitive that way. In any case, it's a good idea. I haven't had my glasses off in a while and I can feel the edge of a headache coming on.

Starting at the burned wreck that used to be Marco's SUV, I pull the glasses from my face and examine the ground as Jimmy distracts Ross and Kip. The familiar malachite green immediately pops from the scorched dust, and I see where he walked to the back of the rig and likely accessed the liftgate. He then walked a slow circle around the vehicle accessing every door and popping the hood. I assume from the encompassing pattern that he retrieved a container of gasoline from the back and was dousing the entire vehicle, inside and out.

A discolored ten-foot trail leads away from the vehicle, marked by the scorched earth of burnt gasoline: here is the wick of this giant Molotov cocktail. I see where he stood to light the match.

I wait for Jimmy to join me so he can collect the spent match, then I continue. The malachite footsteps lead away from the burn site and up a ridge to the west, where I make a most unusual discovery.

It's the answer to the enigma.

Raising my voice so it can be heard below, I say, "It looks like our guy didn't walk down the mountain, after all." I gesture at tread marks on the ground. They can't see the patterns from their vantage point in the draw, but that doesn't matter at the moment.

"He stashed a mountain bike up here and rode out," I shout. "It's all downhill." As if to emphasize this, I rake the air with the back of my hand, sweeping across the long and lonely miles between here and Bakersfield.

It would have been a dark ride on the heels of dark deeds.

When the killer finally lit his match and put foot to pedal, the ritual butcher of Wade Winchell would have been recent enough to leave a slight stench of death on his clothes and in his hair, and the many images and sounds of the man's dying still fresh in the killer's head.

As he rode, did he delight in these? Or did such thoughts haunt him; did they chase him down the mountain and push his feet faster and faster in their orbit around the spindle?

With monsters, it's hard to tell.

# 25

*Tuesday, March 10*

It's just after seven when we arrive at BoBo's Pizza on Niles Street.

The eclectic establishment is just minutes from the coroner's office and has considerably better décor—unless, of course, you're looking for that whole *Dawn of the Dead* vibe that comes with autopsy tables and body coolers. Ben is waiting in a booth when we file through the front door. Ross spots the pathologist immediately, veering off to the left and weaving expertly through the clutter of tables and chairs between us.

After we agree on a large pepperoni pan pizza and a large four-meat pizza, I ask the waitress if they have any *actual* orange juice. She points out the carbonated orange drink in the soda dispenser, hands me a glass, and disappears before I can inform her that orange soda is *not* orange juice.

I settle for water.

Ben waits until we're all settled in our seats before giving us the rundown on Wade. As he begins, his voice is low, so as not to disturb the customers at nearby tables. The particulars of an autopsy can be upsetting to the uninitiated, especially while they're eating.

After running through all the knowns, the things seen with our own eyes and smelled with our own noses, he gets to the "anomaly" he mentioned during an earlier phone call—the reason for our dinner party.

"Remember the laceration to the lung?" Ben leans in to the table and lowers his voice still further.

"The one that was bubbling?" Ross tries to make an effervescing motion with his fingers, but it looks like he's casting a spell on his fork.

"Right," Ben says generously. "I thought the escaping air was from a minor cut, something superficial. Turns out I was wrong."

I exchange a look with Jimmy.

"When I dissected the lung, tracing the wound, it went deeper than I thought. And then, well, I suppose you could say I found a void, a hole in the center of the lung the size of"—Ben struggles for a comparison and picks up the spice shaker from the table—"about like this; maybe three inches long by an inch and a half in diameter."

"Is this a natural void," Jimmy asks, "or something else?"

"It's not natural."

"So . . . something else," I say.

Ben looks at me, his eyes disturbed, and gives a soft nod. "I believe he cut the chunk out after he pulled the lung from the chest and laid it out on the victim's back, probably after our unfortunate victim took his last breath. I suspect this missing chunk was the purpose for his elaborate dissection in the first place."

Our large BoBo's pepperoni pan pizza and the accompanying four-meat pizza choose this exact moment to arrive at our table, landing with all the grace of a crashing, spinning UFO. The waitress gives us a plastic smile and asks if we need anything else. I contemplate asking about real orange juice again, but what's the point?

As she walks away, we stare at the bubbling cheese, the

bloodred tomato sauce, the misshapen slices, and the random chunks of meat. You'd think our appetites would have fled or at least been dampened, but Ross doesn't hesitate. "I'm a four-meat kind of guy." He shovels two slices onto his paper plate and pulls it close.

We eat in silence for several minutes, filling a different kind of void that's been building in our guts all day. Only when our hunger has partially been satisfied does the discussion continue.

"How much do you think was cut out of the lung?" I ask. "By weight, I mean."

I notice the father at a nearby table glance my way and realize my voice may have carried farther than intended. He puts a protective arm across the back of his daughter's chair.

Ben's eyes turn up and to the right in thought. He finishes chewing as he contemplates. "There are a lot of things that could affect the weight," he says after finally swallowing, "but I'd say it's about a pound, give or take."

"A pound of flesh," I clarify.

The statement raises every head.

"What are you suggesting?" Jimmy asks.

"It's Shakespearean. Right out of *The Merchant of Venice*. Shylock and his demand for a pound of Antonio's flesh."

"I'm not a Shakespeare guy." Ross has a bewildered look as he sucks the tomato sauce from his fingertips and waits for clarification.

"*Romeo and Juliet* is the extent of my knowledge," Ben offers. "And that's mostly because I saw *Shakespeare in Love*."

I look at Jimmy, hoping he won't disappoint.

"I only dog-paddle." He mimics André the Giant by cupping his hands and making swimming motions.

"That was *Princess Bride*," I say as if he doesn't know that.

He grins and tilts his head back theatrically, eyes to some distant place beyond the ceiling. "'If you prick us, do we not bleed? If you tickle us, do we not laugh? If you poison us, do we not die? And if you wrong us, shall we not revenge?'"

Finishing, he lowers his gaze to meet mine and gives a triumphant smile.

"Bravo." I clap.

Ross grins and wiggles a finger at Jimmy. "I've heard that 'prick' part before."

"I bet you have," I say with barely suppressed humor.

The whole table bursts into laughter, with Ross leading the pack.

As our party descends into unruly hilarity, the conversation takes a decided nosedive into the gutter, spiraling ever downward, the way a lot of cop banter devolves. This persists for several minutes, until we finally harness our better angels and return to some semblance of good conduct. We take advantage of the ensuing lull to replenish our plates and drinks.

"So, you're suggesting this was revenge of some sort?" Jimmy asks as the feast eventually continues. "That the tissue was cut from the lung as a message, or as payment for some debt?"

"It's just a thought until we come up with a better option."

Ross's latest slice of four-meat is halfway to his mouth when his hand freezes and his eyes set as if working something out. "Did you find the chunk of lung that was cut out?"

Ben shakes his head.

"So . . . he took it with him?"

"I don't know, I can only tell you we didn't find it at the crime scene. The CSIs were still there the last time I talked to them. Maybe they'll find it stuffed in a vent or hidden in someone's desk drawer."

I watch Ross's eyes drift into thought. For a moment he looks like he's going to be sick. "You don't think we have a Jeffrey Dahmer on our hands, do you? You don't think he's *eating* them?"

"He's not eating his victims," Ben assures us. "If he were,

there are far better cuts than the lung. You don't see a lot of people eating cow lung, do you? Not unless they're desperate and starving. Human lungs aren't much different."

"If you say *tastes like chicken*—"

Ben cuts me off with a laugh. "No, no. But the consumption of lungs—human or otherwise—was banned by the USDA decades ago." He takes a quick sip of his beer. "The British government has been trying to get us to drop the ban for years because sheep's lung is a key ingredient of traditional Scottish haggis."

"Disgusting," Ross mutters in disapproval.

"I agree," Ben says, "but Scotland's not alone. There are lung-related dishes from Italy, Hungary, Indonesia, the Philippines, Nepal"—he gives a bit of a smirk and tips his head toward Ross—"even China."

"You seem to know your haggis," Jimmy observes.

Ben laughs. "No, I googled it. I wanted to see if there was a reason someone would want to eat a human lung."

Full on pizza and visions of dripping haggis, we drop Ross off next to his car at the Bakersfield Police Department parking lot and make our way back to the Sierra Inn & Suites. Marty and Les have separate rooms on the same floor, so we stop at each in turn and let them know it might be a couple of days before we can head home.

They take it in stride, asking few questions.

As I'm walking away from Marty's room, he calls, "Hey, Steps. I found this snazzy little jazz bar not far from here. How about we dump the old married guys and go scope it out? See what Bakersfield has to offer."

"Remember that part about me being engaged?" I call back over my shoulder.

"So? It's not like you're married yet. When I buy a car, I don't hang my dice from the rearview mirror until I transfer the title."

"And *that*," I say without turning around, "is why your wives are *ex*-wives." I give him a wave and keep walking.

"They couldn't handle me," Marty calls out with his unending confidence. "I was too much for them. They don't make energy drinks potent enough to keep up with my kind of virility." In a quieter voice, I hear him add, "Poor things were just exhausted." Seemingly satisfied with this proclamation, he disappears back into his room and I hear the door close.

Jimmy's still smiling and shaking his head when he says good night and peels off into his room. Mine is across the hall.

I contemplate a shower but call Heather instead. When there's no answer on her cell, I call home, hoping she's at Big Perch rather than her apartment in Seattle.

"Hello," a British voice belts out on the other end, sounding remarkably like John Cleese.

"Evening, Ellis. How are things?"

"All right, Steps, all right. Are you okay? You sound a bit zonked."

"I'm good. It's just this case. You know how it is; sometimes they're easy, sometimes, not so much."

Ellis is silent a moment, then, dropping some of the accent, he says, "I know I've mentioned it before, but I'd love to come along with you on one of your little jaunts. I may not be FBI, but I was still law enforcement, after a fashion. I daresay I could give Diane a run for her money."

I snort. "Diane would toast you over an open fire and eat you for breakfast."

"Pah! She's all bluster, that one. Besides, she likes me too much. I asked her to go sunbathing with me, you know? Last summer. She *almost* said yes."

"Sunbathing? As in nude sunbathing?"

"Indeed."

"I'm guessing that *almost* is a bit of a stretch," I say pointedly.

"Oh, go ahead and mock the dreams of an old man," Ellis says with good humor. "Was there a particular reason you called or was it just to take the mickey?"

"I was hoping to talk to Heather," I say with a chuckle.

"Heather." He hems and haws. "Well, yes, about that—she's not here."

I nod to myself. "I called her cell and didn't get an answer, but I'll give it another try. Can you let Jens know that we should be back in a couple—"

"Ah-hmm," Ellis interrupts with some exaggeration as if clearing his throat. "She said she may not have cell reception because—how should I say this? Well, the truth of the matter is that she's not at the apartment. There, I've said it."

"Well . . . where is she?"

"I can't say."

"You can't say, or you won't say?"

"A bit of both, I should think." Before I can press further, he says, "Now, don't get spun up, Steps. It's a surprise, you see. And frankly, I've given too much away as it is."

"Given too much—" I stop myself. "The only thing you've given away is that she's not at Big Perch, and she's not at her apartment."

"Well, that's a relief then. Here I thought I'd gone and mucked it all up."

I remain quiet, waiting for him to elaborate, to say something, to say anything. But Ellis is shrewdly silent.

"So you're not going to tell me."

"We, my boy, are at an impasse. I've been sworn to secrecy, and secrecy I'll keep. Now, if you're looking for a sympathetic ear, I've been told that I'm downright therapeutic in my abilities to listen and emote."

"You're no Heather," I say with a chuckle.

With his bushy mustache, practiced estuary accent, and the pith helmet he favors, Ellis often reminds me of hundred-year-old pictures you see of adventurers off to hunt big game in Africa.

I'd known Ellis six months before I learned that he wasn't British at all. He was born and raised in Philadelphia and worked for the US government as a border patrol agent for more than thirty years. He's an odd duck with an affinity for hats and nude sunbathing, but we like him.

"Where's Jens?"

"I believe he's in the hot tub with the triplets." Ellis is then shouted down by my brother, though I can't quite make out what he's saying. "Pay no attention," the mustachioed faux Brit continues in his best estuary. "He's just upset that I've taken thirteen dollars and some change off him in a straight-up game of poker."

"Thirteen dollars isn't bad."

"We're playing for pennies."

"Oh."

After talking to Jens for a few minutes and catching additional grief from Ellis for trying to elicit Heather's location from him, I say my goodnights and end the call.

I miss them as soon as I hit the button.

# 26

*Wednesday, March 11—7:17 A.M.*

Jacob and Isaiah rarely skip school.

Well, they rarely skip school so close on the heels of their last skip day. Today, however, the twelve-year-old twins will make an exception to their normal operating procedures, a deviation born of necessity and curiosity. The mission is—well, they can't talk about the mission. Just know that it's top secret and of the utmost importance.

And if they don't make it back?

That's a risk the boys are willing to take. In such an unfortunate event, it would be left to their CIA handler to deliver the news to their mother, no doubt masked as a training accident or an allergic reaction to seafood.

Their last handler, may she rest in peace, was run over by a car three months ago. They buried her in the backyard with the others; an unmarked grave for a hero of the republic.

It shouldn't have gone down like that, but the stupid cat was always running into the street. It was bound to happen eventually. Now they're stuck with Barney, an okay lookout but skittish as a field mouse. The three-year-old beagle is less than enthusiastic about his new position as CIA handler.

With the kind of devious diligence peculiar to boys, the twins put on all the airs of going to school: getting dressed, making their beds, fetching their lunches from the fridge, and waiting at the curb for the big yellow bus that's bound to be by any minute now.

School mornings have a well-honed routine around their house, so much so that their mother, Penny, sets her internal clock by her boys. When they step out the front door and shuffle to the curb to wait for their ride, she knows that she has five minutes before she has to leave for work.

When she steps outside five minutes later and finds the boys still waiting, she pauses, as if unsure how to proceed, how to deviate from the routine.

"Is the bus coming?" she calls out after locking the door.

"It's just running late, Mom," Jacob says. "It's fine."

"You want me to wait?"

"Mom, we're twelve!" Isaiah says disappointedly.

"I know, but—"

"We'll call if it doesn't show up," Jacob interrupts, waving his cell phone in the air.

Penny thinks on this for a moment but then surrenders to the urgency of routine. It's an eighteen-minute drive to work, with a four-minute margin for lights and traffic. "All right," she calls out, "but if it's not here in the next ten minutes, I want a call."

It was that simple.

When she arrived at work she wouldn't necessarily notice that she was ten minutes early. Even if she did, she wouldn't suspect that the boys had left the house early. Why would they? Certainly not to wait for a bus that was still fifteen minutes away? Not a chance.

As soon as Penny's Lexus turns out of the community, the boys race for the front door, unlock it, and duck inside. They wait another five minutes for the bus to arrive, honk twice, and then move on. Stashing their lunches back in the fridge, they gather their gear from under their beds and, donning the matching backpacks, exit out the back door.

They call it the *Saw* house.

Not because the old place was a former lumber mill, or because the sounds of various saws emanate from within, but because the semi-abandoned house reminds them of the movie *Saw*. Their overactive minds constantly imagine what horrors might lie within, and if the place had a basement—which it doesn't—it would certainly be the center of all earthly evil.

Their cousin Tanner let them watch *Saw* when they were ten, telling them it was just like the reality show *Survivors* but with more blood.

It wasn't. They had nightmares for months.

Now, at age twelve, it seems so long ago, like a decade has passed. When you're young, every year seems so long, and there's so much growing up that goes on between summers. The boys have seen other bad movies since that momentous viewing—maybe not *that* bad, but still terrifying. They like to think of themselves as older and more mature now, no longer the skittish ten-year-olds who were so easily frightened.

The *Saw* house is two lots north.

People have come and gone from the place for a few years now, never staying for long. The boys are convinced it's because the place is haunted—bumps and groans in the night, that sort of thing. The simple truth is that the landlord makes more renting it as a short-term furnished home. And tenants aren't overly picky about the home's condition as long as it's only for a few months.

Creeper has been there the longest.

There were others before him, of course, and before them

all, it had been the lair of a dark witch, an old hag right out of the movies. She'd yell at the twins as they rode their bikes up and down the sidewalks, racing each other from one end of the street to the other. Then one day she was just gone, and the house sat empty for a long time.

That was years ago.

They never heard what happened to the witch, and Isaiah, the oldest of the boys by twenty-three minutes, said that a witch hunter had killed her and burned her body in the backyard. He said he saw the fire from his bedroom window one night.

The witch was the worst thing that ever happened to the neighborhood . . . at least until Creeper moved in.

They call him Creeper because, well, that's what he is. They only see him outside the residence on rare occasions, and when they do, he's always casting about, checking to see if anyone's watching. He wears a hoodie that covers his head and throws his face into shadow so that even if they wanted to, the boys would be hard-pressed to describe him.

One time, they saw Mrs. Mulligan talking to the big man, though the exchange didn't seem overly friendly. More like two spiders squaring off for a leg thrashing. Mrs. Mulligan is a creeper too. It's because of her that the boys stay close to the backyard fences as they approach the *Saw* house.

It's not the first time the boys have snuck into the dilapidated house. If they were honest, they'd admit that it's not even the tenth time. They'd learned years earlier that the latch on the bathroom window doesn't lock. Nobody had ever gotten around to fixing it because, well, the window is so small it's not like anyone can crawl through.

Except for a twelve-year-old boy.

Jacob always gets the dirty job of shimmying through the opening, dropping his feet to the toilet seat, then hurrying around to unlock the rear sliding door. Isaiah says that since he's the oldest, he has to stand guard outside.

Jacob says that's a bunch of bull crap.

When his feet hit the bathroom floor, Jacob crouches for a moment and listens. When no sound comes to him, he rises and peers out into the hall and then down into the living room. Nothing. It's not like they were expecting anyone. They'd watched Creeper leave that morning and had never seen anyone else coming and going from the residence.

Still, as Jacob makes his way down the hall, he pauses and listens a second time, holding his breath for a moment. He thought he heard . . . no, it wasn't anything. Just his imagination. Yet, as his feet carry him the rest of the way to the sliding glass door, his steps are a little more hurried than usual. He glances back over his shoulder at the long hall with its closed doors leading to closed rooms.

The boys haven't been in the house since Creeper moved in. They hadn't dared. But when they saw the giant man applying wet newspaper to the rear bedroom windows two weeks ago, it got them curious. Creeper doesn't look like the type with hobbies, and even at their age they know that you only paper over a window if you're hiding something.

That's what today is about.

They want to know Creeper's secret.

When Isaiah is satisfied that the perimeter is clear, which mostly means that Mrs. Mulligan didn't see them sneaking in, the boys make their way down the hall, big brother now in the lead. They move past the first closed door without interest and stop at the next door on the left. They whisper-argue back and forth over who should open the door, and Isaiah finally relents and turns the knob grudgingly.

The room is dark and there's a soft, rustling sound.

"Rats," Isaiah whispers to Jacob.

The newsprint on the windows blocks most of the light, and Isaiah has to fumble a moment before finding the wall switch. When the naked bulb in the open ceiling fixture illuminates the room, the boys blink a moment against the harsh blaze.

Then their eyes settle . . . and their hearts stop.

Isaiah is the first to scream.

# 27

*Wednesday, March 11—7:34 A.M.*

Noah Long is groggy when he wakes.

He'd been groggy as long as he can remember, which doesn't mean anything because time seems to have shifted out of phase from his reality. Hell, *reality* has shifted out of phase from his reality. The only constant for him is pain; pain and the dark room.

And the demon.

The creature comes and goes, never helping Noah, just laughing at him and saying odd things like "I'm gonna top you off."

Noah struggles with the words every time, unsure what *top you off* means.

It troubles him that he can't puzzle through it, but his mind won't work the way it's supposed to; the way it usually works. He's only ever before felt like this a few times in his life, and that was back in college. Bad decisions that he never repeated.

There's something else about the demon.

He remembers that it once had a name, almost like a man has a name, or a dog or a horse. As he focuses on this single thought, it plays at the edge of his muddled mind. It seems to him that the demon once looked normal like a man, only larger and not a man. He whistled while he secured Noah to the bed. He remembered that part: the whistling. The securing. The *yank* on the restraints, like a sailor making sure a knot is especially tight.

But that was ages ago. Eons.

Now, glancing around at the shadowed room, Noah struggles for something else, some other thought or realization. He struggles for it until it finally takes shape in his mind: Something had woken him. It had stirred him from his stupor, knocked on the door to his subconscious, pried open his eyelids, and demanded he wake.

Wake!

He understands that now—or thinks he does. Was it a noise? A vibration? As his mind tries to clear, he wonders if the demon has returned to "top him off."

He listens as intently as his addled mind will allow, but the house is quiet.

In a fit, he pulls against the restraint on his left arm, knowing the futility of it. He tries to call out to Marco, but the words won't come. His jaw moves and his tongue dances around his teeth, but no sound comes. There's a reason for that, but he can't remember what it is.

Marco was here, but now he's gone.

*Where did he go?* Noah wonders, casting his wild eyes against the gloom.

Summoning every ounce of strength left in him, he shifts his weight on the mattress and heaves hard against the restraints. Whether it's another vain attempt to free himself, or simply to get a better look at the room, even he can't say. But for all his effort, he may as well be a mouse pulling at a railcar. When the little strength that remains has drained from his body, he relents. Exhausted, he falls flat on the filthy bed, causing it to groan in protest.

The restraints remain solid, unconcerned by his efforts.

He's been strapped to the bed long enough that his wrists and ankles are chafed. They've bled and healed and bled some more. The sheets are wet with sweat, vomit, feces, and urine, things the demon cares little about. Noah can feel sores developing on his skin where it lies festering in the filth, and for the first time in his life he understands what bedsores are . . . only this is much worse. It has to be.

Noah has the vaguest sense that he's been propped up somehow, as if the head of the bed is sitting on blocks, elevating it. But, even here, he can't trust his fractured mind. For all he knows, the bed itself is a hallucination.

The thought causes his body to spasm and shiver in the lukewarm filth.

He hears it again!

A quiet disturbance!

Something beyond the door.

It's no hallucination—or he doesn't think it is. The hallucinations seem . . . different from the real. Different in a way that's hard to describe without risking madness. Even with the distinction, it's getting more difficult for Noah to separate the real from the imagined.

The sound is subtle, a low rumble: like something on a track, or distant thunder.

If he could hold his breath he would, but he's hyperventilating again. It sometimes feels like he's suffocating, even when he's not vomiting.

A voice, now.

Whispers.

Noah can almost *sense* the demon on the other side of the door, ready to top him off.

He'll come through at any moment, looming over the room like a mountain, his solid-black eyes looking at Noah, looking through him, beyond him, as if the very act will destroy him in parts. He'll top Noah off and kill him a little more.

The knob squeaks as it rotates, then the door folds into the room. A recess stands in the wall, a place where before there was only blackness. Two shadows linger. Small shadows, not like the demon.

When the light clicks on above Noah, the waves of electromagnetic radiation enter through his eyes instantly and slam into his brain with the velocity of a freight train, causing him to gasp. He blinks dryly against the onslaught, too dehydrated to make tears.

The boys stare at him, trying to comprehend.

He stares back through hollow eyes, his mouth moving as he tries to utter two words, two simple words. Yet try as he might, his vocal cords simply won't cooperate, and before he can issue the plea, the boys scream and bolt down the hall. A door crashes open, striking the wall behind it as if blasted open by an explosive charge. He listens as the screams fade and then disappear somewhere beyond the house, beyond his hearing.

Silence returns. The boys are gone.

Noah's vocal cords relent, too late to do him any good. In a whisper that barely breaks the silence, the two precious words finally bubble from his throat.

"Help me."

# 28

In their long history of 911 calls, the police dispatchers at the Bakersfield PD Communications Center have received more than their share from frightened children—sometimes the worst calls you can get.

So, when Isaiah and Jacob call in a panic, the only thing *not* ordinary is that the boys seem to be *both* frightened and excited, almost comically so. They pass the phone back and forth as they try to explain the *Saw* house and the thing inside. It takes several minutes for them to calm down enough to articulate the main point, that a "zombie-looking guy" was strapped to a bed.

When dispatch asks where, they say, "In the torture room."

When dispatch presses and asks where this room is, they say, "In a torture house." Jacob finally understands that the dispatcher is looking for a street name and house number and has to fight the phone away from Isaiah to convey the information.

That settled, the boys talk incoherently about the movie *Saw* and then become evasive when the dispatcher asks for their names. Isaiah tries to make his voice suddenly older, which doesn't work so well. They finally give up their names when the dispatcher advises them that their phone number and address were displayed on her screen when the call came in.

The boys hadn't counted on that.

She doesn't ask the boys what they were doing in the house, or why they weren't at school. Their obvious distress and excitement make such matters irrelevant, at least for the time being. Besides, if what they're saying turns out to be true, truancy is the last thing Bakersfield PD will be worried about.

It takes ten minutes for the first patrol car to arrive.

When Officer Susie Gwyn exits her marked unit and approaches the house on Tuttle Street, she finds the front door standing ajar and an abiding gloom waiting within. Susie has always had a good sense of smell, and the vapors issuing out the front door give her pause.

It's the stench of human waste . . . and something else.

The home looks vacant and Susie just assumes that squatters have taken up residence. Transients are a growing problem in the city, and they're not exactly concerned about cleaning up after themselves. In many cases, the water to such homes might be disconnected, but that doesn't stop squatters from using the toilets.

At least until they're full.

"Bakersfield Police," Officer Gwyn calls loudly into the house, rapping on the open door for emphasis as she scans the dim interior. When no response comes, she considers whether to enter or wait for backup.

Most police dispatchers, especially those who've been on the job awhile, are intuitive about the calls they take. In their line of work, you quickly develop a feel for what's important and what can wait. Susie learned long ago to ride dispatch's vibe: if they think it's important, she thinks it's important.

Though dispatchers across the country are legendary for their emotionless cadence, those who talk to them every day know otherwise. Susie had detected a sense of urgency in the dispatcher's voice that morning. Maybe the RP—the reporting person—had said something that instilled this urgency, or perhaps it was the way it was said. Either way, this sense of the immediate was carried forward.

Officer Susie Gwyn decides to enter. "Bakersfield Police. I'm coming in. Show yourself!"

Dispatch had said something about a bedroom at the end of the hall, so after clearing the kitchen, utility room, bathroom, and living room, Susie approaches the dark corridor and takes note of the three doors, two of them closed, one slightly ajar.

Clearing the first room, she moves to the door that stands cracked open. Light emanates from within.

"Bakersfield PD," she calls out again.

A sound comes to her, low and indecipherable. With her handgun at the low ready, she gives the door a gentle push with her foot. It creaks slowly inward and stops halfway.

"Oh, God," Susie gasps, almost retching. She fumbles for her radio and somehow finds herself in the hall with her back hard up against the wall as if even the wall conspires to thrust her into the horrors that await through the half-open door.

If she could have pushed through the wall and kept going, she would have.

"Code three," Susie says, forcing calm into her voice. "I need backup and an ambulance. Notify detectives."

It's just after eight when Ross's unmarked screeches to a halt in the portico out front of the Sierra Inn & Suites. Jimmy piles into the front seat and I grab the seat behind him. Five seconds after the first screech of tires, Ross chirps them again as he pulls away and flips on his lights and sirens.

To those having breakfast just off the lobby, the stop-and-go of an unmarked police car, followed by the harbingers of light and sound, draws every eye to the front of the building. Some of those at the breakfast bar rise to their feet and move for a better view, as do two of the clerks at the front desk, watching as the blue and red strobes tear out of the parking lot and race up the street.

There'll be questions for us when we return, I have no doubt.

"The call came in a half hour ago," Ross says after he explains the situation more fully. "I thought they were already on the way to the hospital, but dispatch just advised that the aid crew is working on him at the house. For some reason, they can't transport yet."

"And he's alive?" Jimmy asks for the third time.

Ross shrugs. "That's what I was told."

The drive to Tuttle Street seems to take forever, yet it's just seven minutes from the motel. Time has a mind and will of its own, it seems.

A couple of medics are huddled around the front door when Ross parks. As we spring from our seats, I see the cause of the congestion: they're bringing out the gurney. I hold my breath without knowing it, watching as the feet emerge—covered by a sheet—followed by the torso—covered by a sheet—and finally the shoulders, face, and head—uncovered.

Uncovered means he's alive.

I see Jimmy visibly shudder as he lets out a sigh of relief. I can relate. Following him down the sidewalk and up to the front door, I hold back a few paces and let him do his thing. My eyes connect with Noah for a moment, but I'm not sure he even sees me. His hair is matted and filthy, plastered to one side of his head by God knows what. He's trying to talk, but nothing's coming out. Or if it is, it's so low that I can't hear it.

Jimmy and Ross flash their badges for the medics.

"What's his condition?" Jimmy asks.

Most of the medics look away, but one of them, a rugged Jason Statham type, says, "He's dehydrated and showing signs of organ failure. Whoever did this to him had an IV stuck in his arm and was pumping him full of something we haven't identified. I took a sample for toxicology at the hospital, but the officer"—he dips his head toward Officer Susie Gwyn—"took the rest for evidence."

Noah's right hand slips out from under the covers, and I immediately see the nasty red bands around his wrist, the bloody welts where he tried pulling himself free and failed. And failed. And failed. He tries to lift the hand and manages to tug on Jimmy's shirt.

Jimmy looks down, and his eyes follow the hand and arm to Noah's face. As the hollowed-out man begins to mouth something, Jimmy leans in close and the medics stop the gurney. It takes a moment, but Jimmy finally nods and squeezes Noah's hand.

As he lets go, the medics whisk him away.

In a halo of dust and lights, the three of us watch as the ambulance blasts from the neighborhood, siren wailing. We watch until the lights are gone and the siren is distant and something close to silence settles around us.

"What did he say?" Ross asks.

"Most of it was nonsense," Jimmy says in a distant voice. "Demons and darkness and something about a bear. I'm sure it meant something, but his mind's not all there—probably drugged. He did say that the demon has Marco and that we have to save him."

"Nothing about the others?" I ask, wondering if he even knows.

A dark look crosses Jimmy's face. "He said that Wade's at the dentist's office . . . and Jason's in the ground." Jimmy meets my eye, holds it a moment, then turns to enter the house.

I spot the malachite shine as soon as I slip off my glasses.

Trails lead this way and that throughout the house, though most of the actual coming and going appears to have been through the door leading into the garage. I can see two older tracks through the front door, and perhaps three in and out of the back slider, but that's it.

The oldest shine dates back only months—six months, tops.

"I don't think he was living here," I whisper to Jimmy. "He visits infrequently, and only in the last week or so has he been here regularly."

This conclusion is borne out by the lack of furniture: no table, no couch, no chairs, not even a lamp. More important, there's no TV. I've been in homes where the occupants slept in sleeping bags on the floor and sat on stacks of old phone books, and they still had a fifty-inch TV propped up on wooden crates.

By American standards, without a TV, the place might as well be a cave.

I'm not saying that's good, it's just reality.

Most of the action seems to be at the end of the hall, so I follow Jimmy to the room on the left and peek over his shoulder through the doorway. Three things stand out about the room, and each of them is uniquely and instantly recognized. First, the windows are papered over with newspaper, which would have cast the room into deep shadow but for the weak overhead light and the considerably more powerful crime-scene lights.

Second, the rusty bed frame is topped by a box spring and

mattress. The entire collection resembles something you'd find abandoned alongside the road with a FREE sign taped to the frame. Even then, no one would want it. The bed is at an odd angle, and I realize it's elevated at the head by about six inches. Wondering at this, I lean farther over Jimmy's shoulder and notice that someone has placed several chunks of wood under each side, but only at the headboard.

Third, and of most immediate concern, is the stench.

There's no air movement in the room, yet the smell still comes at me in waves, washing over me with the consistency of smog. Trying not to breathe through my nose, I realize that the sheets on the bed—sheets I took to have a floral pattern—are supposed to be white. They're not. The stench of vomit, feces, urine, and a host of unpleasantries I can only guess at assaults us from the entrenched room.

Anyone wondering at the difference between an aroma and an odor would be well served to step into that room, if only for a moment.

I gag involuntarily.

"If you're going to throw up, go outside," Jimmy says quietly into my ear.

I have no intention of vomiting.

I tell myself that I've seen worse—smelled worse—and know that it's true, but still the saliva gathers in my mouth, the quiet herald of stomach contents soon to follow. Stepping back from the room, from the smell, I wait in the living room as my gut settles and the flow of saliva dissipates.

"How are you?" Jimmy asks as he joins me a few minutes later.

"Fine." I wave away his concern. "When Ross called earlier, I wolfed down the last of my breakfast a little too fast. I don't think it settled well."

"Mm-hmm."

Before I can defend myself further, Ross joins us in the living room. He's holding a small notepad in one hand and a chewed-up pen in the other—old-school. "Gina's the lead on this," he says, gesturing toward a female detective in her midthirties. Her ebony skin is flawless, unmarked by the demands of her harried profession. She walks with a perceptible limp.

"Based on the . . . evidence"—I assume Ross means the stained sheets—"it looks like he's been here at least two days, possibly three. As the paramedics said, they found a needle stuck in his arm and a slow-drip bag feeding some kind of liquid into his body intravenously. They're not sure what was in the bag, but suspect it began as a regular saline solution. Something was added, though, and that's the puzzler."

"How do they know something was added?" Jimmy asks.

"There's a slight greenish tint to the water. Very slight, but you could tell when you placed it side by side with a regular saline bag. Samples are off to the lab, and we should have an answer in a few hours."

Ross flips the page. "He was dehydrated, despite the IV. Guess the drip rate was set too low, either intentionally or otherwise." Ross flips again, then again. "No documents of dominion anywhere in the house. Nothing telling us who the renter is or suggesting he ever actually lived here."

The last part I already know. "So, was this just a staging area?" I ask. "Someplace to hold the men until he disposed of them?"

Ross shrugs. "Seems to be the case. We did find evidence of recent vehicle activity in the garage: imprints in the dust; dirt and debris tracked in by the tires, that sort of thing. It suggests at least two vehicles, one larger than the other. Also, the larger vehicle came and went a lot more frequently. The smaller one might have only been here once."

"Marco's SUV," I suggest.

Jimmy nods. "Probably kept it here until he killed Wade, then disposed of it in the hills." Jimmy looks at Ross. "Any idea what the other vehicle might be?"

"You mean, could it be our mystery van?" the detective replies. "No idea, but there are some good tire prints. Once CSI gets here, they'll take some photos and send them off to the lab. They've got tire-pattern analysis software that should at least tell us the brand and tire model. From there we can figure out what vehicles it fits and then check with local tire shops and see if they have any records that might point us in the right direction."

"Do they keep those kinds of records?" Jimmy asks.

"They must. When you buy tires, they usually have a limited warranty, right? Which means they have your contact information."

"I guess so. I'm thinking that's going to be a big list, though."

Ross doesn't seem concerned. "Depends on how popular the tire is. Maybe we'll get lucky and it'll be a small list. At least it's something."

Jimmy nods and echoes the sentiment. "At least it's something."

"Detectives did a cursory search of the room and house," Ross continues, "but now we have to clear out and leave it to CSI. Maybe they'll have more luck."

"So, what do we do in the meantime?" I ask.

Ross shrugs and smiles. "Curtain lady."

"Curtain lady?"

"Yeah, every neighborhood has one. We just need to find ours."

When Jimmy and I both stare at him without comprehension, he looks almost offended. *"Curtain lady,"* he says with emphasis. "You know, a busybody who hides behind her curtains all day watching the neighbors. In a place like this"—he glances toward the living room window and the street beyond—"I bet there's a half dozen of them."

We're near the front door when something occurs to me. "Does anyone know why the bed was propped up?"

Ross looks around. "What do you mean?"

"The head of the bed was on wood blocks."

"It was?"

"Yeah, about six inches' worth."

"Huh." The detective turns around and continues out of the house.

When I look at Jimmy, he just shrugs and follows.

As we exit, a black Ford Expedition remarkably similar to Jimmy's government-issued vehicle pulls to a stop in front of the house, blocking the right lane of travel. Leaving his semi-covert emergency lights flashing, Special Agent Kip Weir steps from the SUV and assesses the scene.

After asking three or four questions, he all but takes command—assuring Gina and the locals that it's still their investigation—and advocates strongly for activating the FBI's Evidence Response Team (ERT) out of the Sacramento Field Office.

Cupping the SA's elbow in his right hand, Jimmy steers Kip gently away on the pretext of asking about sensitive information. "What has your SAC been hearing?" he asks, referring to the special agent in charge of the Sacramento Field Office.

A sour look crosses Kip's face. "The ADIC out of Los Angeles is pushing to take over the investigation, claiming the Sacramento Field Office doesn't have the resources."

Unlike the other fifty-three field offices around the country, the New York City, Washington, DC, and Los Angeles Field Offices are run by an assistant director in charge (ADIC) rather than by a special agent in charge. This is due to the sheer size and number of investigations handled by those offices.

"It's all political," Kip continues, a defeated tone slipping into his words. "An influential congressman goes missing and everyone sees it as a ticket to advancement. Everyone wants to be the hero."

Jimmy smiles. "But not you?"

Kip takes it well. "Yeah, I admit that when the case was first handed to me, I thought it might move me up the ladder. But then . . ." His voice trails off. "What this guy did to Wade Winchell . . . and Jason Norris."

Kip waves a hand at the house. "And now Noah Long." He turns and looks at Jimmy, a haunted look on his face. "It's not about promotion, jurisdiction, or ego anymore. I just want to get this freak before he does to Marco what he did to the others."

"What about Abel Moya?" I ask.

Kip sighs. "They're still convinced he's behind this."

"You told them about the time line, right? The fact that Abel was smuggling people across the border when Marco was taken?"

"I told them. They're not convinced. They've ordered me to keep after him, and that's where they're going to focus FBI resources."

Jimmy shakes his head in disbelief. "Stupid sons of . . ." He lets the rest of it fall away into indiscernible sounds. Confronted with the ignorance of bureaucracy, all he can do is stand in disbelief with his hands on his hips.

"What do you intend to do?" I ask Kip.

"Screw them," the agent replies indignantly. "I'll hunt Abel, but I'm with you guys as soon as you find something worth pursuing. Promise you'll call me."

"We will," Jimmy assures him. "You've got good people working this case. Bakersfield CSI is on the way, and they know their business. I've seen them at work. Let them do their job."

Kip looks to the house and the detectives and officers securing the scene. Letting out a long breath, he asks, "Anything I can help with?"

"How are you with curtain people?"

# 29

Canvassing the neighborhood is critical to any investigation.

It's surprising how many people never reach out to the police, even when they witness or experience something sketchy or downright criminal. Yet, if you knock on the right doors and ask the right questions, they'll tell you who *really* killed Kennedy, and why the neighbor three doors down has low spots in his backyard.

Ross stays behind to help the other detectives, so it's just Jimmy, Kip, and me. There's no answer at the house next door—on either side—so we cross the street and try again. The first home, another rancher similar to the one where Noah was found, appears occupied because the front door is open and the blare of a TV issues from someplace within, someplace other than the living room.

"FBI," Jimmy calls into the house for the second time, his voice considerably louder on this attempt. He knocks hard on the aluminum screen, but there's still no response. He slips one of Kip's business cards in the crack between the screen door and the frame, and we move to the next house.

At the sidewalk, we shuffle fifty feet to the right and find ourselves standing in front of a salmon-colored cross-gabled rancher. Salmon's not really a color, or at least it shouldn't be. In days past, it might have been called peach or pink or pinkish peach, but not salmon. No one says they painted their living room wolverine, or that they added a little boa constrictor to the master bedroom to make the banana pop.

Or maybe it's just me.

I admit I have a borderline neurotic relationship with colors.

In any case, we find ourselves standing before this peachy house on Tuttle Street, and if houses were people, this one would be ten years past its last checkup and probably in need of a triple bypass. I'm sure the bones of the old house are good, but the rest of it is in desperate need of a makeover.

As Jimmy knocks, the ratty aluminum screen door bangs against the frame, setting up an echo effect.

The old woman who answers matches her house.

Her name, she tells us before we have a chance to ask, is Margaret Mulligan. Not Maggie, just Margaret. She doesn't like the name Maggie because she's known too many Maggies who were as cheap as their shortened names.

"Whores," she explains, in case there was any misunderstanding.

When advised that the local police and the FBI are investigating an incident across the street, she hurries the monologue along impatiently with a roll of her hand, as if we're repeating the obvious.

"This had something to do with the Fenton boys, I imagine? Jacob and Isaiah? I saw them running from the house, you know? Little thieves, those two. Stole the wind chime off my front porch."

When asked if she's ever seen the man across the street, she says, "Oh, sure," overemphasizing both syllables. And when asked if she's ever met him, she says, "Oh, sure." And when asked if she's ever seen what he drives, she says, "Oh, sure."

She's big on *Oh, sure*.

"It was a white van with BLACK WALNUT CATERING stenciled on both sides. I remember it because my granddaughter, Amy, is getting married next summer to this nice boy from Oxnard. He's a marketing director at one of those electronic e-commerce stores."

Margaret shrugs. "I've never been there, but they sell thousands of items, so it must be huge. Like Walmart or Costco, I imagine. Anyways, one day that big man pulls into the driveway and I notice the garage door doesn't come down. This was unusual because he always closes it behind him, very particular about that. Well, I figured I could go over and be neighborly and maybe ask about his catering business."

She shrugs again. "I figured he couldn't be as rough as he looks, least not if he's in the catering business, because *there's* a business that requires a lot of finesse. Anyways, he was yanking on the garage door something fierce when I came up behind him, and I guess I startled him because he said some sharp words I didn't particularly care for, and then he stood there glaring at me as if *I* were intruding, if you can imagine.

"Anyways, he wasn't friendly at all. Not in the least. I asked him what kind of events he catered, and he told me to . . . well, he told me to go do something to myself, if you know what I mean?" She gives us a look that suggests we *better* know what she means because she's not about to explain it.

"And so, I says to him that he's a crass individual—crass—and that with that kind of attitude I rightly expect he won't be in business by the time my Amy gets married anyway." She folds her arms across her chest. "You know what he did?"

This appears to be an actual question because it's not preceded by *anyways*, and she pauses a long moment, waiting for Jimmy to say "What?" before continuing.

"Well, he just stared at me. Stared at me as if his eyes were daggers stripping the flesh from my bones. Gave me the chills, it did. I don't know that I've ever seen eyes like that."

"Mrs. Mulligan," Jimmy says, "if we were to bring a sketch artist to your house, do you think you could describe him?"

"Oh, sure."

# 30

Just before ten, a frail man in his midfifties arrives at the edge of the crime scene and announces in a diminutive voice that his name is Herbert and that he's the sketch artist. Kip and I walk him across the street to Mrs. Mulligan's house, and the old curtain lady ushers us into the dining room, insisting we have coffee and, as it would happen, coffee cake.

We don't argue, particularly since Herbert perks up at the mention.

Over the next twenty minutes, the odd little sketch artist hunches over his large pad and uses a series of pencils and graphite sticks to create an image from words.

Mrs. Mulligan uses some three or four thousand words to paint a thousand-word picture. Brevity doesn't appear to be her strong point. We're left with a thuggish image that could be just about anyone within the criminal element of Bakersfield and the larger Kern County area.

Not much help.

When we escort Herbert off the scene, he carries a canvas bag containing his drawing tools in one hand and two slices of coffee cake on a napkin in the other. Mrs. Mulligan insisted he take the slices, apparently thrilled at his appetite.

He'd already devoured three slices and two cups of coffee in the short time he was drawing.

I guess what they say about starving artists is true.

Around ten forty-five, Gina gets a call from the hospital—not from the doctors and nurses attending Noah, but from Detective Alan Thomas, the unlucky soul assigned to stay with the hedge fund manager every step of the way—or at least every step the hospital would allow, HIPAA rules being what they are.

Ending the call after about three minutes, Gina gives a whistle and waves everyone around, including the CSIs still working the house, the garage, and the yard.

"That was Al. Noah Long is stable. They're still not sure as to the extent of damage, but he may need a liver transplant, and possibly both kidneys. The drip he was being fed, maybe for days, contained a diluted form of antifreeze."

A murmur rustles through those gathered, like so many dry leaves at the edge of a breeze. They understand in a moment the enormity of the statement.

"I know." Gina nods. "The bastard."

Antifreeze.

There are certainly worse ways to die, but not many. It's the ethylene glycol within the green mixture that's the real killer. Of the roughly five thousand cases of antifreeze poisoning in the United States each year, perhaps forty to sixty are fatal. Some jurisdictions have even experienced cases of suicide by antifreeze, though why anyone would pick such a horrible way to end their suffering remains a mystery.

Those so poisoned are usually fine for the first few hours as their body processes and breaks down the antifreeze. Depending on the amount swallowed, symptoms can begin to appear anywhere from thirty minutes to twelve hours after ingestion. After that, things begin to devolve. The afflicted may appear inebriated, demonstrating a lack of coordination and slurred speech. Nausea, vomiting, fatigue, and headache are usually part of the package.

Organ damage takes place from twenty-four to seventy-two hours after ingestion. Rapid breathing, rapid heartbeat, convulsions, and coma are all possibilities.

Death . . . is a possibility.

Gina continues, "The doctors believe our suspect made a mistake and overdiluted the solution. It's obvious he wanted to drag out the effects, but in doing so, he may have allowed us to rescue Noah in time to prevent brain damage. We'll have to wait and see. The good news is that he's responsive, and other than some visual hallucinations that send him into fits of terror, he seems to understand what's going on."

"Has he said anything?" one of the CSIs asks.

"He's tried, but they're not letting him speak. It seems his vocal cords . . ." She's not sure how to describe it. "Well, his trachea, in general, has extensive damage. Irreparable damage, from what Al was saying. It's doubtful he'll ever speak above a whisper again."

"Damaged?" Kip says. "How?"

"Something was rammed down his throat. The doctors think the damage was intentional, a rather barbaric way of keeping him from calling for help."

"Why not just gag him?" a detective asks in disbelief.

Gina nods as if to say she understands his horror. "I asked the same question, but the answer is right in front of us: The bedsheets, the room. This guy did his homework. He didn't want to gag Noah because he didn't want him to drown in his own vomit."

The gathering is silent a moment as that registers, and in that silence, something occurs to me. I give Ross a light elbow. "That's probably why the bed was elevated," I suggest when he tilts his head my way. He thinks on it a moment, then just nods.

No smile. Just a nod.

It's been a rough day for everyone.

"In any case," Gina continues, "they've got him hooked up to a dialysis machine and have him on Fomepizole, so the combination should break down the toxins and sweep them from his system. Again, time will tell what long-term effects he might suffer."

She clasps her hands together. "That's it, so let's get back to work. We still have a missing man out there, and based on the intervals of the killings, we have twenty-four to forty-eight hours. Time is running short, folks."

*Time is running short.*

The words stir a dark spot in my mind, a humorless, vapid place with neither warmth nor humanity. It's not so much the time-running-short part of Gina's pronouncement that pushes me to this dark spot, but rather her estimation of twenty-four to forty-eight hours.

I hadn't put an end cap on Marco's life.

I hadn't supposed we'd fail.

Now I'm not so sure.

# 31

The white van barely slows as it turns off Old Stage Road in Porterville and races up a worn dirt-and-gravel driveway. The mild angle of the path makes this quick entrance possible, but any speed carried from the road is quickly jostled away as the potholes go to work on the undercarriage, rocking the van violently up and down and sideways. The tires kick up a choking cloud of dust, which spills toward the modest farmhouse and the old woman who sits on her wide porch knitting.

*Again!* Barbara Mills thinks, glaring at the van.

The twenty-three-acre farm was once covered with citrus trees, an orchard of green and orange in an otherwise dry landscape. But that was years ago, back when the owners, Otis and Barbara, were young and still believed in dreams.

The farm hadn't fared so well since Otis's passing in 2001. Barbara tried running the place herself for a spell, but what did she know of oranges? It was a hobby farm, after all, and Otis had always handled the crops and the workers and the contracts, taking a few weeks off from his engineering position each year at harvest time. She threw in the towel in 2008 and took a receptionist job at a real estate brokerage to make ends meet.

Most of the orange trees were uprooted or left to die without water, but she kept about fifty trees alive and well tended, scattered in several clusters around the farm. Without them, the place was too flat and dry, she often said. Besides, she could sell the fruit at the farmers' market to supplement her now-meager income.

The barn and half dozen outbuildings at the back of the property had fallen into disrepair over the years, and even the once-proud metal sign arching over the driveway had taken a turn for the worse. Where flame-red letters once spelled out FOOTHILL ORCHARDS, now only FOOT CHARDS remains, the red paint surrendering to rust and the gaps between letters standing out like missing teeth.

The *D* isn't entirely gone.

It's bent at a ninety-degree angle, though, so that it's parallel with the ground, held aloft by one remaining weld spot. The vandals responsible for that indignity likely stood on a ladder in the bed of a pickup to reach it, and Barbara kept her shotgun loaded with rock salt in case they returned.

After a while, she began to hope they'd return.

She hoped they'd finish the job they started and carry off the sad *D*, but it never happened. The sign remains a bent, gap-filled mess of rusting metal. Three bullet holes in the *F*, the *C*, and the *S* seem to have symbolically killed it, putting it out of its long misery.

The corpse remains.

Rising from her rocker on the porch, Barbara yells something at the passing van as it spews gravel and dust and continues to the back of the property, to the barn and the storage buildings and the sorting room. When the van disappears behind the barn, she scowls and shakes her head.

Taking her seat, she returns to her knitting.

The last deputy she'd talked to had encouraged her to get a restraining order . . . or at least ban him from the property.

She'd given it serious thought, but . . . how could she? Even now, after everything, he was still family, and that means something. Doesn't it?

A cold acorn rests in the pit of Barbara's stomach. Even now she can feel it: a realization waiting to sprout, a warning in need of digestion.

The panel van's back door groans as the latch is disengaged and a large hand pulls it open. As a huge mass steps into the opening, blocking the glare of the sun, Noah's demon takes shape. Not a real demon, just a man with a demon's intent. He calls himself Bear, a nickname he seemed proud to share with Marco during the drive as if it were some ancient family name and he the honored recipient. Now, as he pokes his head inside the van and grins, Bear asks, "How are things back here? Comfy?" He takes a quick look at Marco's bindings to make sure he hasn't managed to loosen them. "We'll be spending the night here."

Plucking a black garbage bag from the piles gathered on either side of Marco, Bear unknots the top and extracts two sleeping bags. Marco recognizes them. One belonged to Wade, the other to Jason. Marco catches a whiff of Wade's cologne as Bear reseals the bag.

Marco almost vomits.

He must have told himself a thousand times in the previous days that this isn't real, that it's not happening. As if to repeat the phrase would make it so and land him back in his tent or his apartment, shaken but no longer part of some unending nightmare. His senses keep reminding him that it *is* real—beyond denial.

He can feel it.

He can see it.

He can smell it.

Blathering on about the outbuildings, the stable, and the

old barn in an upbeat, almost friendly voice, Bear pulls Marco from the van with rough hands that don't match his tenor. Placing him on his feet and adjusting his gag, he claps the congressman on the back. "Better, right? Must feel good to stretch the legs."

Grabbing Marco by the upper arm, Bear's fingers pinch down hard. He turns Marco away from the old barn with its weathered timbers and steers him toward a single-story cinder-block outbuilding on the other side of the van. The exterior was once a crisp white, but the paint, like everything else about Foothill Orchards, had faded into a dull shadow of its former self.

"This is my aunt's place," Bear rambles on as if reminding himself. "We passed her on the way in, the old bitch. Her and my mom were peas in a pod." He cocks his head and studies Marco. "You like that saying—'peas in a pod'? Sounds a bit hick-a-billy, doesn't it? Some redneck-farmer saying. My aunt and uncle were farmers, and this is what they got for it: a run-down old farm that nobody cares about."

Bear laughs. "My aunt would have sold the land off years ago, but she's afraid I'll kill her for the money." He turns and nods. "She told me so herself, right to my face, the little bitch. Peas in a pod."

He shrugs. "I spent a lot of time here as a kid, back when it was still a working orchard. They'd make me work in the field with the migrants at harvesttime. I just remember long, hot days trying to keep up with those bastards.

"It wasn't all bad, I suppose. Smoked my first bowl with a kid named Jose, not much older than me. He stole some dope from his dad's backpack—Acapulco Gold, he said—and we lit up in the barn loft. Stuff smelled like a skunk's ass, tasted like it too, but it did the job. Jose didn't speak much English, and I didn't speak much Spanish, but we got by and were pretty tight after that."

Bear stops in front of the building and pulls open an old door. "In here."

The building must have been a storage room or perhaps a packaging room. A single stainless-steel table is bolted to the floor off to the left, and it's immediately evident that four such tables once filled the center of the room, butted one against the other, left to right. All that remains of the other three are a series of lag bolts protruding from the concrete where they'd been bolted down.

The fate of those three is unclear, but some of the lag bolts appear to have been hacked off with a Sawzall, suggesting they were stolen, most likely by Bear. The jagged remnants of the bolts are now rusty spikes rising from the floor, punji sticks waiting for a careless pair of feet.

Stacks of old orange crates fill the back-right corner, occupying the exact spot they'd held when the last worker walked out the door and locked it behind him all those years ago. The labels are now faded but you can still see the words FOOTHILL ORCHARDS in sweeping letters as they flow over the image of rolling green hills and an overflowing cornucopia of oranges.

Better days.

Long ago.

Pushing Marco toward an empty spot under one of the front windows, Bear kicks debris from the area with big sweeps of his foot, then throws down one of the sleeping bags as a spider scurries for a recess in the concrete.

"You sleep here," the big man growls. Any friendliness that had occupied his voice was now gone, and the rumble from his barrel chest hints at darker things lurking within.

He handcuffs Marco to a six-inch C bolt protruding from the wall. Unlike everything else about the room, the C bolt shines as if new. It's attached to the cinder-block wall by a square of fresh concrete that's four inches square.

From the back of his waistband, Bear draws a bowie knife with a foot-long blade. He twists it in the light a moment, letting the rays dance along the surface as he holds it inches from Marco's face. No malice is in his eyes, just a deep fascination with the cold steel.

The blade is clean, but in the crease where it joins the guard, Marco notices a hint of dirty burgundy, a thin line of filth that had flowed there as liquid before hardening into a flaky crust. It survives in its crease only because Bear's idea of cleaning a blade is to wipe it quickly on his victim's clothes.

"I'm going to go pay my aunt a visit," Bear says, loving the knife with his eyes. "Then I've got some business elsewhere." He grins and glances at the handcuffs. "Why don't you wait here."

# 32

*Sierra Inn & Suites, Wednesday, March 11—11:43 P.M.*

Some days are hard; others make hard look easy.

Today was the latter.

If you spend enough time in law enforcement, such days will find you from time to time. If you spend a couple of years with the Special Tracking Unit, such days are known as Wednesday.

When I get back to the motel, the first thing I do is call Heather. When she picks up on the second ring, it's as if a weight lifts from my shoulders, my arms, my head. The sound of her voice doesn't exactly cheer me up, but it does soothe me, if that makes sense.

I imagine it's much like in the westerns when you see some gunslinger with a bullet in his shoulder and they get him sotted up on whiskey before they reach in and pull it out. The whiskey doesn't necessarily make the pain any less; it's just easier to bear.

Heather's my whiskey.

She talks about the wedding and some sleuthing award her website just received for crime reporting. She talks about the price of avocados at the grocery store and a condo in

Hawaii that would be perfect for our honeymoon. We immerse ourselves in talk of all things common sense and nonsense and dollars and cents . . . and time slips by.

The minutes skirt the edge of blissful ignorance, as if the day hadn't included the discovery of an emaciated, tortured, haunted man.

When I finally disconnect the call a half hour later, I'm tired but doubt I can sleep. I turn on the TV and search for something worth watching, settling for a home-makeover show. After only a few minutes I'm captivated. Part of me has always wanted to restore old houses, but after my experience helping Jimmy refinish his kitchen last year, I've decided that I need to better balance my desires against my abilities.

The show is almost finished and I'm just waiting for the big reveal when a loud knock rattles my door. Searching for the pause button on the remote and finding none, I haul myself off the bed and shuffle to the door.

Jimmy pushes through as soon as I turn the handle and charges into the center of the room. He's got his phone in his hand, held horizontally as if he has someone on speaker. I'm just about to ask him about it when Diane's voice trumpets forth.

"Are we there yet?"

"Yes," Jimmy replies loudly—maybe too loudly. "She says she has it." I'm not sure if he's talking to me or Diane, but then he lifts the phone slightly, as if for emphasis, and looks directly at me. "She says she has it."

"Has what?"

"It! The answer! She figured it out; all of it. She wouldn't say anything until we were together because she didn't want to repeat herself."

"I didn't want to repeat myself," Diane's voice says at the same time.

*Diane figured it out.*

The thought—and her voice—sends a rush of adrenaline

through my system. Diane has a little more Tabasco sauce in her voice—a little more fire—when she figures something out. It has to filter through her sarcasm, but it's always there.

It's there now.

"Is this going to help us identify the abductor?" I ask.

"It should. Unless you're stupid."

I roll my eyes, knowing full well she can't see me.

"Tell us," Jimmy says, his pen and pad at the ready.

"I've been looking for the common denominators, the things tying the four men together—other than their friendship and fishing ritual, of course. In some ways, the men have a lot in common, in others, not so much. They have different lives, different goals, different values. Wade and Noah are both Masons, for example, but not Jason or Marco.

"They all learned a few things about investing while building the lure company in college, but they don't share any joint ventures. Noah runs his massive hedge fund, Jason was mostly invested in real estate investment trusts, Wade put some of his profits from the sale of the company into index funds, and some into a nice boat and a truck to tow it.

"As for Marco, he's more of a stock picker, and a pretty good one from what I gather. He bought into Amazon and Netflix early and took a large position in Apple when it was under ten dollars. The guy's shrewd. Those are just a few examples. The point is, I could find no financial common denominator, which is usually the culprit in cases like this."

"Maybe when a ransom is involved," Jimmy points out, "but we've had no ransom—"

"I'm just explaining the process, dear," Diane interrupts patiently. "But, knowing you two as I do, and taking into account your short attention spans, I'll cut to the chase. Failing to find a common denominator, I took a closer look at the crime scenes and the circumstances surrounding them. One man with his head shaved for no apparent reason and buried alive, one man butchered, apparently by way of some

Viking execution method, with part of his lung still unaccounted for, and a third man, almost dead, left strapped to a bed with poison slowly dripping into his vein."

She pauses, letting all this sink in.

"Think about those three outcomes," she urges, her voice almost pedantic. "Tell me what stands out."

Jimmy and I look at each other and shrug but say nothing.

"Who is bald?"

"Old men," Jimmy says.

"Babies," I chime in.

"Cops," Jimmy adds.

"Who else?" Diane presses, her voice suddenly short, borderline peeved. "Maybe the baldness wasn't intentional. Maybe it was a consequence of something."

"Like a fire?" Jimmy asks.

"A hot-tubbing accident," I say.

Jimmy looks at me.

I shrug. "The suction inlet—"

Jimmy waves my explanation away.

"Honestly, how do you two solve *anything*?" Diane says.

"Oh, sure," I say. "It's so easy once you know the answer."

Diane sighs. Loudly. "Let me give you two more clues. What if that same bald person—bald by no fault of his own—had part of his lung removed."

She waits.

No response.

"What if they then hooked that poor man up to a slow drip of poison?" She pauses. "Have I spelled it out enough for you? Here's another clue: it's one of the twelve zodiacs."

"Cancer!" Jimmy barks.

"Sagittar—Cancer!" I say, barely echoing my partner.

"Cancer." Diane lets the word linger in the air, like an unpleasant odor. "He shaved Jason's head and left his hair in his pocket; the coffin, no doubt, was just a symbol of where cancer might take you. A bit of theatrics, I suppose. His version of fun. So, he told us the *what*—that being cancer—and then he told us what *type* of cancer when he carved up Wade and put his lungs on display. To press the point, he cut out a large chunk from deep in the lung, the way a surgeon might. Why he chose to lay him open the way he did is anyone's guess at this point, but I think he likes it. I think he likes bringing fear and pain. Finally, it was Noah who served time in a special kind of hell, hooked up to some perverted form of chemotherapy."

She sighs as this settles in and then asks a pointed question: "What was Marco before he was a congressman?"

"A doctor," I say softly. "An oncologist."

"Correct. That means this isn't about his politics. It's not about Jason, Wade, or Noah. This has everything to do with his medical practice. A disgruntled and disturbed patient. Or maybe the relative of a patient." In a softer voice, she says, "I'd start with a list of those who didn't make it."

Silence takes us.

The enormity of the revelation is staggering and ugly. That someone would use one of mankind's most hideous natural foes and replicate its treatment and consequences is almost beyond belief. That someone had even conceived of this idea, let alone carried it out, is even more horrifying.

Monsters do walk among us.

They wear sneakers and carry smartphones.

"We need a list of his former patients," Jimmy says at length.

"I was in a hurry to call you with the news, but I *did* take a few minutes to look at his work history. Fortunately, it's pretty straightforward. After finishing his residency, he spent his entire career with Price-Baxter Oncology—maybe ten or twelve years. Their new office is on Eighteenth Street and they open at eight A.M. I'll text the address."

"Thanks, Diane," Jimmy mutters as he jots it down.

"One more thing." Diane's voice is hesitant as if she doesn't want to speak of such things. "You should know they moved out of their last office about a year ago. It was on Seventeenth Street. After the interior was gutted and refinished, it was leased out as a dental complex."

"Wade!" I say with a gasp.

"Wade," she echoes.

# 33

*Thursday, March 12—Early*

The night is unforgiving.

I drift in and out of sleep, but it never really takes. A little after four, Jimmy sends a text asking if I want to go to the gym with him. He's having trouble sleeping too. I almost agree, despite my disdain for useless physical activity. Instead, I watch some late-night television—mostly infomercials.

Around four thirty I almost buy a portable urinal called the UroClub. It looks like a golf club but isn't. If you're on the course and don't want to leave the green for a bathroom break, you just pee into the handle, screw the end back on, and you're ready to go.

I want one.

I don't even golf.

At seven, I join Jimmy at a small table next to the breakfast bar. He works on his crossword puzzle silently as I dissect a poppy-seed muffin, entertaining myself by seeing how many individual poppy seeds I can pick out and stack up.

"Thirteen down," Jimmy says after a few minutes, still studying his crossword puzzle. "'Drops on the ground'?"

"Body," I say instinctively.

"Three letters."

"Dew."

He pencils it in and finds it fits.

Just before seven thirty, Ross joins us.

We woke him with an early-morning call around six and gave him the short version regarding Diane's discovery. Now we fill in the blanks, sparing none of the details. When we finish, Ross looks as stunned as we were last night.

"Cancer?"

"Yeah," I say.

We watch him, Jimmy and I, and wait for the same question that came to both of us late last night. Ross doesn't disappoint. Just a few minutes into our expanded conversation, he suddenly stops, a look of mixed emotions on his face: pensiveness, fear, contempt.

"What comes after chemo?" he asks with some alarm. "He's got another victim to put on display, right? So, what is he planning for Marco?"

"That's the sixty-four-thousand-dollar question." Jimmy tosses his unfinished crossword puzzle in the garbage can next to him. "This was about Marco right from the beginning, so whatever it is, it's going to be something . . . unrivaled."

The word is ominous, threatening.

What can be *unrivaled* when juxtaposed against live burial, the full execution of a ritualistic Blood Eagle, and slow poisoning? The answer must be horrific, something beyond reason and understanding.

"We need to find Marco before it comes to that," I say quietly.

Jimmy checks his watch. "Ten minutes until the clinic opens."

Ross rises. "Let's go, then."

* * *

"The cancer business must be good," Jimmy says as we enter the marble-tiled, two-story foyer of Price-Baxter Oncology. "Sweet place they got here."

"Nothing wrong with having a nice office," I observe.

"Not what I was saying . . . just . . . damn!" Jimmy lets his eyes roam from right to left, taking in the waiting room, the acid-stained-concrete reception counter, the plush chairs, the marble floors, and the extrawide halls leading off in two directions. A glass-lined steel staircase leads to the second floor.

Jimmy and Ross flash their badges at the counter while I just linger in the background. I'm good at lingering. I've had a lot of practice.

"Special Agent Donovan?" says a woman in a white lab coat as she approaches briskly from the right hallway. Jimmy takes her hand and she introduces herself as Janet. She turns toward me and Ross, either curious or confused, so we quickly introduce ourselves.

Satisfied that the three of us are together, one big happy family, she cuts straight to it: "I was told you need to look at some records?"

"Yes," Jimmy replies. "We need to see a list of patients that Dr. Marco Perez treated during his employment here. Names, addresses, as much as we can get."

"Don't take this the wrong way," Janet says with a measure of hesitation, "but you *are* familiar with HIPAA regulations, aren't you? Patient records are confidential and inaccessible to law enforcement without a warrant."

"We're aware. We've frequently had to navigate the HIPAA rules. In this case, you'll find that we don't need a warrant because I'm not asking for personal health information. As I'm sure you're aware, patient information can be released to law enforcement—without a warrant—under several conditions. One of those conditions is if the information is needed to help identify or locate a suspect."

Jimmy settles his gaze on Janet. "That's what I'm asking for. I'm sure you've seen it in the papers by now, but Congressman Perez—"

"*Congressman* Perez? The one who was kidnapped?"

"Yes . . . I assumed you knew him."

"No." She seems shaken. "I transferred from our San Francisco clinic last year when they opened the bigger office. I knew that he once worked for us, but when you mentioned Perez, I didn't put two and two together. We have several employees with that last name."

"I imagine you understand why I want to look at his patient records."

"Y-yes! No! You think one of his patients is responsible for his disappearance?"

"Just looking at all possibilities," Jimmy says evasively.

It takes Janet about twenty minutes, but she eventually emerges from a side office carrying a small ream of paper.

"I printed out every patient he counseled and treated during his time with us. It's a lot of names, I'm afraid. You said basic information, so I ordered it by name, birthday, and address. I hope that works."

"That's perfect."

Grabbing a small table in the corner of the waiting room, we pull up three chairs and divide the stack into three. None of us have any idea what we're looking for. Well, maybe Jimmy does, but I'm in the dark, and Ross is rubbing his belly, so I'm guessing he's in the dark as well.

It's not like the patient's name is going to have an asterisk next to it and a footnote that says KILLER OR SON OF KILLER, right? Still, Jimmy wants to take a quick look before we scan the document into a PDF and email it off to Diane . . . the only person who might be able to make sense of it.

Sometimes I'm wrong. . . .

When Jimmy sits erect in his seat, no longer slouching over

his coffee, the move is so sudden and willful that both Ross and I look up.

"I think I have it." Jimmy's voice is filled with wonder.

We're barely two minutes into our perusal and he thinks he's figured it out. I'm about to tell him to stop teasing when I see his face.

Damned if he isn't serious.

"How could you possibly know from a list?"

Ross nods his dubious agreement.

Pulling a page from the stack, Jimmy circles something on it and then turns it around to face us. He places it on the table and slowly pushes it across. The only obvious mark on the page is the circle he just drew around the name Dorothy Smit.

I still don't get it.

Growing impatient, Jimmy reaches across the table.

Instead of pointing at Dorothy's name, he points farther to the right. My eyes follow, and I still don't understand—until the truth of it hits me full in the face. The ugly truth. The bastard has been taunting us every step of the way. As I digest the words before me, a chill walks slowly up my spine, like electricity sparking its way up a Jacob's ladder.

"I think you have it." My mind reels from the discovery. Pushing the page toward Ross, I spare him the intrigue and immediately point to the address, tapping it lightly with my index finger.

Ross is beside himself. "Holy . . . are you serious? The house where we found Noah?"

"Tuttle Street," I say.

"The same," Jimmy replies.

We stare at each other in disbelief for the better part of a minute, processing and trying to come to grips with the enormity of the discovery.

In the end, it's Ross who asks the most relevant question—the only question.

"Who's Dorothy Smit?"

# 34

Some people just *know* they're going to die of cancer.

Some are right.

For Dorothy Smit, it was a given. She'd smoked for forty-five of her fifty-nine years. A lifetime of tar and nicotine, the last half of which was filled with endless media and internet reports of people who did *this* or did *that* and got cancer. Cigarettes were always high on the list of culprits.

How else was it supposed to end?

Diagnosed in 2009, Dorothy fought the good fight for years.

The first surgery was followed by chemotherapy and some limited radiation treatment. Things looked promising for a while, for years, even. Her scans looked good, she finally gave up the cigarettes, and she even started to breathe with more ease, as if the tar pit in her chest was finally loosening its grip on her shriveled and malformed lungs, relenting to the pressure of clean air and clean living.

She had a good run: three years.

The second diagnosis must have hit her particularly hard.

It was so unfair. She'd beaten it once, hadn't she? And after all the progress she'd made, giving up the cigarettes, going for walks, eating healthier meals. For what, an even more aggressive cancer?

Again, there was surgery and chemo and radiation. Her body was cut and poisoned and blasted by invisible rays, and still, cancer marched through her system like a Roman legion, polluting the lymph nodes and reaching its ugly tentacles into her organs, tainting them, corrupting them.

When Dorothy Smit finally died, a mere husk of the woman she'd once been, she was mourned by her sister, her third husband, a niece, and three or four friends. That was it. Some who knew her but couldn't attend the funeral for one reason or another (depending on what kind of excuse they could come up with) would later post a kind word or a remembrance on Facebook.

It was the type of rote gesture expected in polite society, something to make people feel good about themselves while the voice in their head reminded them they didn't like the old bat in the first place. Not at all.

Dorothy had been a bit of a cancer herself.

It was a sad way to end a life—any life. So much potential squandered. In the end, not a single person signed the registry at her wake except her husband, the immeasurably meek Henry Smit, who died himself just two years later.

Dorothy's sons were conspicuously absent.

Both had good reasons, one more so than the other, and those few who took time to gather in her memory whispered of those reasons. Whispered. As if Dorothy's corpse might arise from its coffin and admonish them if she heard a single bad word about her boys.

She loved those boys.

She hated those boys.

And she did both with all her heart.

It was in this purgatory of her own making that she died. And when it was finally done, and the pain of the disease had passed into another dimension, it would be nice to think that somewhere in the world, perhaps, a single blade of grass might have stirred quietly at her passing, recognizing her departing soul, acknowledging that she once lived.

But if this was so, no one took note. Not even the blade of grass.

# 35

We're back at Starbucks.

It occurs to me that for someone who doesn't like the taste of coffee, I spend a lot of time in coffee shops. I have my usual: a Venti mocha, single shot, decaf, with 1 percent milk and no whip. I figure if you can't avoid the coffee, you can at least smother it in milk and chocolate.

The hunt for Marco Perez has taken a decidedly positive turn, but with answers practically throwing themselves at us, an equal number of questions seem to manifest, each begging for attention.

I feel the pressure of time more keenly than at any other point since we started this case. Real pressure, like a clock *tick-tick-ticking* in the back of my brain. How much longer does Marco have—really? We're lucky he's not dead already. Any grace we have left must certainly have expired, and now that the answer seems to be in sight—just beyond our grasping minds—I have to wonder: How many hours do we have left? How many minutes?

And what do we tell Ella if we fail?

The six interrogatives of any good investigation are who, what, where, when, why, and how, the most important of these being *who*. Once the *who* is determined, the rest often follows. Regarding the disappearance of the four men, where the *who* was such an insurmountable question mark, we now have an answer.

Now we just need to find him . . . and Marco.

"That was Diane," Jimmy says, returning to the table after a lengthily huddle with his phone in the corner of the room. "She's still digging, but it looks like Dorothy Smit had two sons that were always in trouble with the law. The oldest, Michael Graves Jr., was shot and killed during a botched robbery in 1998. He stabbed a store clerk in the neck with an eight-inch drill bit and then tried to ambush the arriving officers. He lost."

"Don't bring a drill bit to a gunfight," I mutter.

Jimmy cocks his head in agreement. "Safe to say we can cross him off our suspect list."

"Safe to say," Ross replies. "What about the other son?"

"Angus Graves." Jimmy slides his phone across the table so the detective can view the latest in a series of mug shots. "Diane downloaded that from JBRS, but I imagine you have access to a much larger assortment of booking photos. The guy's been arrested twenty-seven times. Just finished a six-year stretch at Ironwood State Prison for robbery and assault after a drug deal went sideways. He was released eleven months ago."

"Ironwood," Ross says. "Yeah, that's about three hundred miles southeast of here, not far from the border with Arizona. I've had to make the drive a few times to interview suspects." He shakes his head. "Not a fun drive."

"Maybe you should call Kip," I say to Jimmy.

"We don't know this is our guy yet."

"Yeah, but they're wasting his time having him chase down Abel Moya."

"Let's just see what we can confirm before we jump the gun."

Jimmy can tell I'm not happy and tries to give me a

reassuring smile. If I were Kip, I'd be pissed at being ordered to pursue leads that I know are irrelevant, especially with a congressman's life on the line.

Jimmy says I have a touch of oppositional defiance disorder because I don't like clueless, micromanaging bureaucrats.

Like that's a problem.

Setting up his MDT, or mobile data terminal, Ross uses his AirCard to access Bakersfield PD's secure database. His stubby fingers peck away at the keyboard with surprising agility, and a moment later he mutters, "Uh-huh." A comment that seems meant for his own gratification because he doesn't elaborate. More keystrokes follow, along with a *hmm* and another *uh-huh* as his fingers continue to putter.

Finally satisfied, he pushes back from the terminal and adjusts the screen so he can see it better from his new position.

"There's a lot here," he mutters. Then, almost apologetically, he asks, "Can I have our records department forward a bunch of reports to Diane? See what she can do with them?" He pauses. "We've got people, but between Marco's disappearance, the murders of Jason and Wade, and the rescue of Noah—"

Jimmy holds up a hand. "You don't have to explain."

"It's just . . . maybe Diane can hit all this with fresh eyes, especially since we now have a suspect."

"Anything specific you want her to look at?"

"No. That's the problem. It's not just one thing but a whole bunch of things. Angus Graves is thirty-nine and he's been offending since he was eight. Our database displays fifteen one-line record entries per page, and I've got thirteen pages of contacts on him. A bunch of the early entries are runaway reports, juvenile problems, stuff like that, but there's also an assault when he was eleven, burglaries and car prowls when he was twelve, thirteen, and fourteen, attempted suicide when he was fifteen, and the hits just keep coming."

"Do you have narratives with all the reports or just the basics? The dates, times, places, and people?"

"I'm guessing it's probably going to be about fifty-fifty. The real meat is in the narrative, I know, but these records go back thirty years, so . . . I just don't know."

Jimmy scribbles an email address on a Post-it note and pushes it across the table. "Have them send it here. I'll text Diane and let her know it's coming."

"Tell her I'm sorry to dump on her like that."

"Are you kidding?" I turn to Ross. "She'll be ecstatic. She's freaky that way."

As the detective notifies his Records Department about the substantial records request, and Jimmy shoots off a text to Diane, I drag two chairs around and place them on either side of Ross, claiming one for myself and leaving the other for my partner.

With the email and text sent, we get down to the business of scrubbing the database. The very first record, as Ross said, is from over thirty years ago. Little Angus Graves, it seems, had gotten angry at a neighbor boy who took his bike. And what does the average boy do when someone takes his bike? Well, he hits the kid over the head with a baseball bat, of course.

Just once, though.

Little Tommy from two houses down had a concussion and the desperate need for eight stitches. He never touched Angus's bike again.

That was the beginning of a criminal life that established Angus as a bona fide frequent flier, an outlaw so prolific in his criminality that he should get bonus miles for every night he stays at the county jail or state pen. Double miles when physical injury is involved.

We spend the next twenty minutes perusing the reports chronologically, eventually reaching one labeled ATTMPT SUIC, cop shorthand for an attempted suicide.

"Fifteen years old and he's trying to kill himself." Ross shakes his head. "How much do you have to think the world sucks to even contemplate such a thing?"

"Hard to tell when it comes to suicide," Jimmy says. "Could have been a cry for help or a bad trip on whatever drugs he kept getting arrested for. Things tend to snowball when you make bad choices."

"Where was this?"

"It says Ranch Hill Road, out in the foothills northeast of Bakersfield. There are some good hiking trails in that area, but not much else. Well, except for the old silver mine. Kind of a ghost town, if you ask me. Most of the old buildings are still standing, and it's been used for one thing or another through the years. Abandoned these days, last I heard."

"Seems an odd place to commit suicide," I say, having seen my fair share.

"Maybe his family was camping in the area?"

"I suppose. Does it say how he tried to kill himself?"

Ross scans the five paragraphs that constitute the report. "Hanging." A thought seems to occur to him. "That might account for the scar."

Jimmy perks up. "What scar?"

Ross makes a swiping motion across his neck. "The 'Scars-Marks-Tattoos' section indicates he has a burn scar around the front and sides of his neck. A good hanging attempt will do that."

"That doesn't sound like a cry for help."

"No, that takes commitment," Ross agrees.

Continuing through the myriad reports, we find that Angus's crimes seem to have taken on a more sinister tone after the failed suicide attempt, as if, failing with the rope, he intended to get the job done by other means, mainly through dangerous deeds with dangerous people. By the time he turned seventeen, he was the main enforcer for a local drug dealer. And when Angus came around, people always paid.

One way or another.

Three weeks after his eighteenth birthday, Angus was finally booked into the county jail for the first time. It was a far cry from juvenile detention, but at six foot three and almost three hundred pounds of mostly muscle, Angus was a force to be reckoned with. His juvenile career had been impressive, no doubt. It included convictions for burglary, car prowl, rape, assault, robbery, drugs, and more. But that was just the warm-up act.

Angus Graves had finally come into his own. Some might say it was a bit like Lucifer finding hell and taking his throne. Others would forgo the simile and say it *was* Lucifer—the devil himself—in all his three hundred pounds of menace and malice.

Noah called him a demon; he wasn't far from the mark.

After viewing all the local records, Ross logs into NCIC—the FBI's National Crime Information Center—and pulls a Triple-I on Angus. The Triple-I is just one of many features of NCIC and is similar to the return from a local law enforcement database, but with a wider reach. It doesn't record every contact with Angus, but it does include all of his arrests, whether in Bakersfield, California, or Bakersfield, Vermont, as well as any warrants, restraining orders, missing person reports, and other information that might be relevant. It's the bread and butter of law enforcement, and cops all across the country run millions of queries a day.

"As you said, he was released from Ironwood State Prison eleven months ago and is currently on supervision." Ross points to a notation on the screen. Picking up his pen, he writes down the phone number for Angus's community corrections officer, or CCO, then reads her name aloud: Crystal Baum-something.

He puts the phone on speaker and dials the number.

# 36

Marco lies on his side, his hands fastened securely behind his back with not one but two heavy-duty zip ties. He's gagged—a pointless gesture, all things considered. Tired from trying to hold his head up, it cocks to the side, the crown resting against the dry California soil. The tactile caress of the cool earth is almost comforting, a reassurance of the cycle of life.

*Ashes to ashes, dust to dust.*

From his vantage point, he can see everything; which is, he imagines, exactly as intended. The big man named both Bear and Angus intends for him to see what he's doing, see every moment of it.

The hulking figure is in high spirits, moving about as if preparing for some great spectacle that he's very much looking forward to. It's all a game, a festival. Pouring gas into a two-thousand-watt generator, Angus looks at Marco and announces that he got the portable unit brand-new from a tweaker who stole it from Home Depot.

"I gave him fifty bucks, and he just walked in, put it in a shopping cart, and wheeled it right out the door." A look of mischief is in Angus's eyes as he relays this to Marco as if the congressman is supposed to laugh with him and talk about how ballsy it was. When he doesn't, Bear's eyes grow suddenly cold—the lifeless orbs of something staring up from the abyss, something not human.

He watches Marco with those brutally cold eyes, then turns away.

A moment later, he returns with a pair of brand-new sawhorses, a circular saw with a pawnshop sticker still affixed to the blade guard, an impact drill that's seen better days, and a cordless Sawzall with one extra battery pack. There are also some hand tools: a pack of chisels, a mallet, some files of different sizes.

He positions the various tools to create his work space as if the location and purpose of the tools are immensely important to what's coming. Satisfied, he takes the Sawzall in hand and turns to face Marco.

With a maniacal look on his face, he holds the tool aloft, revving the blade. Then, with a sneer, he turns and walks into the nearby stable. A ruckus ensues, the type of noise generated by one not familiar with power tools but determined to use them nonetheless.

After about twenty minutes of this, Marco hears the distinct splintering of wood, a timber getting ready to give way. And not just any piece of wood, but one of substance.

A *crack!* shatters the air.

Something heavy crashes to the ground with the noise of a train wreck, breaking other things on the way. The ancient stable convulses and shakes. A cloud of dust drifts out the open door, suspended momentarily in still air.

When Angus emerges from the building a few minutes later, he's covered in wood particles and old dust. The structure has taken on a decided lean to the right as if threatening to fall over at any moment. With the help of a bright yellow nylon rope, the big man drags a large timber from the building, heaving it a foot at a time in jerks and starts. The hundred-year-old beam is stout, at least eight inches on each side and a good twelve feet long.

The wood is dense and heavy, hard from age.

"See this?" Angus pats the timber solidly with his palm. "This is a special piece of wood. I cut it from the rafters myself—probably not the safest thing to do since the building is like to fall over, but I had to have it. The rest of the wood can come from elsewhere"—he pats the timber again—"this one is special."

He studies Marco a moment, waiting for acknowledgment.

When no such sentiment comes, the mountainous man's voice grows tight, as if displeased by the congressman's lack of appreciation.

"It's been in that building since before I was born," Angus admonishes. "This timber might have been cut from old growth a hundred years ago. That in itself makes it special."

His body language changes and he sounds almost nostalgic when he speaks next.

"Oh, this timber and me, we have history. Yes, we do. I carved my name right here when I was but a boy." He runs his fingers through the deep grove where the word ANGUS is still visible and glances over at Marco. "I guess you can't see it from over there, can you? No worries. I'll let you see it up close soon enough."

A broad smile creases Angus's face.

Evil.

Maniacal.

After checking the oil on the generator and flipping the switch to ON, he pulls the starter cord once, then twice, and the engine sputters to life. It's quieter than Marco would have imagined, but Angus still has to yell to be heard.

"Have you figured it out yet?"

He gestures toward the timber.

Marco just stares at him.

"I bet you have, haven't you?" Angus grins broadly. "You know, I've been looking forward to this. If it's not clicking yet, just wait, you'll figure it out. I've got some more work to do, but you'll see the bigger picture soon enough."

The big man shivers with anticipation.

"It's going to be so good," he adds in a wondrous exhalation. "And"—he turns to Marco with all seriousness as if making a life vow—"I promise to stay with you through the night, through the whole ordeal. I do. I'll light a little campfire, maybe play some music, drink some beer. Maybe you can have some. Do you like beer?" Angus quickly waves the question away. It doesn't matter.

"I even brought my chair," he says, suddenly remembering.

He hurries to the van, which is parked next to a nearby outbuilding, and rifles through the back, emerging a moment later with a folded mess of blue fabric. "This is my lucky chair," he shouts, holding it aloft.

When he returns, his gait and mood seem to have grown suddenly somber, as if by regret or empathy. He contemplates Marco as if seeing every part of him with utter clarity for the first time. With a worrisome downturn of his mouth, he sidles up to the congressman and crouches, so they're eye to eye.

It's all a ruse.

Men such as Angus are incapable of empathy. Yes, they can wear it the way some might don a costume or slip on a mask, but it's just as phony.

Placing a massive hand on Marco's shoulder, Angus gives the congressman a gentle shake, the way one might comfort a distraught nephew. With sympathy in his eyes that could pass for genuine, he leans close, the rancid stench of old pepperoni issuing from his mouth in grunting huffs.

"Don't worry," he says soothingly. "I'm going to make you famous."

# 37

Using a cell phone on speaker mode isn't something one would normally risk when discussing a sensitive criminal case in public, but the coffee shop is mostly empty, caught between the breakfast and the lunch rush. Besides, it's better if all of us hear the information at the same time rather than have Ross try to recall what he can after the fact. Time is running short and we can't afford to have anything lost or jumbled.

Marco's life depends on it.

Angus's community corrections officer answers the phone with a flourish of words that encapsulate her name—Crystal Baum-something—her title, and her organization in a rapid-fire three-second string of words that would make an auctioneer proud. The CCO's barrage momentarily stuns Ross, but then he identifies himself and explains the situation.

Jimmy and I have a side bet—a blueberry scone—that Crystal's not going to give out any information over the phone, not without being able to verify Ross's identity. I luck out when she immediately remembers him—their paths having crossed on other cases. She mentions meeting him at the courthouse and the police station, neither of which Ross seems to recall, but he plays along.

He must have made an impression on her.

"I'd like it warmed up," I whisper into Jimmy's ear, referring to the scone. He puts his finger to his lips and points at the phone.

"I've been Angus's CCO for ten years and three prison stints. What do you need to know?"

"Everything," Ross replies in a rush, but then settles on the basics. "How about a possible location, for starts. You guys still do residence checks, right?"

"Not as much as we used to." We hear the sound of a filing cabinet opening and then papers shuffling. "I still try to do regular checks on all my clients, but the caseload is too much. We just don't have enough CCOs."

"But you have to approve his residence before he moves in, right?"

"Yes, but that doesn't always mean they're living where they say they are."

"How about Angus? Is he living where he says he is?"

"I'm not sure," Crystal replies with a hint of hesitation. "I've been to his apartment several times, but I've never actually contacted him. He has a roommate that tells me he's living there, and I've seen his bedroom, which contains his personal effects, but other than the day he was released, I've never actually contacted him there."

"When you visit," I ask, "is it scheduled or a surprise?"

"Oh, surprise visits. Always. It's the best way to make sure they're complying with release conditions. In Angus's case, that means no alcohol, no drugs, no weapons of any kind. He's also supposed to be holding down a regular job, but we're more flexible on that part. Some of these guys just aren't employable. They end up in government housing, living off food stamps and other assistance programs."

"Nice, our tax dollars at rest," I mutter.

Ross chuckles.

We hear paper shuffling again, then Crystal exclaims, "Ah!

Here it is." Her voice is suddenly louder, closer to the phone. "Looks like he's living in the Benton Park neighborhood, on Terrace Way. Got a pen?" When Ross tells her to fire away, she rattles off the street address and apartment number, which he scribbles into his old-school notepad.

"Is Angus employed?" Jimmy asks when Crystal finishes.

"He's had several jobs with different landscaping companies, but none seem to last more than a couple of months. For the most part, he seems to be complying with his release conditions. I know that he's a regular marijuana user, but we tend to look the other way for pot. His UAs keep coming back clean, so I know he's not using meth, heroin, or any of the hard drugs."

"How about his demeanor?" Jimmy asks. "How would you describe him?"

"Mean," Crystal replies pointedly. "He's dangerous, and not all that stable. I'm sure you've met the type. We release them back into society because they've served their time and we have no other reason to hold them, but we know full well that they're going to re-offend. It's a matter of *when,* not *if.*"

She grows quiet, then confesses, "That's what keeps me awake at night. Wondering just how bad the next incident might be. In Angus's case, that *next incident* would have likely been the murder of his mother . . . if the woman wasn't already dead."

"Murder?" Ross says. "His mother?"

"Dorothy Smit?" Jimmy blurts at the same time.

"Oh, yeah! He hated her. The woman had been dead for years by the time Angus got out of prison, yet he could barely speak her name without spitting." Papers shuffle and there's a silent moment as Crystal seems to be searching for something.

"Here it is," she says, more to herself than for our benefit. "When he wrote out his formal request to attend her funeral, it was immediately denied. The official reason was officer safety concerns. The real reason was that he threatened to piss on her coffin."

"Jeez," Ross mutters, "model son."

"You have no idea," Crystal assures him.

"So, in your mind," Jimmy probes, "is there any way he'd want revenge against Dorothy's oncologist?"

"For what? Not saving her? He'd probably buy the guy a beer."

I'm on my feet at this point; none of it makes sense.

"Let me explain it this way," Crystal's voice rasps forcefully through the speaker. "The first time I met Dorothy Smit was a month after Angus went to prison the last time around. She wanted me to know that she'd visited him, or, in her words, she'd gone to *redeem his soul*, which seemed important to her. In any case, Angus told her he was going to kill her when he got out, told her in the same tone and with the same face one might ask for a glass of milk. She wanted me to know in case something happened to her. She never went back, as far as I know."

Crystal sighs. "When he was released, I asked Angus if he was going to behave himself. He told me, 'Sure,' saying that since his mother was already dead, he wouldn't have to kill her. He seemed disappointed." She pauses, perhaps wondering how such creatures exist. "Prison was never a problem for him," she adds as an afterthought. "He's a first-class animal, a top-level predator. If anything, he thrives behind bars."

"Any idea why he hates his mother?" I ask.

"I can send you a copy of his psych profile if you want something disturbing to read, but I'm guessing you want the abbreviated version?"

"For now, yes."

"Bear—that's Angus's nickname—was conceived, it seems,

after a one-night stand that started in some bar that Dorothy couldn't even remember, having frequented so many of them."

"I thought she was married to this Michael Graves—"

"Yeah, she was."

"Oh."

"Yeah, she was a bit of a free spirit. A party girl who took her sex, drugs, and alcohol wherever she could get them. It was a shame because by all accounts Michael—her husband Michael—was an okay guy. Steady job. No drugs. In the end, he hanged himself from the rafters in the garage with an extension cord. Angus found him. He was four."

"Jeez!" Ross hisses.

"Yeah," Crystal says, echoing his astonishment. "After that, Dorothy found God and Jesus, but some twisted form of it—cultish if you ask me. The more Angus and Michael junior acted out, mimicking the very actions they'd learned from her, the more she *purified* them in the mercy of God."

"Purified?" Jimmy asks, the burgeoning horror evident in his voice.

"Uh-huh. She may have been a bit mentally unstable at this point, we don't know. Several members of her church were later arrested for child abuse on a massive scale, including statutory rape. Instead of learning about Jonah and the whale, David and Goliath, and Lazarus being raised from the dead, like most Sunday schoolers, Michael and Angus learned that God demands penance, and penance means pain.

"One of the forms of ritual punishment that Dorothy used frequently involved strapping the boys to a mocked-up cross in the basement for hours at a time."

"Like . . . crucified?" I ask, wincing at the words.

"Exactly, but with leather straps. She'd have them stand on a chair while she bound their wrists to the arms of the cross, and then she'd pull the chair away. There was a small block for them to put their feet on, but it was so far down that they could only touch it with their outstretched toes. Hardly a relief against the weight of their bodies and the strain on their stretched lungs."

Crystal lingers on the thought a moment as if contemplating it for the first time. "I think she looked on the boys as if they were sin incarnate, especially Angus, as if he'd been the cause of her philandering rather than the by-product. She felt it was left to her to remedy the sin of their existence. She told the boys as much."

Crystal sighs. "There were other punishments, of course. Other trials and tribulations, none of them having anything to do with the Christianity I know."

"Doesn't sound like my church either," Jimmy replies.

"Don't get me wrong. Dorothy punished herself too, but it was always the boys who took the brunt of it. In addition to being hung from the cross, they'd be forced to lie prone before it for sometimes a whole day. Other times they'd kneel and pray for hours.

"Angus once told his social worker that, during those times of prayer, he asked her God to take her, to strike her down like in the Old Testament. He prayed that she'd have a car accident or fall down the stairs or be butchered by a serial killer. He never prayed for a peaceful or painless death, only one filled with fear and agony. Eventually, he became angry at her God for not answering his prayers and began to imagine doing these things himself."

Crystal pauses. "Are you sure you want to hear all of this?"

It's Jimmy who answers, "We have to."

After a hesitation on the other end of the line, Crystal continues, "Angus once admitted to one of his caseworkers that he practiced his mother's death on neighborhood animals: small dogs and cats. He broke necks or strangled them. In one case he tied down a Chihuahua, doused it in gasoline from the shed, and burned it alive. He was never caught, but we were able to confirm that a dog was burned to death and dumped two blocks from his house. Angus would have been eleven at the time."

"Was that on Tuttle?" Ross asks.

"On what?"

"Tuttle Street? His mother's house."

"I'm not familiar with that street name," Crystal says hesitantly. "Angus and Michael grew up in south Bakersfield, mostly on Footman Avenue."

I give Jimmy a look.

The Tuttle Street address has bothered me since we first found it in the medical records. Angus's unmistakable malachite shine had been plentiful in and around the home when we found Noah, but only recently so. There was no long history, none of the deep layers and prolific quantities I'm used to seeing at a longtime residence. Nothing, that is to say, that would indicate he'd been anything more than a common and recent visitor.

"The boys were taken away by Child Protective Services several times," Crystal continues, "but they were always returned. When they were finally pulled from the home for good, Michael was sixteen and Angus was fifteen. Of course, at that point, the damage was already done."

After a silence, Jimmy asks perhaps the most important question. "What . . . would possess him to go after . . . ?" He almost says *Marco* but catches himself. The CCO doesn't know that Angus might be a suspect in the congressman's disappearance, and right now that's the way it has to stay.

"Is there any reason he might go after someone who had tried to help his mother, maybe during her illness?"

"I don't know," Crystal replies in a small voice. "He once told me that if his mother's God stood for love and compassion, then he would become the god of hate and destruction. I asked him if he thought he was the Antichrist, and he laughed at the notion. He said he was something different from the Antichrist. Something apart."

"What the hell's that mean?" I ask.

"I don't know. It may mean nothing; idle comments carelessly spoken. But with Angus, you just never know."

# 38

As we roll into Angus's neighborhood, malachite-green footfalls tread here and there, polluting the sidewalk, street, and parking lot with tainted shine. Rather than appreciating the magnificent color for what it is, I've come to despise it, viewing it the way one might look on black mold or some fungal spore under the magnification of a microscope.

I love green, but I'll never again look at this particular shade with the same eyes. The color is forever linked with Angus and Blood Eagles and exhumed corpses. I'm sure the gremlins that administer my nightmares will have a field day with it. Little bastards.

As we exit the car, I get close and whisper, "Malachite," to Jimmy.

He pauses, takes a deep breath, and nods his understanding.

Angus's apartment is on the bottom floor and has a first-rate view of the overflowing dumpster next to the concrete barrier wall separating his complex from the one next door.

Jimmy knocks while Ross takes up position to his left, hand on the butt of his gun. The door opens enough to reveal a diminutive man cast in shadow, who takes one look at us and says, "He's not here."

"How do you know we're here for him and not you?" Ross asks.

"Are you? Here for me? Because my CCO—*deep*—was just here two weeks ago."

We all stare at him.

"What . . . was that?" Jimmy says with a puzzled look.

The man shrugs. "I got a tic. It's like that Tourette's thing, only I got just the one word, and no cusswords. I woulda liked some cusswords," he adds wistfully. "I don't say it all the time, only—*deep*—when I get nervous, or when my hypoglycemia kicks in."

"*Deep* is your one word?"

"Yep—*deep*!" The utterance sounds like a dismembered hiccup, a sound with no legs to stand on.

"What's your name?" Jimmy asks the odd man.

"Delmont."

"Delmont what?"

"Just Delmont. I'm a mononym. It means someone—*deep*—with just one name, like Madonna and Sting. Cher and Bono."

"Okay . . . Delmont. What would your name be if I checked your criminal record?"

"Deep." The little man screws up his mouth at this and stomps a foot the way a spoiled child might after not getting his way. "Delmont Wilson," he replies nastily.

"That's more like it. Now, what about Angus? Is he home?"

"Didn't I just say he's not here?" Delmont replies, exasperated. "I know somebody said it, and I'm pretty sure it wasn't the voices."

Jimmy pauses at this, and I know his inclination is to ask about the "voices," to get their opinion, but we're in too much of a hurry. The voices will have to wait.

"You know, I'm pretty sure that lying to us would violate your release conditions, right? Sending you straight back to prison? Before I ask to come in and check for Angus, I want to make sure you don't want to change your story. Like maybe you forgot that he came home late last night and he's asleep in his bedroom, or he's taking a shower. Something like that?"

"He. Ain't. Here."

"So you say. May we come in and check?"

Delmont's behind the door now, looking like he might slam it on us.

"You got a warrant?"

"No. But you're under supervision, same as Angus. If it's a problem, we can have your CCOs join us. In case you forgot, they can do spot checks of the residence anytime they like."

"No, I didn't forget," Delmont mutters. Then, in a louder voice: "Fine! It's no problem—*deep*! Come on in. I got—*deep*—nothing to hide."

He throws the door wide, and in the enhanced light I notice that he's wearing nothing but a white tank top—a wifebeater—and a skimpy pair of red underwear. Women's underwear, as it turns out.

He flicks his hand toward the back of the two-bedroom apartment.

"Angus is on the right. Mind the—*deep*—toys." By which he means the sex toys and porn magazines scattered around a worn beanbag chair on the floor behind him.

We give the collection a wide berth.

There's no attic or basement, and Angus is simply too big to hide in a hamper or under a kitchen sink, so we limit our search to closets, the shower stall, and a massive pile of used and soiled blankets on the floor next to his naked mattress.

The blankets look nasty, and we argue briefly over who gets the honors. Ross finally sighs and extracts a pair of nitrile gloves, settling the issue. Using a baseball bat that was stashed behind the bedroom door, he pokes at the pile and flips the blankets over and around, dislodging a pair of off-white underwear big enough for two men. They look soiled.

Satisfied that no one's hiding underneath the pile, we beat a hasty retreat and decide that the apartment is clean. Well, clean of Angus. The rest of it—filthy!

Disgusting.

As we leave, Delmont boldly grumbles, "Get the hell out of here," and goes about whatever he was doing before we arrived.

I'd rather not dwell on it.

Back in the car, Jimmy retrieves his phone and dials a number. I hear the faint ring and then the indistinguishable sounds of someone answering.

"Kip, it's Jimmy."

# 39

Ross is just pulling his unmarked away from the curb when the theme song from *The Pink Panther* issues from Jimmy's phone. Diane's ringtone. He puts it on speaker.

"How are you doing with the reports Ross sent over?" Jimmy asks by way of greeting.

"It's going to take a while. Some of the reports are lengthy, while others are brief or have no narrative at all. I should be done with the first pass in another hour or two."

"Anything jumping out?"

"No, but every page I read only reinforces the thought that this is one dangerous man." The sound of rapidly flipping papers comes through the phone. "Take this for example: In 2004 he was listed as a suspect in the death of a rival drug dealer's girlfriend. She was shot execution-style in the living room of her apartment. No witnesses, at least none that would testify.

"He's a suspect in one other murder and listed as a possible suspect in another. I mean, we're talking top-tier stuff. You could fill a book with his other crimes. I think he's broken every law in the state of California except bestiality, and I'm not even sure about that one."

"All right, well, call us when you get something."

"Wait!" Diane says before Jimmy can disconnect. "That's not why I called. I just got off the phone with some lady—Carol, or something—from California DOC, who said you gave her my number and told her to call if she had any new information." Diane leaves the statement hanging in the air like a question.

"Yeah, that's Crystal," Jimmy confirms. "Angus's CCO."

"I'll take your word for it," Diane says briskly. "In any case, she said she remembered something after you talked. It seems she gives all her clients a little extra attention and walks them to their cars after their scheduled in-office visits. A little bit of the personal touch, right? Anyway, she mostly does this to see what they're driving and get the plate number in case something comes up. You know, like the abduction of a congressman."

"Does that mean she has the plate number on Angus's van?

"It does. She said on his last visit, he was driving a white 2005 Ford Econoline panel van—a work van. No windows, but big barn doors at the back. When she ran the plate through DMV, it came back with a report of sale from several months back, but it's still registered to the previous owner."

"But the report of sale lists Angus as the new owner, right?"

"Not directly."

"What does that mean?"

"It means that I don't think Jimmy Hoffa is cruising Bakersfield in an old work van."

"That would be something," Ross says with genuine amusement.

"Okay, what about the original RO?" Jimmy says, referring to the registered owner.

"The former owners are Tobias and Jackie Harlan, owners of—"

"Black Walnut Catering," Jimmy says with a nod. "We ran that van after finding Noah. It was seen coming and going from the house on Tuttle Street."

"Well, that would have been nice to know earlier. . . ."

"Oops!"

"Mm-hmm. I'm glad I could help," Diane retorts. "Crystal also wanted me to tell you that she ran a check through California DMV, and there are no vehicles with current registration in Angus's name. Despite her reassurances, I ran my own checks."

"Yeah, Ross ran a vehicle check a little while ago and came up empty."

"Did he?" Diane replies with exaggerated enthusiasm. "Did he also look at *expired* registrations?"

"I . . . don't know."

"Hmm. Because I did, and I happened to notice something rather interesting." Diane pauses, an intentional delay meant to force a question. Her way of chastising us for not sharing the van data sooner.

"What's that?" Jimmy asks compliantly. After years of working with Diane, he knows how this goes. You don't stomp all over her turf without paying for it one way or another, and data—information—is her turf.

When she replies, her tone is not as harsh, and the didactic flow of her words has returned, implying that she's satisfied with the modest supplication offered by Jimmy. "It seems that over the years, Angus has had several vehicles registered at an address on Old Stage Road in Porterville."

"Where's that?"

"It's due north of Bakersfield; about fifty miles, give or take."

"Any idea what the connection is?"

"Still checking," Diane replies, "but the property is an old orchard of some sort. I pulled it up on Google Earth and you can see some of the trees are still there. There's a house, a barn or stable, and numerous other outbuildings. Some might be migrant housing for the workers, but others are clearly production related. The assessor's office indicates it's owned by Otis and Barbara Mills, but I haven't found anything in CLEAR or Accurint showing a link between them and Angus."

"Well, if he's registering cars there, there must be a connection."

"Obviously. I just haven't found it yet." There's a pause. "So . . . maybe you should start heading that way . . . ?"

"It's fifty miles—"

"All the more reason to get started." Then Diane says in a softer tone, "It's the only real lead we have. We already know he's not at his apartment—he couldn't hide four hostages there if he wanted to. Unless the locals have a better location for him in Bakersfield, this might be as good as it gets. The orchard has everything he'd need to hide out, and, well . . . "

"Well, what?"

"Well . . . I've got a feeling about it. I've been crunching data a long time, and sometimes it doesn't tell you exactly what you want, but it does steer you in the right direction."

"And you think this orchard is the right direction?"

"I do."

"This is life-or-death, Diane. We're running out of time."

"Don't you think I know that!" she replies sharply, and for a moment I detect dismay or fear or heartbreak in her voice. Perhaps all three. This from a woman who doesn't easily rattle.

"Okay," Jimmy says quietly. "We're heading to the orchard. Feed us updates as you get them."

"I will."

Jimmy waits for her to disconnect, but she doesn't. The

open line lingers as if waiting for a final assurance or admonition, something to speed us on our way and deliver hope to a place where hope has fled. In the end, Diane can manage just a single world.

"Hurry!"

Then the line goes dead.

# 40

The weather is mild, but Angus Graves works up a sweat as he notches and shapes the massive timber from the stable. He only needs to work the side of the beam facing skyward; no need to heave it onto its side or back. Even with his great strength, Angus is thankful for this: the beam nearly killed him as he cut it from the roof structure and dragged it free of the building.

Once finished with this portion of his immense task, he fishes an icy beer from the cooler and falls into his favorite camp chair, which looks perilously frail under his bulk. With a gulping pull that seems ridiculously long, he empties the beer and then rubs the cold bottle against his forehead. A sigh of contentment escapes him.

After a small rest, and without a glance or word shared with Marco, Angus rises and gathers his tools. He walks to a separate building about sixty feet away and disappears inside. A disjointed orchestra of sawing and hammering soon issues from the old structure, which was probably once a mess hall.

As a reciprocating saw hums to life, Marco yanks hard against his bindings, pulling and straining and searching. His eyes scour the surroundings for something—anything—to cut the ropes. It's pointless. By the time the sawing stops, his forehead is damp from the exertion, his wrists are bloody, and he's no better for the effort.

When Angus returns, he's dragging a second beam. It's considerably shorter than the first, but still has a substantial girth, maybe six inches by six inches.

Marco watches quietly as Angus notches the very center of the second beam and fits it crosswise over the larger beam. Finally satisfied with the fit, he removes the beam and sets it aside.

Wiping his brow, he strolls over to the back of the van and opens the cooler, fishing around inside for another beer.

"Thirsty?" He casts a look at Marco.

The gag in the congressman's mouth prevents a response. He could nod or shake his head if he chose to . . . but he does neither, casting his eyes defiantly to the hillside instead. It's a small victory, but he'll take it, for now he knows the suffering that's heading his way. He can see what Angus has crafted and understands the significance.

More important, he understands the terrible part he'll play.

How a man like Angus—even if utterly insane—could come to this is beyond Marco's comprehension. He remembers Dorothy Smit, just as he remembers *all* the patients he lost. If Angus blamed him for that loss, he would understand, but the man clearly detested the woman and felt cheated at not killing her with his own hands, as if cancer had been an easy out.

This . . . spectacle that he seems bent on creating is nothing more than a sacrifice to the hatred he still carries for a woman now years in the grave.

If she had survived, it would be *her* sitting in Marco's place.

The thought gives him no comfort.

"Sure. You gotta be thirsty," Angus says, ignoring the congressman's insolence. "How about"—he picks up a Coke and then a Sprite, but sets them aside and digs deeper—"ginger ale," he says triumphantly, pulling first one can, then two, from the bottom of the cooler, where the ice has melted into a cold slurry.

"Great for the digestion." He makes his way toward Marco. "My mom used to give it to me to settle my stomach when I was a kid. Did your mom do that?" Angus brushes aside the question. "Of course, she did," he says with assurance. "Everyone's mom does that."

Removing the tight gag from around Marco's mouth, he runs a rough finger along the impressions left on the skin, the furrows where the fabric had dug and pressed itself into Marco's checks, rubbing the corners of his mouth raw and bloody.

"Little tight, I suppose." Popping the top on the soda, Angus says, "Tilt your head back."

When Marco doesn't immediately comply, the big man gives him a perplexed look, then violently grabs a tuft of the congressman's hair and yanks his head back as if he were a Pez dispenser.

Angus pours ginger ale into the congressman's mouth as if from a fast-flowing faucet until he gags and sputters for breath, amber liquid flowing out the sides of his broken mouth and down his chin.

"Best if you do what I say." Angus's words are hard with purpose. After allowing a moment for Marco to catch his breath and clear his lungs, Angus once again orders him to open his mouth and tilt his head back.

This time he complies.

Angus cuts the restraints that bind the congressman to his chair, first at the feet in front of him and then at the hands, which are pulled tightly behind his back, cop-style. Marco entertains the brief hope that the man is going to release him—a change of heart for some reason.

It's not to be.

Handing Marco a shovel, Angus leads him to a spot halfway between the stable and what appears to be a bunkhouse of some sort.

"Dig here," he orders, kicking the toe of his boot into the dirt at his feet.

"Dig what?"

"A hole."

"How-how big of a hole?"

Angus grins broadly, understanding Marco's fear. With the same booted toe, Angus outlines a dig spot, dragging his foot this way and then that. Though he holds a menacing Smith & Wesson .357 Magnum in his right hand, he keeps a respectable distance between himself and the smaller man with the shovel. He knows what thoughts desperation can spark, for he has sparked some himself. Crazy plans that, in hindsight, were patently stupid.

When Marco hesitates, Angus waves the gun casually toward the outline on the ground, implying that Marco should get started. When he still doesn't move, Angus uses the massive thumb to pull back the hammer on the stout revolver, doing so with slow deliberation, as if to let the moment unfold with a conjured sense of the surreal.

Marco starts digging.

# 41

Porterville is in Tulare County, which is way outside Ross's jurisdiction. That wouldn't be a problem if we were just checking an address or scoping out the vehicles parked in the driveway, but we're not. There may be a hostage on Old Stage Road, an important hostage, and that changes everything. We're going to need help.

That means Ross has some calls to make.

The first will be to Detective Sergeant Alcott at the Tulare County Sheriff's Office. Ross scrolls through his contact list as we walk. "I'm going to ask that they have some guys on standby just in case we need them. I'd feel better, though, if we also had one of their guys with us when we contact the house."

Jimmy nods. "I think I know a guy."

The canary-yellow Mustang convertible is parked next to Ross's unmarked. As we approach, all three of us hesitate, unsure whether we should veer left to the Mustang or right to the police interceptor. Ross points at the phone, which is now ringing, and then at the Mustang, making it clear that he's going to be too busy to drive.

Jimmy, it seems, has a call of his own to make.

Uncharacteristically—*unfathomably*—he tosses me the keys to the smoking-hot muscle car. I stand like an idiot looking at the fob in my hand as if I were Charlie Bucket staring in disbelief at the golden ticket that will buy me access to Mr. Wonka's wondrous chocolate factory.

Pulling out of the parking lot, I goose the engine. The immediate result of this—and I do mean immediate—is that the tires squeal and spin in place, curling off smoke and, much to my consternation, causing the rear of the car to walk sideways in the road.

Jimmy gives me a glaring, concerned look—but at that moment his call connects. Thank God for small miracles.

"Can I speak with Sergeant Joe Mingo?" he asks briskly.

Mingo.

I suddenly understand.

He and Jimmy had seemed to hit it off, so it makes sense. I don't doubt that Ross will have a lot of talented connections from Tulare County to bring to the party, but Mingo's the only local *we* know—tenuous as that connection is.

Besides, he has a Humvee.

# 42

On the way out of Bakersfield, we swing by and pick up Kip, who retrieves a rifle case and a bag from the gun vault in the back of his Expedition and stows them in the trunk of the Mustang. As we head north, we fill him in on the details. When we finish, he just pushes back in his seat, shakes his head, and mutters, "Abel Moya," as if it were a profanity.

We meet Joe and his decked-out Hummer in the gravel parking lot of a steepled church about two miles down the road from the questionable house on Old Stage Road. By this time, the sergeant has had ample time to surveil the old homestead. With most of the orchard cut down and hauled off years ago, he accomplished this with nothing more than a pair of binoculars and by parking in three or four discreet spots scattered along the surrounding roads.

There's no movement at the house, nor on the rest of the twenty-three-acre property.

"I saw a couple of vehicles up near the house," Joe explains. "Most look inoperable, but the blue sedan parked closest to the front door looks newer and is in decent shape. Couldn't get a good look at the outbuildings at the back of the property. Must be eight or ten of them, plus a barn or stable, though I didn't see any livestock."

We're still discussing strategy when Jimmy's phone rings: *The Pink Panther.*

Connecting the call on speaker, he says, "Hi, Diane—"

"I found the link. The property owner, Barbara Mills, is Dorothy Smit's sister—Angus's aunt." She explains that she found it in one of his many juvenile records. A case where the boy's mother, Dorothy, was too busy or disgusted or angry to retrieve her lawless son and asked her sister to do it instead.

"Nice work, Diane."

"Mm-hmm. Where are you?"

"Two miles from the orchard. Trying to figure out our next move."

An audible sigh issues from the speaker, as if from relief.

"Well, best get back to figuring," she says a moment later, and without waiting for a response ends the call.

"I hate when she does that," Jimmy mutters, pocketing his phone.

"So . . . what's our play?" Ross asks, glancing from face to face.

"It's your show," Joe replies, "but I say we make contact at the house. See what's what."

"Works for me," the detective says with an approving shrug.

As we pull into the driveway off Old Stage Road, home of Barbara and Otis Mills, we pass under an arched metal sign like those you sometimes see on ranches. This one looks like it was dragged out of a scrapyard and propped up with baling wire.

It's a place from a bygone era, from better days long since passed.

All that remains of the once-noble sign are the uprights,

which seem barely capable of holding the arch aloft, and the scant letters needed to spell out FOOT CHARDS—a considerably less noble proclamation.

It sounds like something you might get after walking on broken glass.

My initial reaction to the farm is a sense of nostalgic melancholy, a sense of sadness at what once had been and is no more. This is punctuated by the sign's inability to remember its own name, as if the farm had fallen into dementia.

Soon, there'll be nothing left to remember.

Time and technology are never ceasing, never retreating.

They leave in their wake a littered landscape of corpses—the husks of businesses, ideas, and systems that have outlived their relevance. With the growth of industrialized farming, this includes many of the mom-and-pop farms that once filled the land.

A few survive.

Those who've adapted to the new normal and found new ways of packaging, modifying, marketing, or otherwise making their product special. Some went the other direction, gobbling up land and farms and joining the steady march toward ever-larger farms and ever-expanding farming corporations.

It's not all that bad, I suppose.

If not for more efficient farming, billions of people around the world would die of starvation in short order. The amount of food we now coax from the soil, and the relative ease with which we do so, would stagger our forebears.

This fact, sobering as it is, does nothing for my melancholy.

I remember seeing *A Walk in the Clouds* when I was younger—perhaps ten or twelve years ago, though the movie came out long before I saw it. It's a Keanu Reeves film that's set in a vineyard in California in the mid-1940s.

Oh, the romance.

The promise—*the hope*—of such a life was compelling

beyond measure as if someone had enchanted that younger version of me with visions of an idyllic life among the vines and vats, a Spanish villa for a home. The movie doesn't necessarily depict the hard work that goes into such a venture, but that mattered little at the time. It was the possibility of living such a life that pulled at me. That was the fantasy, the hope of hopes.

Foot Chards, I imagine, is the reality.

Reality, it seems, is a brutal mistress when compared to her pleasing cousin, Hope.

Jimmy and Joe approach the front door cautiously, scanning the windows, the vehicles, and the outbuildings as they go—anyplace, that is, that might conceal a gunman. Kip and Ross take cover positions at opposite corners of the house so they can observe all four sides of the house. I remain near the Humvee.

Well, *behind* the Humvee, if truth be told, basically using the monstrous vehicle as a shield between me and any lead that might fly from the general direction of the house. The former military vehicle is pulled into the driveway far enough that I have a sideways view of both the front and the back.

There's real danger here; I feel it in my bones.

Upon our arrival, even before stepping from the Mustang, I had slipped off my glasses and cast my eyes along the driveway, the yard, the path to the house. It didn't take much of an effort to realize that Angus has been coming and going from the orchard for decades. Most of the shine is old, probably from his youth. With a silent glance and a single nod, I conveyed this to Jimmy, who visibly tensed but otherwise maintained his composure.

It's the recent shine that concerns me, some of it so fresh that, even now, I find myself glancing about, half expecting to see Angus step from behind a tree.

I shiver at the prospect.

Diane was right.

She's always right; it's maddening.

At the front door, Joe raps several times and loudly announces, "Tulare County Sheriff's Office." He gets no answer.

Jimmy takes a go at the door, using the bottom of his fist to give it a good pounding while announcing, "FBI! Barbara! Otis! We just need to ask you some questions. It's important."

After several minutes of pointless knocking and pounding, Joe moves to a nearby picture window and presses his face to the glass, hands on either side blocking out the light. Finding nothing, he moves to another window, while Jimmy does the same going in the other direction. They work their way along the front of the house in this manner, then down both sides, with no sign of the occupants.

As Jimmy disappears behind the far side of the house, the only place I can't see, I feel the anxiety run up my legs and settle in my chest, but he soon emerges unscathed at the back of the house. I'd like to say that was the last of my anxiety on this day of days, but I'd be lying.

At the back door, Jimmy is just moving up to the glass when he freezes. His right hand finds the grip of his Glock, but he doesn't pull. As Joe approaches from the other direction, Jimmy halts him with a gesture, then directs his attention through the glass with a jut of his jaw. Joe moves quietly to the side of the glass and does a quick scan inside. By this time, Ross and Kip are also collapsing on the house.

I remain with the Humvee, unarmed and feeling wholly inadequate. My Walther P22 is tucked safely away at the bottom of my travel bag back at the motel.

I have no idea what Jimmy sees, so I do the only thing I'm qualified and equipped to do: I watch. I watch the rear of the house, I watch the front of the house, I watch the one side of the house facing me. I look for runners, faces in windows, shifting shadows that might threaten or harm.

I don't like guns.

That said, I've been shot at more than once and can say with absolute certainty that there's nothing worse than needing a gun and not having one. It kind of feels like . . . now.

Damn.

Jimmy tries the door handle and finds it unlocked. Cautiously, the three men move into the house. I see their flitting shapes and hear their commanding voices as they move through, clearing room after room, ordering occupants to show themselves.

But there are no occupants.

None living, anyway.

When Jimmy steps out onto the back porch and waves me forward, I see the truth of it spilled out on the kitchen floor. An elderly woman—Barbara, I'm assuming—is sprawled out on the tile, a dozen large knife wounds in her stomach and chest.

There's also damage to her head and face; damage that's . . . indescribable.

More disturbing, the lack of blood around the head suggests this damage was postmortem, unlike the stomach and chest wounds. It's as if someone stood over her corpse and rained hell down upon her face. The instrument that carried this wrath to the skull and visage of Barbara Mills was no knife, however. This was blunt-force trauma, something heavy that was lifted and dropped a dozen, maybe two dozen, times.

The bloody culprit lies beside the body.

An urn.

A small brass plaque at the bottom of the urn, smeared

with gore, suggests it holds the ashes of one Otis Mills, who died in 2001.

Angus is no longer in the house and nothing can be done for Barbara, not even the dignity of a towel over her head because such a gesture would contaminate the crime scene. We back out of the house and retreat to the Humvee. The first patrol units should be here soon. It'll take longer to mobilize CSI and the contingent of detectives needed to process such a scene.

The only saving grace is that we're in Tulare County. Bakersfield PD and the Kern County Sheriff's Office already have their hands full. The last thing they need is another heinous crime scene and the budget-killing overtime needed to process it.

As Joe coordinates the response and both Kip and Ross inform their superiors, I slip my glasses off and have a quick look around. The malachite shine inside the house is mostly old. The only exception seems to be the tracks and impressions that Angus left in the kitchen during the commission of his most recent crime.

With my glasses gripped hard in my right hand, I note that this new shine doesn't enter or exit through the front door but through the back. As I step onto the rear porch, I note one more anomaly: the tracks don't come from the driveway.

Instead, Angus appears to have strode directly across the orchard from the direction of the barn and outbuildings at the back of the acreage.

One path approaching, one path leaving.

A sliver of fear runs up my spine as the realization settles. For a moment, I imagine the killer watching me from around the corner of a building or peering out through the unwashed window of one of the old processing rooms, hidden in shadow.

*What better place to hide hostages.*

I'm suddenly aware of my heartbeat as it *thump-thump-thumps* in my ears, the result of a sudden adrenaline dump, no doubt. I've never had blood pressure issues, but if you ran a cuff around my arm right about now, I'd bet the pressure could kick-start an old steam engine. Fight or flight, that jittery sensation that comes with adrenaline, quivers its way through my system.

Every part of me wants to run—not toward the buildings, but away from them. There's an ominous sense about the structures, buildings remarkably convenient if one is up to no good. And as Barbara Mills can attest, Angus is certainly up to no good.

Waving Jimmy over and trying not to look frantic about it, lest I draw unwanted attention, I quickly explain what I'm seeing.

Like me, his eyes dart to the distant buildings.

Without a word, he turns sharply and calls out to Ross, Kip, and Joe. "What about the outbuildings?"

The question needs no elaboration.

Ross and Kip look at each other, then at Joe, who gives a dismissive toss of his head and says, "Go ahead. I'll wait here for patrol."

We're halfway to the barn when Jimmy points out a series of tire tracks coming and going through the field. On closer inspection, we can see the impressions of an old road, a whole series of roads that once connected the various buildings.

While the driveway is gravel and ends just beyond the house, the old farm paths were never graveled—why go to the expense? They remained dirt tracks during their useful life, and once abandoned, their compressed earth was easily reclaimed by nature—to an extent. The impressions remain, like a scar, but covered now by grass and weeds and underbrush. The ruts are an almost indistinguishable blemish on the otherwise level orchard.

Only someone familiar with the orchard would know the paths even exist.

That *someone* has, it seems, been making recent use of them.

Ahead, the flattened path of weeds turns to the left, disappearing between a weathered barn and a couple of the outbuildings. Even from here, I can see Angus's shine on the ground, on the barn, on the buildings.

Most of it is old, but a scattering is more recent—days, maybe hours.

"The barn," I whisper to Jimmy when Ross and Kip fall behind.

We pass a locked man-door at the rear of the classic farm building, with its two-story central structure and wings coming off both sides. At the center of the rear wall, two massive doors hang on metal sliders, one designed to pull open to the left, the other to the right. Traditionally, these would be used to let livestock in and out, but in this case, I'm guessing it was tractors and production equipment that passed through the massive doors.

The doors are secured to each other at the center with a length of heavy rusted chain and a padlock. From the looks of it, the doors haven't been opened in a great while.

The chain is a momentary setback. Locking a barn against someone determined to make entry is about as effective as keeping water out of a leaky canoe by patching it with chicken wire.

After rattling the chain in his hand and testing the lock, Jimmy grabs both handles and tries to pull them apart. A black strip of midnight opens between the doors before they reach the end of the slack chain. It's enough.

Pressing his face to the five-inch gap, Jimmy peers inside, cupping his eyes so they adjust to the shadowy gloom within. He holds his gaze for a full minute, silently perceiving what we cannot. You would expect him to cough from ancient dust or grunt from holding his position so tightly pressed to the wood, but he doesn't. He may as well be dead and propped up against the door for all the life and movement he shows.

"I don't see anything," he finally whispers.

Pulling back, he squints at the brightness for a moment, then eyeballs me up and down, assessing my girth. "If I pull out the bottom"—he motions with his head toward the base of the left door—"do you think you can squeeze through?"

"What? No!"

"The man-door is right there." He gestures behind us. "All you have to do is get inside and unlock it."

"Why don't I hold the door—"

"My chest is bigger than yours."

"Since when?"

"His chest does look a bit bigger," Ross chimes in. When I glare at him, he just shrugs.

"Why don't you go?"

He just rubs his protruding stomach and raises an eyebrow.

Point taken.

I'm about to make a more vigorous argument—leaving out my obvious and logical hesitation to enter a dark and creepy barn while hunting for a sadistic killer—when a distinct *clank!* echoes nearby.

Not from the barn, but from beyond the barn, from the other side . . . somewhere. It comes again, louder this time: *clank!* It's followed by some smaller sound, a barely audible nothing.

Jimmy and Ross draw their handguns instantly, instinctively, and move quickly to the corner of the barn. Satisfied the way is clear, they move forward along the wall of the barn, stacked one on the other as they advance on the next corner. I follow a few steps behind, my hand searching uselessly for my diminutive Walther P22 . . . but then I remember.

Damn!

Near the far corner of the barn, Jimmy extends his Glock and steps away from the side of the barn. With measured steps, he slices the corner in small wedges, clearing the area on the other side without overexposing himself. He's halfway through the practiced maneuver when his body language changes abruptly. With an audible sigh, followed by a small, nervous laugh, he drops his hands, letting the handgun hang at his side a moment before holstering it.

Goats.

Friggin' goats.

A pair of them are staked out between the buildings, no doubt to keep the vegetation under control. The little beast on the left bleats at us pathetically, its tongue hanging over its teeth, white foam at its mouth. I don't know goats. I don't *want* to know goats. But the galvanized water trough nearby is bone-dry, and it looks as if the animals haven't had anything to drink in some time.

Jimmy finds a hose attached to a spigot and drags it over. We stand by for a couple of minutes as he tops off the trough, the goats seeming to empty it as fast as he fills it.

Our respite among the goats allows us a moment to compose ourselves before continuing our sweep of the various buildings. It doesn't take long, and when we finish, we have nothing to show for it. Or so it seems.

I know better.

In one of the buildings, and on the ground just outside, I find Marco's shine. He was here for an extended period—hours, maybe a day. The intensity of the shine tells me we just missed him, but there's something more: his shine is still pulsing, meaning, wherever he is, he's still alive.

Angus's shine is all over the place, including the barn and several of the other outbuildings.

He liked the goats.

I see where he took the time to pet them and hold their

chins in his hand, perhaps speaking to them as one would a dog or a favorite cat. It makes me wonder what a psychopath would have to say to such an animal. Perhaps he was just sizing up their necks for a knife and decided against it.

Who knows.

Sirens approach as we make our way back to the house.

# 43

Time stands still.

The sun continues to move in the sky, the wind caresses the remaining trees at Foothill Orchards, and the hum of activity in and around the house continues . . . but time stands still.

Diane has nothing new for us.

The despoiled home on Old Stage Road, it seems, was her last hurrah. She continues to dissect records, query databases, and make phone calls, but finding another possible location for the psychopath Angus Graves remains beyond her reach.

When they roll Barbara Mills from the house on a gurney, her frail frame barely inflates the body bag that contains her; just a couple lumps zipped up inside. It seems undignified because it *is* undignified.

Graceful exits are a hard thing to come by.

When the soul departs, the earthly remains don't simply wave a hearty goodbye and wander off to find themselves a grave. Something is always left behind, and unless one dies in the wild, where nature tends to take care of its own, someone has to deal with the bag of bones that nobody wants to touch.

I feel sorry for Barbara Mills.

She seemed a good woman, a hardworking woman, unworthy of the death she was dealt. I feel sorry for Otis. The man is going to have to listen for all eternity about how Barbara was brained to death with his ashes. Poor bastard.

Jimmy, Ross, and I are gathered near the Mustang while Kip hovers impatiently nearby. A cluster of trees provide some small measure of shade, and we've commandeered some of Barbara's outdoor furniture to set up a temporary office. Not much can be done here until CSI finishes with the house and gives us the okay to enter, so we do what we can.

We watch—all three of us—as the gurney is loaded into the ambulance.

"Did you know that Walmart sells body bags?" I ask as Barbara makes her slow departure. I don't know why I say some of the things I say. Words just come out and then I have the rest of the day—or of my life, depending on how outrageous the statement—to regret them.

"Huh?" Ross replies. "Body bags?"

"It's true. Google it."

"I don't remember seeing *that* in the clothing section," Jimmy scoffs.

Ross chuckles. "I wonder if they let you try them on in the fitting room? You know, in case it's too big or too small."

"Too tight around the waist," Jimmy suggests.

"Body bags for muffin tops!"

They both laugh at this before they remember that they're at the scene of a rather bloody homicide and rein themselves in.

"I don't think they have them in the *store* store," I say with mock disgust. "You probably have to order them online."

Ross ponders this. "Can you return them if they've only been worn once?"

"That's disgusting." Jimmy laughs, throwing a wad of paper at the detective.

It's almost 4:00 P.M. when we finally get the go-ahead to examine the interior of the house more closely. CSI has been through the place thoroughly, leaving traces of fingerprint powder on doorknobs, countertops, the toilet handle, the fridge, and anywhere else the suspect might have touched.

The smell of blood and death hangs in the air, though the corpse of Barbara Mills is conspicuously absent. I can see where she lay from the blood. The larger pool is where her chest had been—largest because, for a few moments at least, her heart continued to pump, pushing out the vital fluid through the numerous two-inch gashes in her chest and stomach.

I suspect she bled out quickly, a godsend considering what came next.

Though the head is a notorious bleeder, there is relatively little blood where hers had come to rest because by that time her heart had given out. With the body now absent, all that remains is a smear upon the tile, a mix of brain and tissue matter congealed with a scant amount of blood.

Angus's shine litters the floor and walls of the old farmhouse from top to bottom, but almost all of it is decades old, perhaps from his childhood. The only recent tracks enter from the back porch and appear to immediately confront Barbara in the kitchen. They move this way and that as if a conversation took place, and then he ends it—quickly and with force.

From the kitchen, he walked into the living room and plucked the urn from a shelf. I know this from the shine leading to the shelf, and the void in the dust where it once sat, a void in the shape of the urn's base.

He paused here.

His feet shuffled sideways a step and it seems he picked up a framed picture. Shine from his thumb glows on the front of the frame's glass. There's also blood—his hands must have been dripping with it.

He didn't try to wipe the blood clean, as some might—those interested in covering their tracks and hiding actions. Instead, he laid the picture faceup on the shelf. He wanted us to find it, wanted us to know of his interest.

"Why didn't CSI bag this for evidence?" I say to no one in particular.

Ross shrugs. "If they took everything with blood on it, they'd have to cart off half the house. Don't touch it yet. I'll check and make sure they got pictures of it."

He's gone less than a minute. When he returns, he's snapping on a pair of gloves.

"They got seven pictures, including a close-up of the image in the frame. Some sort of boys' camp. He said they placed it back the way they found it."

With the blue nitrile gloves snuggly in place, the detective picks up the frame and rights it, setting it back on the shelf facing out. The image certainly looks like a camp. Two boys wearing jeans and T-shirts—and looking none too happy—are side by side next to a large wooden sign with rustic letters that spell out RANCHO COLINA BIBLE CAMP. In smaller letters below, it says FOR BOYS.

"Rancho Colina?" I say.

"Ranch Hill," Jimmy interprets.

"Where's that? And why would Angus pause to stare at *this* picture while he's in the middle of an unspeakable homicide?"

"Good questions," Jimmy replies, but provides no answers.

Ross points at the two boys. "You suppose that's him and his brother?"

Jimmy shrugs. "We don't know yet if Barbara and Otis had

boys of their own. It could be kids, grandkids—hell, it could be a friend's kids."

We spend another ten minutes in the house, making sure we don't miss anything. While Jimmy, Kip, and Ross linger in the kitchen, the scene of the crime, I spend my time in the hall and living room. Barbara loved Otis, that's for sure. Pictures of them adorn the walls: wedding pictures, anniversary pictures, pictures of them at the Grand Canyon and at some tropical beach—probably Hawaii.

They were not camera shy, and I suspect that somewhere in the house photo albums are bursting with moments in time—microseconds of life frozen for posterity. I don't know what those photo albums might show, but I can see more than thirty pictures on the walls and shelves, images spanning decades.

Only one shows a pair of boys.

Back at our makeshift tree-shaded "office" in front of the Mustang, Ross flips open his mobile data terminal and waits for a signal. Accessing Google, he does a broad search for Rancho Colina Bible Camp and gets several returns, all of them linked to 1000 Rancho Colina Road, a private road off Route 190, east of Porterville.

Ross studies the map on his screen. "It's past Camp Nelson, which is maybe thirty miles from here but an hour's drive."

"You haven't seen Jimmy drive," I say under my breath.

Ross ignores the barb and seems to be fixated on the screen. "Rancho Colina Road . . . ?" He suddenly begins typing frantically. Connecting the MDT to the Bakersfield Police Department's records management system, or RMS, he types in the address exactly as presented. When the screen refreshes, he sucks in a breath that would empty heaven.

"Remember the suicide?" he asks, the words falling over

one another. "When he was fifteen—Angus tried to hang himself and we were wondering what would cause a boy that age to do such a thing?" Ross taps the MDT's screen hard. "It was at Rancho Colina Bible Camp. I thought I recognized the address."

A look crosses Jimmy's face: stern and hopeful and desperate all at the same time.

"An hour's drive, you say?"

Ross closes the laptop and stands. "Maybe less."

# 44

When Marco finishes digging the hole, he places the shovel against the side of the van as Angus instructs and then returns to his seat, hands behind his back. Before surrendering the shovel, he calculated his odds of braining the big man with the business end before Angus could shoot him.

The odds weren't good.

*I'm dead anyway,* he told himself. Despite this, something stayed his hand, something that Angus had said as Marco pitched dirt from the growing hole. It was a casual, offhand remark: "They're figuring it out."

Angus had said it with a sense of urgency as if time was running out and all might end in ruin if he didn't accelerate his plans.

Marco didn't know who *they* were, though he assumed it was law enforcement of one variety or another. Perhaps Secret Service.

*How close were they to figuring it out?*

Based on what he'd discerned of Angus's plan, Marco had another hour, maybe two, before things got . . . well, nasty. He'd live considerably longer, he was sure of that, but, dear God, he didn't want to think of it.

Angus is feeling the pressure. His words and actions

speak volumes. His wandering glances as he looks to the trees and hills with increased frequency. He now has but one purpose before his pursuers reach the old Bible camp: kill Marco in a spectacular manner that's worthy of eternal praise or condemnation—it doesn't matter which.

One way or another, he was going to make the congressman famous.

"Hell, we'll both be famous," Angus says, the words spilling out as if the two of them just won the first billion-dollar lottery or discovered the lost city of Atlantis.

*We'll both be famous.*

What an absurdity.

After securing Marco's compliant wrists with a fresh pair of black zip ties, Angus steps back and then thinks better of it. Retrieving another zip tie from his bag, he adds it to the others.

"Can't be too careful," he says with a grin.

Since their arrival at the camp that morning, Angus had spent his time—hours upon hours—building what he refers to as his "project." Most of this involves a network of beams and supports that stand thirteen or fourteen feet tall. To this, rigging has been attached.

The steady *click-click-click* of a ratcheted pulley now issues from the top of the structure as the big man slowly hoists a timber into the air—the very timber he'd cut from the stable; the special timber that Angus seems to hold in such regard.

As the end of the beam rises into the air, it drags its trailing end in small steps across the ground, leaving an impression in the soil, a scar. When it's close to its apex, Angus gives one long pull on the rigging and the timber clears the ground, swinging gently in the air, like a dead man at the end of his rope.

Angus barks his victory and wipes the sweat from his brow with his dirty sleeve. He pauses for a long drink of water, and then, still breathing heavily, points at the swaying timber. It's the gesture of one about to reveal some insight or secret . . . or one simply talking to himself, reminiscences of glory past.

"I carved my name in that beam."

Walking over, he reaches out and steadies the beam, then runs his fingers through the grooves once more, the crude letters spelling ANGUS. His fingers are alive as they explore the cuts, but his eyes are dead, dead to the timber, dead to the boy who made the cuts, dead to the world.

"I hanged myself from this old beam," Angus mutters, patting it affectionately. "Hanged myself and almost succeeded." His voice grows low and cold. "Imagine the people that would be alive today if they would have just left me strung up like I wanted. If they would have let me die. They're to blame, not me. It's their fault, not mine."

He seems to remember Marco.

With his dead eyes, he finds the congressman in his seat.

"She made me come here, you know? My mom. She made me and Mikey come here every summer after she joined her crazy cult. We told her we hated it, but she said we were sinners and had to be *cleansed* before the Second Coming."

He nods as if that somehow makes sense.

"She beat us with a length of rope—what she called her rod—and made us lie all night facedown before a cross because her *soul guide*"—he frames the words in air quotes—"told her that was the way to righteousness. But it was never enough. She looked at us and saw herself, like looking in a mirror. I hated the old bitch. I hated her, and I hated her crazy doomsday cult. I hated her almost as much as Mikey did—and that boy had a *powerful* hate."

Angus looks directly at Marco.

"I was going to kill her, you know? When I got out of prison?" Angus sighs. "I figured it was about time. Besides, she's the one who turned me in the last time around. Bitch!"

Marco's confused. "I thought this was because I couldn't save her?" he manages to say between dry, chapped lips.

"It is."

"I . . . I don't understand."

"It's because you didn't save her!" Angus barks impatiently as if restating the obvious. "If you had, I could have killed her my way, the proper way. But you failed, didn't you? What kind of worthless doctor are you?"

"My God," Marco mutters in hopeless desperation. "You're mad!"

Angus smiles with malice and spits on the ground. "Oh, I'm a genius. You'll see."

After lowering the timber into the hole, Angus packs dirt tightly around it until he's satisfied it'll stay upright. Earlier, before building the rigging supports, he cut a half joint into the beam. The notch now faces outward, about two feet off the ground.

It's the perfect height.

Picking up the second beam, a six-footer that he'd prefitted, Angus manhandles it over to the upright and drops it horizontally onto the ground at the base. Like its larger brother, the smaller beam has a half joint cut into the wood, though this cut is dead center.

With one final groan, Angus bends at the knees and deadlifts the beam so that the two halved joints slip easily together. Pushing the smaller crossbeam hard against the timber, the two ancient slabs bind together as the two cuts embrace and hold.

For good measure, Angus drives four six-inch spikes into the joint. Stepping back, he takes a moment to admire his creation. He glances over at Marco with a satisfied look, as if to say, *See what I made? See what I made . . . for you?*

Marco looks away.

One last measure of defiance.

The grin fades from Angus's face and hard words rumble from his throat. "This next part's going to be difficult for you." Angus nods. "Great things take great sacrifice."

Over the next few minutes, several things happen, each progressively worse than the one before. Knowing that a cornered animal is dangerous, Angus uses caution as he ties Marco's feet together at the ankle with a half-hitch knot. A good length of the rope remains after he finishes, so he stretches it out from the chair in a line, giving a good tug to make sure it's tight around the ankles.

Marco's hands are already bound behind him, but Angus takes the extra step of fastening his right hand to the back of the chair before he cuts loose the left hand and brings it around to the front. As he begins to fasten it to the arm of the chair, Marco yanks it from the big man's grip and tries to eye-gouge him with his thumb. Angus backhands him, sending the chair spilling over backward.

"Shouldn't do that," Angus says, then lifts the chair upright, lifts it as if it were a piece of toy furniture occupied by a doll or a stuffed panda.

Fastening the offending hand to the chair, he next brings around the other, but instead of fastening it to the right arm of the chair, he brings it across and zip-ties it to Marco's left hand, once again binding the hands together.

Then he cuts the tie holding the left hand down.

"You'll want to take this like a man," Angus says, and without warning he jerks the chair out from under Marco, dropping him to the ground with such force that it nearly knocks the wind from his lungs.

He gasps.

When he tries to rise, Angus pushes him down with his foot, holding him in place until he stops squirming. "It doesn't matter now. It's done. Accept it."

Walking away several feet, Angus fusses with the rope attached to Marco's feet, securing it to a second rope extending from the pulley system he'd rigged. Once satisfied that everything is secure, he begins ratcheting. Inch by inch, the rope and pulley drag the congressman across the ground, feetfirst.

Toward the beam.

Soon, his feet rise into the air, then his hips and lower back. In less than a minute, Marco feels his shoulders lifting, and finally his head. He finds himself suspended upside down with the beam and its crossbeam at his back.

Wrapping a heavy leather weight-lifting belt around Marco's waist, Angus pulls it until it's uncomfortably tight and fastens it. What Marco can't see is that the belt has been modified with a large eyelet punched through the back.

Angus turns Marco's swaying body slightly to the left and then gives an upward jerk on the belt. The eyelet catches something on the upright beam and hooks into place. Angus could release Marco's feet at this point and the man would just hang there, hooked to the slice of timber by some unseen mechanism.

Angus could do this, but he doesn't.

Using a Velcro strap, he runs it around Marco's neck and pulls the slack out, not enough to restrict breathing, just movement. This accomplished, Angus cuts the vinyl ties holding the congressman's hands together.

Dragging his right hand to the right side of the crossbeam, Angus fastens it in place with another length of Velcro and repeats the process on the left.

"I suppose you know what comes next," the giant says.

From a pouch, he extracts two five-inch spikes and shows them to Marco, letting him feel the points against his skin. With a carpenter's hammer, he delivers a carpenter's fate. Shrieks of agony tumble over the hills as the first nail drives through Marco's right palm, and a second nail pierces his left.

Angus had heard that the Romans might have done it through the wrist, but he also knows the hands are more sensitive, capable of delivering unbelievable pain, so through the palms it is.

The upside-down cross is almost complete now.

With the nails in place and Marco drifting toward shock, Angus walks slowly to the van and rummages around a moment, moving things aside as he retrieves an eight-foot stepladder.

"Gotta do your feet," he explains to Marco. The congressman's body shudders and convulses from the pain, and for a moment Angus worries that Marco might die too soon. *All great things come with risks,* Angus tells himself, then he climbs the ladder.

With great care, Angus lines up the feet so that the heels are stacked one on top of the other. Using a small maul, he drives the single nail through both heel bones with three strong whacks.

A brief, eerie silence follows, then a startled intake of oxygen fills Marco's lungs and he vomits forth a calamitous wail that seems to shake the very cross upon which he hangs.

Angus drops the maul and covers both ears against the sound.

Even the nearby leaves seem to cower and shudder, not from the noise but from the presence of the hammer-wielding man. It's as if he were Death incarnate and the van his pale horse.

Marco's cries shake heaven itself.

And if angels exist, they surely wept.

# 45

Sergeant Joe Mingo blasts his Humvee out of the driveway on Old Stage Road and wheels it to the north, lights flashing and sirens wailing. Detective Ross Feng, his only passenger, clamors for a handhold as the rugged ex-military vehicle quickly accelerates away from the sad farm that was once Foothill Orchards.

Jimmy's at the wheel of the Mustang and wastes no time catching up to the Humvee, putting the car into a powerslide as he hits the pavement. I'm sure my screaming doesn't help, but some things are unavoidable. Meanwhile, Kip is in the backseat, taking it all in stride. Behind us, twenty feet off our bumper is a Tulare County patrol car occupied by two deputies that Joe pulled off the crime scene.

He introduced them, but I already forgot their names.

That's it. That's our team.

For the first twenty miles we run lights and sirens and keep the speedometer pegged at over a hundred miles an hour—the full-meal deal. As we get closer, however, the lights flicker off and the sirens go quiet. Per department policy, this also forces us to reduce speed. It can't be helped. Lights and sirens are meant to draw attention, put people on alert. That's the last thing we want right now.

"It was a Bible camp for three different churches between the late forties and the late nineties," Diane's voice grumbles through the speaker. "It's mostly a ghost town now. The property was passed back to the National Forest Service in 2008, but all they did was secure the buildings and set up NO TRESPASSING signs."

"The picture we saw in Barbara Mills's living room wasn't dated," Jimmy says, "but from their ages, I'm guessing Angus and his brother attended in the early 1990s."

"Mmm. I was afraid you were going to say that."

"Why?"

"You've heard of the Danielites, I assume?"

"Yeah, the group that keeps predicting the Second Coming—"

"And keeps getting it wrong," I interrupt in my snarkiest tone. I jab a finger at Jimmy. "You wonder why some people have a problem with religion? It's because of people like that."

"Don't lump everyone who goes to church—including me—into the same camp," Jimmy replies disappointedly. "I'm pretty sure God's not happy about it either."

"Yeah, well . . . he should turn them into brimstone or something."

"Salt," Jimmy says, his disappointment growing.

"Boys!" Diane's voice pleads.

"Sorry, Diane," Jimmy says, leaning closer to the phone. "Theological disagreement."

"Yeah, well, can you take it up later?"

"Sure."

"As I was saying, the Danielites owned the property from 1984 until it closed in 1998. The road leading to the camp is gated, but there's enough room to drive around. I wouldn't advise it, though."

"Too exposed?" Jimmy guesses.

"Too exposed. It leads from Route 190 right up to the camp and there's not a lot of cover. Your better option is to circle around behind. There's an access road that'll take you to a ridge just a hundred yards beyond the outermost building. Probably not an easy hike, but you'll have a view of the whole camp. I'm sending an overhead image . . . now."

With nothing else to add, Diane says, "Be careful," and then, "Hurry."

The call disconnects.

Jimmy hands me his phone and I forward the image to Joe and Ross.

In the brooding quiet of the car, the last miles unwind before us. The silent solemnity is broken only by the rush of air around the Mustang. Jimmy gives my shoulder a light shove.

"Heathen," he says, never taking his eyes from the road.

"Zealot."

He smiles.

Diane was right about the ridge.

The view from the top takes in the whole camp, though great parts of it are obscured by the buildings themselves. Still, the front corner of an unrecognizable white vehicle peeks out from the edge of a building near what looks to be a stable, and the occasional murmur of voices—or perhaps just one voice—rises up now and then, caught on the scant wind, yet indiscernible.

As we lie prone at the peak, Jimmy breaks out his Steiner 10x42 tactical binoculars and studies the various buildings, the access gate farther down the driveway, the stables, and the woods and trails beyond. At last, he focuses on the vehicle, studying it for long seconds.

"Does that look like the front of a 2005 Ford Econoline van to you?" he whispers, handing me the binoculars—like I'm going to know the difference.

Peering down at the abbreviated white fender and black bumper, my first impression is that it reminds me of a boxer, as if the vehicle had taken one too many hard smacks to the nose. My second impression is that it looks like a white fender and black bumper. I adjust the binoculars, hoping that this will magically bestow the power to discern between vehicle makes and model.

It doesn't.

Handing the Steiner field glasses back to Jimmy, I whisper, "It could be a Ford van." He looks at me for a little more confirmation. "It could be a Subaru," I add, a resigned shrug sloughing off my shoulders. "I'm not a car guy."

"It's an Econoline," Joe confirms, peering through his own set of binoculars. "The amber blinker at the front of the fender is the giveaway."

Jimmy and I share a surprised glance.

Joe gives a slight tip of his head. "I was a plumber before I was a cop. That's pretty much what we drove."

Ross—binoculars now pressed to his eyes—suddenly flails his hand wildly, smacking me on the shoulder and then pointing.

As every eye turns and follows his gesture, a large man looms at the front of the van. He pauses and stretches out his back, the way a weight lifter might between sets.

"His lips are moving," Ross narrates. "He's talking to someone."

We don't hear the words from our concealment on the ridge, but when the big man lifts a hand in gesture, we all see it. No binoculars required. It's the type of grand gesture one might make when driving a point home, or when explaining the intricacies and majesty of dark energy to an eager pupil.

"Marco's still alive," Jimmy murmurs. "He's talking to him."

"Or it's an accomplice," I offer.

Jimmy squints at this. "We've seen no evidence of a partner. It's *got* to be Marco."

"Just a concern," I say. "Can't be too careful."

Kip shifts his body closer. "What's the plan?"

Jimmy eyes the 5.11 urban sniper bag lying on the ground next to the special agent. It contains a fully automatic M4 assault rifle with a 6920 upper, an aftermarket quad rail and forward grip, a Streamlight laser-light combo, a collapsible stock, and a sixteen-inch barrel. It's some serious hardware.

"How good are you?" Jimmy asks, gesturing at the bag and the gun within.

"Better than most; not as good as some."

"How are you at a hundred yards?"

"Tight. I'm running a holographic sight with an EOTech magnifier."

"What's your load?"

"Standard FMJs," Kip replies, indicating full metal jacket rounds.

Jimmy turns to Joe and asks, "What about them?"—indicating the two deputies just now working their way up the slope, having paused at the patrol car to add round-trapping trauma plates to their body armor.

The term *bulletproof* is a misnomer when it comes to body armor. *Bullet-resistant* is more accurate, especially when the offending round is fired from a handgun. That's why standard body armor is fine when responding to normal day-to-day calls.

This is far from normal.

The deputies have heard the stories—tales of the butcher who kidnapped a congressman and slowly killed off—or tried to kill off—his friends in horrifying ways. There's no telling if Angus is armed, but no one's taking any chances.

A round from a hard-hitting rifle like an AK-47 would punch right through both sides of a standard law enforcement vest. The plates help but aren't a guarantee.

You won't hear anyone complaining about the extra weight, though.

Joe glances at the deputies as they approach at a low crawl. "I imagine they're set up similar to Kip," he says, referring to the M4s they each carry.

Jimmy seems satisfied. Turning to Kip, he says, "I want you on overwatch."

Kip glances along the line of the ridge until his eyes settle on a spot. "That looks like a good perch. I'll adjust if needed."

"Do we have a green light on this guy?" Joe asks.

Jimmy nods. "Follow your department policy, but I'd say any aggressive move, drop him." Waving the deputies close, he says, "Here's what we're going to do."

It takes Deputy Pete Eagan ten minutes to descend to the patrol car, backtrack to Route 190, and return to the gated entrance to Rancho Colina Bible Camp. When he arrives, it's with lights flashing and sirens blaring; the full show. A regular Broadway production.

By this time, Jimmy, Ross, Joe, Deputy Jason Bullard, and I have descended the ridge and secreted ourselves among the buildings close to the Ford van—but not too close. We still can't see Marco, but Angus is seated in a camp chair facing away from us at a slight angle. He has a beer in his hand and he's talking as if telling tales around a campfire.

Oddly, a long spear rests against the chair.

When the first wail of the distant siren breaks the air, Angus stiffens in his seat. Setting the beer down, he turns his head and follows the noise. Rising, he moves perhaps thirty feet to the north of us and casts his eyes toward Route 190, shielding them against the low sun.

A moment later, he's running back.

We hear him say, "Cops!" Then he rummages through the van. We hear the van door groan and then slam closed, followed by the sound of running feet.

"He's entering the stable," Jimmy whispers to us as Kip feeds him intel from the ridge above. "He's out the other side now and climbing the water tower." To Kip, Jimmy says, "He's going to try and snipe. Tell Pete to take cover behind his vehicle and keep a low profile."

Turning to the four of us, Jimmy says, "You all know what you have to do."

Jason peels off to the left, followed by Ross. Jimmy pats me on the shoulder, glances at the borrowed Sig Sauer in my hand, and says, "Make sure the safety's off."

Then he's gone, trailed by Joe.

I'm alone in a ghost town with a psychopath on the loose.

I've had better nightmares.

Working my way up to the rear of the van, I keep the Sig at the low ready. As I clear the interior of the vehicle, I notice the keys in the ignition. Pulling them free, I toss them into the brush. If Angus manages to kill all of us, at least he'll have a long walk home.

A shot cracks from the water tower.

Another.

Down at the gate, the windshield of Pete's patrol car spiderwebs from the impact of the first round, while the second shot shatters the window on the open driver's door, dropping pebbles of safety glass to the ground.

Pete's at the rear of the vehicle hunkered down low. The angle of the parked car allows him to use the rear passenger wheel for cover. Still, it's no fun being in the scope of a shooter, especially one who knows what he's doing.

When a third shot erupts from the water tower, it's followed almost instantly by a shot from the ridge: Kip returning the courtesy. A barrage of gunfire erupts from the tower, and I see dirt kick up on the ridge. The rounds are wild, however, impacting along a fifty-yard stretch of the hill.

Angus has no idea where Kip is.

Realizing the clock is ticking, I move past the van, eyes scanning. We've yet to see Marco, but he has to be here. Building equipment, sawdust, and scattered chunks of wood tell me that Angus was building something. I barely notice the gallows-like structure, mostly because there's no corpse hanging on high.

I should have looked lower.

"Help . . . me."

The cry is weak, spent.

It's coming from the direction of . . . and then I see it: Not a gallows, but a massive upside-down cross. On it, bloody feet pointing to the sky, is Congressman Marco Perez. Alive, but only barely.

More gunfire.

Rushing forward, I kneel beside Marco, hissing words of encouragement to a man I feel I already know. Studying his hands, I quickly realize there's no way I'm getting the spikes out by pulling them. I don't even want to think about his feet.

Jimmy's only instructions were to find him and get him out of here. None of us were counting on crucifixion.

A thought occurs to me.

It's desperate, but it might work.

Running back to the van, I toss items around in a desperate search. I spot it under a coil of thick rope: a Sawzall in a carry bag. The blade is for woodworking—that much I know—so I swap it out for a metal-cutting blade I find at the bottom of the same bag. Checking the battery, which seems to have enough juice, I run back to Marco.

"I'm sorry if this hurts," I whisper. "I don't have any other option."

Marco nods and sets his jaw. "Do it."

Slipping the blade between the back of his hand and the wood, I rest the blade on the thick nail and—holding my breath—squeeze the trigger. The racket that issues from the blade and the electric motor driving the Sawzall is enough to wake the dead, but it can't be helped.

*Angus will know something's up.*

With fatalistic acceptance, I realize that if he makes his way back to the stable, and therefore back to the site of the crucifixion, I won't be able to hide behind Marco and his cross when I return fire. I'll have to place myself between them, Secret Service–style.

Oddly, I'm at peace with that.

The Sawzall bounces a few times on the hard steel and then makes short work of the nail. The metal is hot from cutting. It sizzles as I pull it from Marco's hand and toss it to the ground. The open wound drips blood, but any real medical attention will have to wait until we're clear of danger.

I turn my attention to the other hand.

Another burst of gunfire erupts, with return fire not from the ridge but from someplace off to my left.

When his second hand comes free of the cross, Marco holds it up next to the other and stares in blessed joy and utter sorrow. Joy, because he's free and he still breathes. Sorrow, for all he'd lost in the preceding days. These wounds, his personal stigmata, are a testament to all he'd suffered.

Marco weeps.

"I don't know what to do about your feet," I say in desperation. "If I cut the nail, you'll fold over in half around the belt at your waist. If I cut the belt, all the weight will shift to your feet. The pain . . ."

I leave the rest unspoken.

"There's . . . a pulley," Marco manages.

My eyes dance around—then I see it.

Quickly looping the rope around Marco's ankles, I ratchet

the pulley until the smallest amount of pressure is on the rope. Even this causes Marco to writhe with pain.

"Steps!" a voice cries from perhaps fifty yards away.

It's Jimmy. His voice is urgent.

Jumping to my feet, I turn toward the sound but see nothing.

Then I see everything.

With an explosive outward thrust, the door to the stable bursts open. A mountain of a man steps through with a rifle in his hands. I recognize Angus from his many booking photos . . . but only barely. People always seem so different in real life.

*Here we go again,* my mind says.

In slow motion, I watch the barrel of the rifle rise in my direction. Near the top of its rise, it swings wildly off to the right as Angus jumps suddenly and dodges a Sawzall flying in his direction. It barely registers with me that *I'm* the one who threw it. Instinct, I suppose.

As the barrel of the scoped hunting rifle slowly swings back to find me, a hand rises in front of me and spits off a round from a Sig Sauer pressed into its palm. My hand. My Sig.

The shot goes wild, and I fire in slow motion again and again. One of the rounds punches through Angus's thigh, but the man barely flinches.

I can see the black, bottomless hole at the end of the rifle now; the eternity hole.

I'm surprised to find Marco at my back. Somehow, I'd managed to throw a Sawzall, fire several rounds, and throw myself between a lunatic and a congressman. I suppose there are worse ways to die.

Angus jerks as his rifle cracks.

The bullet whistles past my left cheek.

The big man stares at me for a moment, a look of surprise on his face, as if he's never missed a shot before. Then I see it. A growing patch of crimson just above his heart. He drops to his knees.

Either determined or possessed, he tries again to lift the rifle, his eyes now fixed on Marco. There's nothing left in him.

The lifesaving shot from Kip's M4 has done its job. The bullet may not have pierced Angus's heart, but it's close enough. As he falls face forward to the earth, Angus jerks spasmodically once, then twice, yet I feel no pity.

There are humans and there are monsters; Angus was the latter.

Irredeemable, unsalvageable, unrepentant.

He dies as he lived.

With a little help from Jimmy and Ross, we free Marco from the cross and are just lowering him to the ground when the ambulance arrives. Joe had called for it shortly after our arrival, requesting that it approach with no lights or siren and stage two miles down the road until given the all clear.

At the gate, Pete somehow cut his hand slightly on the broken window glass but is otherwise uninjured. He seems pretty pleased with himself and is already cultivating the story of the shoot-out at Rancho Colina.

In his version, he shoots back.

As for Marco, the medics don't waste any time whisking him away. One moment they're loading him on the gurney, the next he's jumbled in a wash of lights and siren and headed for the nearest hospital. Halfway to Porterville, they'll rendezvous with a helicopter air ambulance that'll transport the congressman to Bakersfield.

He'll be a different man after this.

Haunted.

He may never have served in combat, but he'll have the thousand-yard stare nonetheless. He'll have the nightmares and the PTSD; the fear and the guilt and the anxiety. But he'll also have life. He'll have his sister and a dog named Roller.

We all break when stretched too far. Some pick up the pieces and trudge on, others don't. I'm hoping Marco is the former.

I'd bet on it.

In the calm aftermath, all of us, in ones and twos, take a turn standing in front of the cross. The bloodstained monstrosity seems to mock us, and I'm sure I'm not the only one who wonders about the type of mind that could conceive of such a thing.

I find myself staring absently at the ground, at the cast-off pieces of nail from Marco's hands and feet. I wonder if he'll want them, a reminder of what he endured, what he had lost, what he had suffered. Would I?

Part of me says yes, but part of me wants to vomit at the thought.

I turn away from the sad remnants, from the bloody cross. I glance at the corpse of Angus Graves where it lies on the ground, my bullet in his thigh, Kip's in his chest. That a man could go so wrong shouldn't surprise me, I suppose. Not after everything Jimmy and I have seen. It still makes you wonder, though.

# 46

It's just before midnight when Jimmy and I stumble from the elevator and shuffle down the hall toward our rooms at the Sierra Inn & Suites. Les's room is dark and quiet as we pass, but Marty's room has all the sound and hum of a five-star party. Not *too* loud, of course, otherwise management would be up here pounding on the door.

Jimmy just shakes his head as we pass and mutters, "Marty."

Our carefree copilot has a way of attracting people wherever he goes. Some people are like that; the life of the party. That's never been me. I'm a sit-in-the-corner guy, the one looking at his watch and wondering when things are going to wrap up. That's what happens, I suppose, when you have a kaleidoscope constantly spinning in your head.

My life is a permanent glow party—a rave of unusual colors, every day, every night.

Whether I like it or not.

"Good night," Jimmy says as we reach our respective doors. I return the parting words as he turns his way and I turn mine. I hear his lock chime and disengage as he swipes the electronic key, followed by the turning of the door handle.

"Steps . . ."

I turn to find him paused in the doorway.

"Good work today." He gives a tired smile. "I mean it."

We share a moment and I smile back, giving a slight nod. As we turn once more to go our separate ways, it's my turn to pause.

"I'm thinking of upgrading to a Glock or a Sig."

Jimmy laughs. "What about your Walther?"

I shrug. "I'll give it to Heather."

He seems to like the idea, but as he opens his mouth to reply, a voice comes from down the hall—from the half-open door to Marty's room.

"Did someone say my name?" It's the most beautiful voice I've heard in days. The words wrap around me like a blanket, and I sigh as Heather smiles and then bursts toward me.

Throwing her arms around my neck, she draws me into a kiss that nearly takes us to the floor. The cryptic conversation I had with Ellis on Tuesday evening starts to come into focus.

In a flurry of words—kung fu utterances too fast to fully comprehend—Heather spills the details of her last two days in the type of eloquent, exquisite monologue that only she can muster. Sadly, this lush storytelling is lost in the fog of my exhausted, spent mind.

The important takeaways are that she was scheduled to interview a witness for an article she was writing about the Nolan McMannis homicide. Instead of flying down, she decided to drive. The logic being that she could meet me in Bakersfield, and when I was finished with the case, the two of us could take a mini-vacation as we make our way back to Bellingham.

She talks excitedly about vineyards and Napa Valley; about Monterey and Carmel-by-the-Sea; about other places I've only heard of—or never heard of.

Jimmy's just smiling, having known about this all along.

While Heather and I are tooling through California and Oregon, he's taking Jane and Petey over to Victoria, British Columbia, for a much-deserved vacation.

Apparently, they have cool gardens.

And a couple of castles.

# 47

*Friday, March 13*

Jimmy and I say our goodbyes incrementally, but all at one location: Kern Medical.

It seems that anybody who's anybody is here. Ross and Ella shuffle back and forth between Marco's room and Noah's room, which are side by side. With the help of some complicit nurses, they even snuck Roller in for a visit.

These are the survivors, all of them, in one way or another.

Graves will be dug because of this case. Funerals will be attended: Jason Norris, Wade Winchell, Barbara Mills . . . Angus Graves.

William Johansson shouldn't count in the tally of funerals, having already been buried once. He'll need to be returned to his coffin, and since his god-awful sky-blue burial suit is locked away in evidence, maybe he'll get some decent clothes for the great beyond.

The media is having a field day with the Perez story. News is big business I suppose, especially when it's bad.

I haven't exactly had time to watch much TV recently, but the Marco Perez story has soaked up the ratings this last week. From all the fuss, you'd think a busload of kids had fallen down a well or something.

Marco's probably a shoo-in for reelection.

Legions of media are camped around the hospital, like flies on a carcass. Their masts and antennae give the place a prickly feeling. The reporters, for lack of anything else to say, breathlessly report the minutiae of daily hospital life, everything from the switch to chocolate pudding on the dinner menu to the odds of catching MRSA or some other ailment that's worse than the thing that brought you to the ER in the first place.

Jimmy and I join the congressman in his room. With him are his sister, Canela, and that funny wheelchair-bound dog, Roller, who recognizes me right away. He demands a pet, putting his head under my hand and lifting up until I comply—slave that I am. Then he looks at me and gives a low woof.

I didn't know this, but *woof* is Doggish for "feed me."

This becomes clear when Canela reaches into her purse and pulls out a beef-flavored Pup-Peroni, handing it over with an apologetic grin.

"There you go," I say to Roller as he takes it from my hand, leaving a dripping deposit of slobber behind, the currency of dogs. I can almost hear him say, *Keep the change,* as I wipe it off on my pants.

Dogs!

Marco looks remarkably well considering his near week in captivity. He extends a hand to shake, but the thick bandage reminds him of the holes in his palms, the unholy stigmata. He can't seem to stop thanking us—both him and Canela. Part of me wants to accept this, but the vision of Jason and Wade on the autopsy table clouds my vision. It's hard to hear such words when you only half succeeded.

I've always had trouble with the balance sheet between wins and losses.

There was a time I kept track of such things in two photo albums, my own *Book of the Dead* and *Book of the Living*. The tally of the dead always seemed to exceed that of the living, no matter how hard we tried. Jimmy eventually convinced me to set them aside. I still have them; I just no longer add photos to them.

Canela gives each of us a hug before we leave, insisting that we call if there's anything they can ever do for us. Not that we'd ever abuse that privilege, but the thought of having an influential congressman on speed dial is kind of nice.

We stop by the room of Noah Long, but he's in surgery. A liver and a pair of kidneys from the same donor became available overnight. I can only imagine how conflicting such moments are for the recipients of such a gift, knowing that they have a shot at life because some unfortunate soul perished.

And for the family of the departed—how odd to know that some earthly part of their loved one lives on in some other form. There must be some comfort in that, some sense of salvation from loss. I can't even imagine.

We're quiet on the way back down to the lobby.

The hardest goodbye is yet to come.

Jimmy and I are in a unique profession that throws us into life-and-death situations with perfect strangers. Within days, these men and women become comrades in arms.

We've been with Ross for almost a week now, through things none of us could have imagined. I still think he looks like a belly-rubbing Teletubby, but he's our Teletubby, and I don't want to let him go.

"Kip wanted to be here to see you off," Ross says, "but he got a tip on Abel Moya. After what we found in the warehouse, he's pretty hot to get his hands on him." Ross pauses, rubs his belly. "I think I might join him."

We stand in the parking lot, not awkwardly, but in the way friends do when trying to avoid the inevitable, no one wanting to make the first move. When I see the glassy sheen in Ross's eyes, it almost breaks me. Shaking his head and smiling through the building tears, he says, "Steps," and embraces me, as if no other words are necessary. Jimmy is next, and they embrace as brothers.

Will we ever see him again?

I don't know.

Law enforcement is a strange profession, especially our version of it. Now that Ross knows what we can do, I have no doubt we'll be the first ones he calls if something comes up.

At least I hope so.

Heather is waiting in front of the Sierra Inn & Suites when we return, leaning against the trunk of her sleek little Honda S2000 and looking like a goddess. I notice the top on the convertible is down, which is fine by me. This is California, after all. Besides, after a week with the Mustang, I think my windburn is building calluses.

"I checked out when you called," Heather says, giving me a peck on the cheek. "Your stuff's already in the trunk."

I turn to Jimmy. "I guess this is my ride."

He nods . . . then does something rare. He extends his hand. When I clasp it in my own and hold it for a moment, he places a hand on my shoulder and says, "Great job."

"You too."

Winking at Heather, he turns and strolls toward the motel entrance, my brother, unhurried by demands or needs. Untroubled.

Rare.

Heather and I spend the next week like vagabonds. We visit Disneyland and Universal Studios because I've never been to either and I guess that's a moral imperative (I didn't get that memo when I was a kid).

We swing through Monterey and some of the most stunning scenery I've ever beheld, particularly along 17 Mile Drive. We stop at the aquarium—Marty's always going on and on about this aquarium—and while we're waiting in line, Heather swears she sees Johnny Depp drive by in a red Maserati.

I'm not so sure; the guy looked nothing like Captain Jack Sparrow.

We visit Alcatraz in San Francisco, the vineyards of Napa Valley, Bodega Bay, which was the setting for Alfred Hitchcock's 1963 film, *The Birds*, and then it's on to the Redwood Forest.

In Oregon, we stop at the Sea Lion Caves along Coast Highway, then linger at Cannon Beach before moving on to Astoria, near the Lewis and Clark National Historical Park.

It wasn't so much the places we visited as it was the shared memories we imprinted. Spending time together is one thing. Spending time on an adventure—even one as simple as a road trip—is a completely different animal. The impressions and memories scratch deeper, making themselves permanent: tattoos on the brain, only in color and ever moving.

Such deep memories make two souls one. They're bonding moments that make it easier to get through the inevitable rough spots down the road.

It's a good beginning.

For the last six years, my life has mostly been about death. Death and the causes of death. Death and the perpetrators of death.

Only now do I start to see that there is, in some sense, life after death.

I mean to grab it.

# EPILOGUE

Cold case.

It's a benign enough pairing of words for something that causes such angst for so many investigators. Every agency has them. It's just a fact of law enforcement that there will be cases that can't be solved regardless of the diligence brought by those seeking answers. For some, these cases are an open wound, an ever-present, festering reminder of their presumed failure. After all, justice denied is not justice; neither is justice delayed.

Cold cases represent both.

Diane has no idea what she's about to step into as she pulls into the Hangar 7 parking lot. She believes it'll be a brief stop to check email and water her plants. With Jimmy and Steps a week into their respective vacations, there's little for her to do, yet she can't help herself. If she is steel, the office is a magnet.

Collecting her purse and a fresh container of chocolate-covered macadamia nuts from the passenger seat, she exits her car and makes her way to the man-door on the side of the building.

As she draws near, she notices a Ziploc bag attached to the

door handle with a rubber band. It contains a piece of white paper that she assumes is an advertisement, community notice, or some other rubbish, so she pays little attention. Removing it, she punches an access code into the cipher lock and turns the handle. As she does, the Ziploc also turns, revealing a pencil-drawn image on the piece of paper inside.

Diane freezes.

Her hand betrays the slightest shake as she stares at the image, perhaps disbelieving her eyes. As the initial shock passes, she rips open the top of the bag and removes the folded piece of paper. On one side, crudely drawn, is the image of Leonardo da Vinci's Vitruvian Man.

Unfolding the letter, Diane's face turns to ash as she reads the words within. Instead of entering Hangar 7 she retreats to her car, locks the doors, and starts the engine. Turning the car around so she can see any unexpected approaches, she sits like a sprinter in her starting block, ready to burst out at the first sign of trouble.

She dials 911 and requests an immediate response, then calls the FBI's Seattle Field Office to request agent support and an Evidence Response Team (ERT).

The Leonardo case is the oldest cold case in the Special Tracking Unit's files, predating the establishment of the team. The serial killer Leonardo was so named for his habit of posing his victims to look like the iconic Vitruvian Man. When Steps was sixteen, Leonardo abducted and killed one of Steps's classmates, setting the two on a collision course that was eventually going to come to a head.

Diane knows enough about Leonardo to be afraid, enough to sigh with relief upon hearing the approaching sirens.

Deputies from the Whatcom County Sheriff's Office clear the building and find no evidence of entry or attempted entry into the highly secure facility. When the forensic team arrives from Seattle, they dust the door and handle for prints and find none, but the effort isn't a total waste. Written across the door, presumably by Leonardo's finger, are the words I SEE YOU. Though invisible to the naked eye, they were meant to be found.

Diane nearly faints as the dusting powder reveals them.

Despite pressure from every level of brass between herself and the director, she refuses to call Jimmy and Steps. Leonardo has no way of knowing where they are, and Diane has no intention of interrupting their first real vacation in years.

They'll be back in a week.

Maybe she'll have answers by then.

For now, she'll move into a hotel. Against her pointed objections, the director assigns a security detail to her, and another to Big Perch to watch over Steps's younger brother, Jens, and Ellis, the eccentric groundskeeper.

Temporarily forgotten in this burst of activity, Leonardo's letter lies faceup on Diane's desk. Words glare up from the bleached paper, a repeated proclamation:

DEATH COMES FOR US ALL.
DEATH COMES FOR US ALL.
DEATH COMES FOR US ALL.

# ACKNOWLEDGMENTS

I owe a great deal to my editor, Keith Kahla, and probably more to my agent, Kimberley Cameron. Between them, they breathed life into this book and made it real. I also want to thank my assistant editor, Alice Pfeifer, who keeps the publishing wheel rolling with patience and grace.

Finally, I want to tip my hat to the art department at Minotaur Books. A lot is riding on a book's cover, and they've just delivered amazing art again and again. They have my deepest respect.

# ABOUT THE AUTHOR

SPENCER KOPE is the crime analyst for the sheriff's office of Whatcom County, Washington, where he provides case support to detectives and deputies. Prior to that, he was an intelligence operations specialist with the Office of Naval Intelligence. He lives in Lynden, Washington.